AMBUSH BAIT

"I like bein' next to you," Laura Renault said. "You're the first real man I ever met."

The girl smiled and snuggled closer to Pete Houston, and as she did her warm body sent a thrill through his muscular frame. But when he looked at the girl he saw what seemed like a tinge of regret in her eyes, and he couldn't understand it.

And then suddenly from above the rock they were sitting against, the point of a rifle touched Houston's head, and a hard voice said:

"Don't move, Mr. Bounty Hunter, or you're dead."

Houston froze and stared at the girl who had leaned over and extracted the six-shooter from his holster. Yet he was more angry with himself than with Laura Renault. He should have known better, and now he had made a mistake that would surely cost him his life!

TRAIL OF THE BOUNTY HUNTER

BY LAWRENCE CORBETT

ZEBRA BOOKS
KENSINGTON PUBLISHING CORP.

ZEBRA BOOKS

are published by

Kensington Publishing Corp.
475 Park Avenue South
New York, NY 10016

First printing: September 1987

Printed in the United States of America

CHAPTER ONE

By the time the sun rose in the east, Pete Houston and his prisoner, burly Colorado McIver, were already five miles away from the campsite where they'd spent the night. Houston had been on the trail for almost two days with this rustler and the bounty hunter was anxious to reach Buffalo, Wyoming, to claim his reward from the Wyoming Cattlemen's Association. Houston squinted at the rising Black Hills to the east that had become more distinct with the brightening morning. His prisoner sat on his horse with a sullen look on his pudgy, unshaven face. Now and then he glared at his captor, but said nothing.

Houston did not speak either as he loped leisurely northward, occasionally glancing at McIver or staring at the swift-flowing Crazy Woman River to the east that snaked between the Big Horn grasslands and the craggy hills. When Devil's Peak loomed into view, Houston knew that Buffalo lay but a few more miles ahead. Within a couple of hours he would reach town, stop at the

5

sheriff's office for his voucher, and then go to the Buffalo branch of the cattle association to collect his bounty.

Once more Houston looked at the glum-faced McIver to make certain that the man's hands were still firmly tied to the saddlehorn and that his legs were still securely bound to the stirrups.

As the duo continued north on the dusty Johnson County Highway, the prisoner finally spoke. "Like I said, mister, you're crazy. Do you know that?"

Houston did not answer.

"When my friends learn that a bounty-hunter snake is takin' me in, why, they'll come after you and shoot you dead."

But still Houston made no reply.

"How much am I worth to you, anyway?" McIver continued. "I don't think it's very much. Are you willin' to trade your life for a few dollars?"

"Shut up, McIver!" Houston finally barked. "I've been hearing the same talk from you for the past two days, and I'm still hearin' it. Now that I think of it, it isn't the fear of your friends that irritates me, it's your constant talk."

"I'm only tryin' to steer you straight."

Pete Houston scowled at the man and then squinted at the road ahead. He tipped his hat, exposing thick strands of dark hair, before he wiped the sweat from his square face and deep-set brown eyes. Next, he straightened his tall, muscular body in the saddle, loosening some of the kinks in his back muscles; they'd become quite discomforting after two days on the trail.

Suddenly, Pete Houston stiffened when he saw two riders coming toward them. He pulled the rein of McIver's horse, bringing the outlaw closer to him before winding the rein around his saddlehorn. Then he extracted his Winchester rifle from his saddle scabbard and cocked the weapon, ready to defend himself and his prisoner. For a full minute Houston remained steady, waiting for the oncoming riders. The bounty hunter did not recognize them, but they appeared to be a pair of drifters on the trail. Finally, the two horsemen slowed to a lope, approached Houston, and stopped a few yards from the bounty hunter.

"Mornin'." One of the strangers doffed his hat. "My name is Hank Beaudoin and this is my partner, Snake Dawson." He cocked his head at the second rider. "We're on our way to Egleston. Can you tell me how much further it is?"

"You're a long way; maybe another forty miles, and I'd say you can't make it there in less than four or five hours."

The second rider, Dawson, eyed Houston and his prisoner and then grinned. However, he said nothing while he worked his way slowly to the left of the bounty hunter. The first man, Beaudoin, remained in front of Houston, while he shuttled his glance between Houston and McIver. The bounty hunter noted that both of them wore battered hats, dirty shirts, denim trousers, and dusty boots. Unshaven faces and stringy, unkempt hair completed their seedy appearance. Houston became suspicious. If they had come

7

from Buffalo this morning, only a few miles to the north, they would have at least cleaned up. Also, they could have easily learned in town how far it was to Egleston. No! These men had been on the trail for some time, roughing it outdoors at night, and simply ignoring personal hygiene.

"Egleston is about forty miles, did you say?" Beaudoin asked.

Pete Houston nodded, but he noticed that a sudden change had come to Colorado McIver's face. A smug glint had replaced the anger in his gray eyes, and the slightest hint of a grin had softened his hard face. These two riders were apparently the friends of whom McIver had spoken. Houston did not know if they were acquaintances of the outlaws or part of the rustling gang that had made off with more than four hundred head from the Starlight Ranch. The bounty hunter did not recognize the two horsemen as any outlaw gang members that the law or the cattlemen's association had thus far identified.

Houston looked at the two men again, even more warily this time, and he noticed that about him was only a stretch of empty, desolate terrain: no ranch houses nearby, no people about, and not even a sodbuster's hut. If these men intended to rescue Colorado McIver, they had certainly picked the right place to do it. Houston's suspicions grew when he saw the second rider, Snake Dawson, working himself to the bounty hunter's rear, while Hank Beaudoin remained in front of Houston.

"I see you got a prisoner there," Beaudoin grinned, "but I don't see no badge. You must be a bounty hunter."

"What I'm doing is none of your business," Houston answered. "You stopped to ask me how far it was to Egleston and I told you. Now I suggest you go on your way and I'll continue on mine." He stared at the men with a hard, vigorous look, and Beaudoin recoiled slightly but managed to grin.

"We don't mean no harm," Beaudoin said, suddenly raising his arm in a gesture. "We was only curious, that's all."

Houston surmised that this first man was holding his attention while the second man got behind Pete to draw his gun and get the drop on the bounty hunter, or even kill him. Houston whirled just as Snake Dawson hoisted his gun from his holster and Pete shot quickly and accurately, striking the man's fingers, drawing blood, and skidding the weapon out of his hand. Before Beaudoin could bring down his arm to draw his own gun, Houston had whirled around and aimed his Winchester at the rider's chest.

Beaudoin's arm stopped in midair and he gasped as his companion held his bleeding hand and winced in pain. "G-goddamn, mister," Beaudoin stammered, "I told you we didn't mean no harm."

"Then, why was your partner going for his gun?" Houston glared. Then he gestured to Beaudoin. "Nice and slow—take your gun out of your holster and hand it to me. I wouldn't want to

9

kill you."

"Sure, sure," the man answered. Then Beaudoin carefully lifted the gun from the holster and handed the weapon to Houston, who shoved the six-shooter into his waist.

"Leave those rifles in their scabbards and get down from those horses," the bounty hunter said. "That means you too," he cried to Snake Dawson, who held his bleeding fingers.

The two riders complied, getting off their mounts. Houston took the reins of the animals and tied them to his own horse. The two men, standing on the trail, looked at Houston in near panic.

"Y-you ain't gonna just leave us here, are you? Unarmed? No horses?"

"I suspect you planned to leave me dead out here," Houston said. You're at least alive. You can go back to Buffalo. It's only a few miles and it's a nice morning for a walk. You might even go to the sheriff's office to claim your guns and horses, because that's where I'll leave them. But, when you tell Sheriff Angus that you tried to free a wanted man, he might take offense and put you behind bars. He's got no sympathy for people who do things like that in his jurisdiction." Pete leaned from his saddle and grinned. "I suggest you keep going south on foot, and maybe you can reach Egleston in a day or two."

"Y-you expect us to walk all the way to Egleston?" Beaudoin gasped.

"Unless you go north and face Sheriff Angus."

"Wait," Snake Dawson cried. "Please, mister, don't leave us here. My hand is bleedin' bad and I

10

need medical help. If I don't get it, why, I could lose the use a this hand."

"That wouldn't be such a bad thing," Pete said. "It would mean there'd be one less of your kind around to waylay people on this highway." He raised his rifle and pointed at the two men. "Start walking."

The duo stiffened but then started plodding southward. When they had gone about a hundred yards, Houston turned to Colorado McIver. "That was dumb, McIver. If they were friends of yours that'll make it worse for you, adding attempted escape with armed accomplices to your cattle-rustling charge."

"Honest, mister, I don't even know them," McIver cried. "I swear I don't know who they was. Maybe they was just highwaymen who wanted to rob us."

"Maybe," Pete said. He kicked the flank of his horse before starting off again with his prisoner and the two riderless horses.

Houston said little more as he rode, and he only occasionally glanced at his prisoner. In turn, McIver had reverted to his somber mood, certain now that he would soon find himself behind bars. Now and then the rustler would glance at his captor and then squeeze his face irritably. He inwardly scolded himself for allowing this bounty hunter to take him in Egleston, south of the Hole In The Wall country. He realized that he should have listened to Dude Rawlings, the rustler gang leader. An informant had come into the gang's hideaway and told Dude and the other members of the gang that the law had identified five of them, including McIver, after the Starlight Ranch job.

Dude Rawlings had then warned McIver and the others to stay put in their hideaway until things cooled off, but McIver had insisted on going into Egleston for a good meal, some cold beer, and a woman. When he had reached the town, he had indeed enjoyed food and drink. However, as he had started for one of the brothels, this damn bounty hunter had caught up with him, surprised McIver, and taken him prisoner.

McIver's two friends, Hank Beaudoin and Snake Dawson, had seen the incident and they had slyly signaled Colorado that they would meet him and the bounty hunter on the trail to rescue the rustler. Actually, Beaudoin and Dawson were not a part of the Rawlings gang, but merely petty thieves and longtime friends of McIver. But, as this rustler had just witnessed, the hope for rescue had failed, and now his friends were weaponless and abandoned on the highway.

News of Colorado's capture had probably reached Dude Rawlings by now at his Hole In The Wall hideout, but even Rawlings was unlikely to liberate McIver. Colorado knew the reputation of Sheriff Angus at Buffalo. The lawman and his deputies were tough, determined men and no one had ever escaped from the Buffalo jailhouse.

Perhaps, if McIver had realized this bounty hunter's ability, he might never have come to Egleston.

Pete Houston belonged to one of those rare

breeds in the west, a man quite educated, who was also endowed with the finesse to handle himself in this wild country. Houston had schooled himself well to survive against the hordes of roving, conscienceless men who had only contempt for the law and disdain for the properties and well-being of others. He had been educated at the public school in Casper, where his father had been a clerk for the cattlemen's association branch office there. He had also learned to shoot well during his youth, reaching a point where he could pick off a cougar at two hundred yards and knock over a deer speeding across the rugged landscape of the Tongue Hill country. Since age five, when he'd gotten his first pony, Houston had been riding horses; and by age fourteen he had grown tall and strong, able to subdue with his fists other boys who were quite older than himself.

For a time, Pete Houston had worked as a clerk in a Casper general store, but he had always possessed a restlessness that made him incompatible with an indoor job. But he had also never liked the hard work and low pay of farmhands or cowpunchers. At age nineteen, he had worked as a deputy in Casper, but after a year, even this work seemed too restrictive to him.

Then, two years ago, Pete had seen posted notices of two wanted men in the Casper sheriff's office: two Wells Fargo robbers for which the company offered a $500 reward, dead or alive. By chance, he had learned of their whereabouts from some drifters in a saloon and he had decided to track them down. The job was not hard, since it was much easier to follow the trail of horses and riders than that of mountain cats or deer. He had caught up to the pair in a rickety rooming house at the hamlet of Liefer on the Buffalo River and the two wanted men had given up without a fight.

A thousand dollars! That's what Pete had been paid when he brought the Wells Fargo bandits into Casper. From that moment on, Houston realized the lucrative return available to bounty hunters. Further, such an occupation enabled him to roam freely, to go where he pleased, and still have enough money to live quite comfortably. True, he had found that most people disliked bounty hunters, considering them mercenaries who fed on the lives of others, despite the fact that such lives were those of outlaws. However, Pete had brushed off these criticisms. He was doing what he liked. Also, he was potent with his fists and deadly with his guns, enough so that most outlaws were out of their class when they faced him.

Houston had brought in about fifteen or twenty wanted men over the past two years and he had earned himself close to $4,000 during this period, much better than any clerk, cowhand, or farmer. His keen mind and his good education had given him an inner sagacity and sense of logic that abetted his physical strengths and thus made him an even more deadly adversary.

By midmorning of this fall day, Pete Houston finally loped into Buffalo with his prisoner and two trailing horses. As usual, the cow town teemed with people, wagons, and riders, for

14

Buffalo lay in the middle of the Powder River cattle country and thus was the center of activities for surrounding ranchers, farmers, and their hands. Its main street, Gillette Avenue, nearly twenty yards wide, had been laid out to accommodate ranchers who often drove cattle herds through town to the cow pens at the far end of Buffalo. High, wooden boardwalks ran along both sides of Gillette, crossing the street at intersections, for the convenience of pedestrians.

On both sides of this main street, merchants, liverymen, boardinghouse owners, cafe managers, shopkeepers, and saloon operators maintained their establishments. From daylight until late in the evening, these businesses thrived because the hundreds of cowpunchers and farm hands had nowhere else to spend their money except in Buffalo. Cattlemen and farmers, of course, had long displayed an animosity toward each other, with the ranchers protesting the encroachment of homesteaders who built farms on this once-free range land.

Farmers, in turn, protested the incursions of cattle herds on their planted fields. Remarkably, Sheriff Red Angus had done a good job of keeping the peace here, but he and his deputies spent most of their time breaking up saloon brawls between ranch hands and farm hands who, following the lead of their bosses, had developed an unfriendliness toward each other.

With the wide, mired Gillette Avenue so jammed with freight wagons, riders, and even some cattle, no one noticed Pete Houston come into town with his burdens. He loped through the crowded street until he reached the office of Sheriff Red Angus, where he dismounted, tethered the four horses, and then untied the prisoner before having him dismount.

"Inside," Houston gestured. McIver then preceded the bounty hunter into the office, where Sheriff Angus had been sitting at his desk while scanning some papers. When he looked up, he grinned.

"Goddamn! Houston! You brought in one of those rustlers?"

"Colorado McIver. I found him in Egleston."

"You're likely to find a lotta wanted men in that outlaw roost."

Angus stroked the cheeks of his round face and then twitched his thick, red mustache before he rose from his chair. He reached behind him and pulled some keys from a rack before he walked to one of the five cells. He needed this many, for hardly a night went by that he and his deputies did not lock up at least a dozen drunks, carousers, or disorderly visitors. When the sheriff opened the door, Pete shoved his captive inside. Angus locked the cell after the prisoner and then returned to his desk. He fumbled through some wanted posters on his desk and then pulled out one on William Colorado McIver. He squinted at the prisoner and then at the photo on the poster before he nodded.

"That's McIver, all right."

"I'd appreciate my voucher, Sheriff, so I can cash in at the association office."

"Sure thing, Pete," Angus nodded. He opened a drawer and pulled out a pad of printed forms, on one of which he filled in the name of the prisoner, the date and time he'd been brought in, the name of his captor, and a request for $250 in payment. After he signed the sheet, Angus handed it to Houston.

"Thank you, Sheriff."

"Did you get any leads on any of the others in the Rawlings gang?"

"No," Houston said. "I suspect they're hiding out in the Hole In The Wall country. I may go back to Egleston and smoke some of them out."

"We only know four others from that rustler gang besides this prisoner," Angus said, "—Rawlings himself, that ex-churchman Ralph Rogers, that safe-cracker Frank Sparks, and that wetback Pedro Anias. The Pinkertons are still doin' some investigatin' up in Sheridan and they might learn the identity a the others. There's a rumor that some army deserter is also runnin' with 'em." The sheriff sighed. "What are you goin' to do when you cash in?"

"Rest up for a couple of days and get me a nice hot bath," the bounty hunter sighed. "I got a nice soft bed at the Mercer Hotel and I can't wait to stretch out on it.

Angus grinned. "Take care of yourself."

"Yeh." Pete nodded. "Oh, by the way . . ." He suddenly gestured. "Colorado's horse is outside along with two mounts I took away from a couple of would-be waylayers about five miles south of here."

17

"Waylayers?"

"I think they were friends of McIver, hoping to get him loose from me. I doubt if they'll come into town to claim their animals, guns, and gear, so you can probably sell them off at the next auction." He glared at McIver, and then looked back at Angus. "You can question him, Sheriff, although this prisoner claims he didn't know them. The two men on the trail called themselves Hank Beaudoin and Snake Dawson."

"I'll question McIver," Angus said. Then he tapped Houston on the shoulder. "You did well, Pete. We just don't have the time to run down all of these wanted men. There's so many of 'em. I know a lotta people don't like fellows like you, but your kind are needed in this country."

"Can I leave my horse outside until I come back from the association office?"

"Sure, Pete, sure."

Pete Houston nodded and left the sheriff's office. He walked up the boardwalk, weaving through the crowd of pedestrians and stepping around the storekeepers who were setting up displays or loading wagons for customers. After walking about two blocks, he reached his destination and looked up at the sign hanging over the door of the neat one-story brick building: Wyoming Cattlemen's Association, Buffalo Branch. He walked up the smooth concrete steps and then through the rich oak front door before coming into the neatly paneled anteroom.

The association building was new and ornate. But then, the wealthy and influential ranchers of

Wyoming contributed liberally to the organization, which continually fought for their interests: lobbying legislatures, seeking out rustlers, and conducting legal battles against homesteaders. When Pete got inside, he slapped away some of the dust on his tan chino trousers and brown cotton shirt. He took off his hat and dusted that as well before he walked up to the counter.

A girl looked up. "Yes?"

Pete simply stared, mute for a moment. She was one of the prettiest women he had seen in a long time: a trim shapely body, creamy oval face, long, shiny, light brown hair, and sparkling blue eyes. The girl could not help noticing the examination and she smiled, revealing rows of neat white teeth. She then rose from her chair.

"Can I help you, sir?"

Pete Houston jerked and then grinned. "I'm sorry, I didn't expect to see anyone as pretty as you in here."

"I started about a week ago."

"I must apologize for my appearance," Pete said. "I've been on the trail for the past couple of days and I haven't had time to clean up."

"It's all right," the girl said. "You still look a lot cleaner then most of 'em who come in here. How can I help you?"

"Is Joe Simeon in his office?"

"Can I ask who wants to see 'im?"

"Houston; Pete Houston."

The girl gaped and her eyes widened. "Ain't you the man who's been trackin' them rustlers from the Rawlings gang?"

19

"I haven't done too well so far," Pete said. "I only managed to bring in one of them."

"They told me you were good, but they didn't tell me you were also good lookin'." She smiled. "Wait here, I'll get Mr. Simeon." Pete stood and watched as the shapely girl disappeared into the inner office. Only a moment later, the door opened and Simeon came outside, a wide grin on his big, round face.

"Come in, Pete, come in," he said as he motioned with his arm.

As Simeon went back inside his private office, the girl returned to her place behind the counter. Pete looked at her. "I don't suppose there's a chance I could take you to dinner tonight—after I clean up, I mean?"

"Maybe," the girl said. "I'm here 'til five; then I'm free."

"And your name, miss?"

"Jane Clemons."

"I'm really happy to meet you, Jane."

"Pete, are you coming in here?" Simeon's voice boomed before he came outside and saw Houston talking to his clerk. He grinned. "You can talk to her later."

"I'm coming," Pete said, grinning at the girl before joining Simeon.

The Buffalo association director sat at his desk, tapping the thick fingers of his big right hand on the top. His huge bulk seemed almost as big as the desk and completely hid the chair on which he sat. Big Jim was by no means fat. He was simply huge, over six feet tall, with a frame that was massive and muscular. At 225 pounds, he looked like a trim heavyweight boxer.

"I brought in one of those rustlers, Colorado McIver," Houston said. "I got my voucher right here."

"Good," Simeon said. "Did you get any leads on Rawlings and the others?"

"Not yet."

Simeon took the voucher, nodded, reached into a drawer, and peeled off $250 in ten- and twenty-dollar bills. As he handed the money to the bounty hunter, he rose from his chair and leaned over his desk, almost looking down at Pete who himself was nearly six feet tall. He handed the bills to Houston and then spoke.

"Pete, the association would sure like to get the rest of that gang as soon as possible."

"I'll go after them," Houston said, "but not right away. I want to spend a little time in town, relax for a while."

Joe Simeon grinned. "Jane Clemons is a real pretty filly."

CHAPTER TWO

Harry "Dude" Rawlings was not a big man, only five feet four inches tall, and was as slim as a rail, weighing only about 120 pounds. His narrow face tapered down to a sharp chin, so that his face looked like an elongated triangle. His sharp, pointed nose was another, miniature triangle, and his small, beady, dark gray eyes lay in their sockets like two lustrous marbles, emitting a perpetual aura of sadism. But, like so many small men, the Dude maintained an air of firmness and resolve to control those under him. And, as a successful leader, his followers obeyed him almost religiously.

Rawlings had gained the vernacular name Dude because of his immaculate dress, despite a profession that kept him in a saddle and dealing with stenchy cattle caked with grime and filth. He wore spurs, denim trousers, and rawhide shirts on the range, but when his work was done, he quickly washed these work clothes, bathed, and shaved himself thoroughly, and then donned fashionable, custom-cut attire: shoes, socks, silk shirt, tie, neat suit, and bowler hat.

On this fall morning, the same day that Houston was bringing McIver to Buffalo, Rawlings rode northward from his Hole In The Wall hideaway. He stood out conspicuously among his companions because his riding clothes were unusually clean.

Among the Dude's cohorts, Ralph "Preacher" Rogers had been a former church elder who had given up religion because he had seen too much hypocrisy among the church members. Besides, black-market cattle dealers paid a lot more than the pennies and nickels a flock put into a collection box. Frank Sparks, a former safe-cracker and drifter, had skills neither with a gun nor with his fists, but he was willing and fearless and he could ride well. He was a tall, thin man, whose gaunt face made him look like a walking cadaver. He had no previous experience with cattle, and why Rawlings wanted him in his gang was a mystery, although Sparks supposedly did have the knack for sighting night-time guards who watched over a herd.

Pedro Anias was a wetback from Mexico who had crossed the border some years ago as a wanted man. He had extensive experience as a cowpuncher, and he was good with a gun and better still with a knife. He had been a rustler in Mexico and he had learned the art of directing stolen herds away from the searching eyes of posses and ranchers. So, the Mexican was a key man in the gang.

Among those the law had not yet identified was

Big Val Henry, well over 200 pounds and nearly six feet four inches tall. None too bright, he had been an unsuccessful housepainter by trade, and he had willingly joined Rawlings as a cattle rustler. Clint "Wild Man" Eliot had formerly worked on cattle ranches, and few men in the cattle country could steer cattle as deftly as could Eliot. He had no use for morals or cleanliness, only carnal pleasures, and his reckless disposition had earned him the tag Wild Man.

Jerry "Cap" Roseberry had been an army captain who had left the service because of disagreements with superiors. He was the man suspected of being the army deserter, but he had not been identified. In truth, he was not a deserter, but had simply quit when it had come time for reenlistment.

Roseberry was smart, lithe, strong, suave, and gentlemanly. He dressed only slightly less neatly than the Dude. He was ever cautious, acting with care and logic despite a battle-scarred past in which fellow soldiers or renegade Indians had often been killed or maimed in combat. Roseberry abhorred violence and he had persuaded gang members not to hurt or kill victims. Thievery brought only routine efforts by lawmen, but murder aroused fervent responses.

Roseberry enjoyed almost as much prestige among the men as did Rawlings himself. The ex-army captain, in fact, was so glib, that the Dude rarely did anything without first consulting Roseberry.

And finally, there was the slim, shapely Laura

Renault, whose dark hazel eyes on a smooth, light-complected oval face enhanced her beauty. Her dark flowing hair added to her good looks, but she always kept these locks in a bob when on the job. Laura had been a waitress and a store clerk in Sheridan, but she had always been an adept rider. When the Dude met her in Sheridan, he had been attracted to her beauty and riding skills, and he had asked her to join his gang of rustlers. As a lark, she had agreed, and after the first job had netted her nearly $500, she decided that stealing cattle paid a hell of a lot more than waiting on customers. She displayed a cool exterior, forcing the male members of the gang to keep their distance. She had joined this gang strictly for business and she intended to keep it that way.

As the rustlers rode northward, Jerry Roseberry came up to the gang leader holding a map in his hand. He gestured to Rawlings. "We should be at the river bend by midafternoon and the RX range is about five miles to the east of there."

"We'll make camp at the hollow," Rawlings said, "and get a little sleep. We'll have a long night."

"You don't think Eliot and Sparks made any mistakes, do you?"

"No, they were pretty accurate," Rawlings said. "The RX Ranch keeps no more than four men on the range at night, and they bed down the herd two or three miles from the main ranch house and bunk houses. That leaves the animals near plenty a grass and water. Them steers will be so groggy and full-stomached they'll move along

25

like lambs."

"You know where the sentries are posted?" Roseberry asked.

Rawlings nodded and then yelled, "Sparks! Eliot! Get up here."

The two outlaws quickly loped forward and settled next to Rawlings and Roseberry. "You're sure them guards are where you marked them off on this map?" the Dude asked.

Wild Man Eliot looked at the map and nodded. "That's right. Two of 'em is always at the Powder riverbank camp. The third patrols on the north side a the herd and the fourth on the south."

"At about midnight, the two punchers at the camp relieve the other two," Frank Sparks now spoke. "In fact, Dude, even the two on horseback are jes' loafin' most a the time, half-asleep in the saddle."

"Then, we'll take out the pair on the north and south at the same time we deal with the two at the riverbank camp," the Dude said. "We'll then take the herd north along the grassland skirtin' the river and we should be in Spotted Horse by dawn." He turned to Roseberry. "What do you think, Cap?"

"Yes, that's the best way," Roseberry answered. "Are you sure your man will be waiting for us?"

"Oh yes." Rawlings grinned. "Balfonte is expectin' at least three hundred head, and he's already got a team a men near Recluse Ridge Canyon to change the brands. He'll pay us the usual ten dollars a head, so if we can move at least three hundred of those steers, we'll earn a good

26

night's pay."

Ex-army captain Jerry Roseberry nodded.

By two o'clock in the afternoon the eight gang members reached a grove of trees in Crazy Woman Hollow. Here, they unsaddled and brushed down their horses. They needed these mounts fresh and strong by late evening because both horses and riders faced a long, tedious night. Frank Sparks, along with Clint Eliot and Laura Renault, prepared an almost festive meal, cooking slabs of bacon, potatoes, hot rolls, and even heating up jerky. The gang members enjoyed the satisfying repast, which was even topped off with sugar to sweeten the coffee. Then they settled into their bedrolls to sleep through the remainder of the afternoon and into the early evening. The men took turns on watch, each on a one-hour stint. Laura Renault was exempt, since she had cleaned up after the meal.

Soon, Jerry Roseberry noted that an irritation had returned to Dude Rawlings' face, and he knew that the gang leader's mind had again drifted to their lost companion, Colorado McIver. Roseberry reached over and tapped Rawlings on the shoulder. "Dude, you've got to forget Colorado."

"I can't help thinkin' about that fool."

"You warned him clear enough," Roseberry said. "He wouldn't listen and he got himself caught. We've got a big job tonight and you mustn't concentrate on anything but that."

"It ain't even so much that he was caught," the Dude scowled, "but I'm burnin' when I think that

27

a goddamn bounty hunter took 'im. Houston, Brake told us his name, Pete Houston. I got no use for men who hunt down others for money. It wouldn't 'ave been so bad if a lawman got McIver."

"If you keep steaming about it, it won't do us any good," Roseberry said.

"You're right, Cap." Rawlings nodded. "Right now, I got to think about tonight and nothin' else. But I'll tell you one thing"—he gestured—"as soon as this job is done, I'm going after that bastard Houston."

"Now you're talking as stupidly as Colorado did," Roseberry said. "They know about you, Anias, Sparks, and Preacher. They've got your pictures on wanted posters. Not only lawmen, but Pinkerton agents and bounty hunters, are on the lookout for you. Outside of anywhere but maybe Jaycee, somebody would spot you and arrest you.

"Cap is right, Dude." The two men looked up to see Laura Renault suddenly squat next to them. "I'm sorry about Colorado, too," the girl said,"but at least he's strong and he won't talk. I'd hate to see you taken in, Dude. Some a the others with us might run off like madmen to save you, and get taken themselves. The Preacher adores you and he'd be the first who tried to break you out of a jail cell. But if he got caught, he might get religion again, and then some brim-and-hellfire reverend might convince him to confess all to save his soul. And then there's Sparks. He also worships you, Dude, and he'd also go stampedin' into Buffalo or Sheridan to save you. Now, we all know that he ain't got much brains, and some smart sheriff or Pinkerton agent could easily wheedle a confession out of 'im."

"You really think those boys would do that?" The Dude grinned.

"They'd surely go off hell-bent to free you, and in that kinda mood, they'd get caught without a doubt."

"What about Cap, Laura?" Rawlings asked.

"He's too smart to jump into any fryin' pan," the girl said.

The Dude shuttled his glance between Cap Roseberry and the girl. "I got a coupla real counselors in you two, ain't I? But, I got to admit, there's a lota sense in what you say, Laura. Still, somethin'll have to be done about that Houston. If he's as good as Nebraska Brake says he is, and if he's as dogged as Brake says, he'll surely come after the rest of us."

Roseberry leaned closer to the gang leader. "That's the best part, Dude—letting that bounty hunter come after us. Then we can take care of him on our own terms."

Rawlings scowled. "Maybe he won't try to get any of the rest of us."

"He will, Dude," Laura pointed. "Once he collects that bounty on Colorado, he'll like the feel of it. If he sees a chance for more easy cash, and the price is right, why, he'll walk through a field a rattlesnakes to find us."

Dude Rawlings grinned.

"The price will surely go up after tonight," Laura Renault continued. "When we clean that herd off the RX Ranch, the bounty on you and the others will double, maybe even triple. That'll draw that bounty hunter right into our nest."

The Dude nodded. "You're a smart girl, Laura. Too bad you don't have some warmth in you to go along with your smarts." The girl said nothing and the Dude leaned forward. "Are you ever goin' to warm up to a man? Don't you ever feel a desire or a need for a man?"

"When or if I want a man, I'll pick 'im out," the girl answered. "Everything has been fine so far. I'm doin' my part and earnin' good pay. That's how I want to leave it right now."

"Sure, Laura, sure." Rawlings nodded.

"Get some sleep, Laura," Jerry Roseberry said. "It'll be a long night."

Laura Renault looked at the ex-army captain, studying his thick mop of sandy hair, his deep-set blue eyes, his strong oval face, and the broad shoulders on his tall, muscular frame. He was the gentleman in this crowd of rustlers and she felt a deep respect for him. If there was a man in this gang she could get close to, that honor would go to the intelligent, sensitive, modest ex-army captain. She smiled at Cap. "That's good advice."

By nine P.M., when darkness had completely enveloped the rough open country of northern Wyoming, the eight gang members had saddled their horses. The octet studied the map once more before dowsing the campfire over which they had only boiled some coffee. Then Dude Rawlings looked at his followers.

"Now, does ever'body know what to do? You,

30

Pedro, make sure you and Sparks take care a the guard on the north, but don't kill 'im. And you, Big Val, make sure you don't cause no stampede when you and the Cap get that guard on the south. The rest of us will take care a the two on the riverbank, while Preacher stays with the horses. Anybody got any questions? Anybody who don't know what to do?"

No one answered.

"Then, let's move out."

Within an hour, the rustlers had come within a mile of the herd and reined up in a clump of trees. Rawlings had the others wait while he and Roseberry crouched down, moved cautiously into the open, and slithered to a knoll for a good view of the herd. In the moonlight, they could see the huge mass of cattle already bedded down for the night. The animals appeared relaxed and content, so they would be no problem if Rawlings and his cohorts moved quickly and noiselessly against the guards. The pair could also see the silhouettes of the two mounted guards, one on the northern perimeter and the other along the southern side of the herd. And finally, the gang leader and his companion caught sight of the campfire down at the riverbank where two more men loitered.

"It doesn't look bad," Roseberry said. "Those guards are half asleep in their saddles, just as Sparks said. They aren't expecting anyone tonight."

Rawlings nodded before the two men returned to the clump of trees. "Pedro, you and Sparks move on that guard to the north. Big Val, you and

31

Cap get after the guard on the south. Laura and Wild Man will come with me and we'll move on their campsite from the riverbank. Preacher, keep a good hold on the horses. I'll signal you from the camp on the river and then you bring the mounts down there."

"I'll be watchin'," Rogers said.

The four sentinels, meanwhile, continued their leisurely pace in their flannel shirts, leather chaps, Levi trousers, high-heeled boots, and six-guns strapped around their waists. Only their spurs made any sounds, jingling lightly as the cowpunchers moved about.

While Rogers remained in the grove of trees with the horses, the others worked quickly and effectively. Pedro Anias and Frank Sparks crawled stealthily up to the cowhand on the north. They waited until he paused to roll himself a cigarette. Then, Anias whirled a lasso around him and yanked him to the ground before Sparks rushed up to him and pistol-whipped him into unconsciousness with his six-gun. The two outlaws then quickly bound and gagged the man and left him next to his horse.

Roseberry and Big Val proved equally adept as they snaked up to the guard on the south. Here, Roseberry also lassoed the man in surprise and yanked him to the ground from his horse. Big Val Henry then came up quickly and stomped on the man's chest, knocking the breath out of him and almost rendering him unconscious. He might have stomped the cowhand again and perhaps killed him if Roseberry had not intervened. The duo quickly gagged and tied the dazed guard and left him wiggling helplessly on the ground.

Meanwhile, Rawlings, Laura, and Wild Man had worked their way quickly to the riverbank where the other two sentinels sat on a log, relaxing and drinking coffee, while they peered into the darkness at the huge herd that lay quietly like a glob of big black rocks. Rawlings and Eliot, both wearing bandannas over their faces, suddenly came up a slight rise from the river and pointed the barrels of their guns at the two cowpunchers.

"Don't move and don't yell," Rawlings cried in a harsh command, "or we'll blow your heads off."

The astonished sentinels stiffened in terror and sat like carved statues. "Get 'em up," Rawlings continued. When the duo complied, Eliot yanked the six-shooters from their holsters, while Rawlings cried out, "Come out!" Laura Renault suddenly emerged from the trees. "Tie them and gag them."

The two cowpunchers remained immobile, while Clint Eliot and Laura Renault, who also wore a bandanna over her face, quickly tied the ankles of the two men. Then they tied their wrists, while Rawlings stood erect and held a gun on the prisoners. As the outlaws began gagging them, the cowpunchers studied their captives in a mixture of fear, awe, and curiosity. They looked hard at Laura, at the sparkling hazel eyes, the clean skin of her upper face and forehead, the eyebrows, and the slender body. The guards guessed that this interloper was a girl, a very pretty young woman.

One of the cowpunchers then stared hard at Eliot, at his disheveled mop of hair, his thick eyebrows, wide forehead, and dark, sadistic eyes. The cowhand then pursed his lips hard to hide his astonishment. He recognized this second captor as Clint "Wild Man" Eliot, a former cowpuncher with whom he had once worked.

When Wild Man and Laura finished gagging the two cowpunchers, the captives looked at Rawlings. The outlaw leader could not hide his long, narrow face, despite the bandanna that came just below his eyes, and the sentinels knew that he was the rustler gang leader, that Dude Rawlings who had stolen other herds from other ranches. Yet, the recognition had relaxed them, for they also knew that the Rawlings gang had never killed or seriously harmed anyone, and that they also could expect to come out of this unscathed.

When the trio finished with the two men, Rawlings ignited a piece of brush, hurried into the open, and waved the improvised torch. A moment later, he heard the clop of hoofs as Rogers came out of the trees with the horses. By the time the Preacher reached the campsite, the other four men had also arrived.

"Did you take care of the others?" Rawlings asked Roseberry and Sparks. The two men nodded. "Okay, then, let's move this herd," the Dude gestured.

The two bound guards watched the octet mount their horses and lope out of the campsite. A moment later, they heard the cattle stir and bawl, they heard the stomps of horses and they heard the yells of men. Rawlings and his gang had roused the huge herd of cattle and were now urging them off on a northerly course in a loping, endless line. These rustlers were moving in near silence, and since they were some two miles from the ranch and bunkhouses, no one there would hear them. By the time any relief arrived in the morning, the rustlers would be long gone with over three hundred head of cattle.

Rawlings and his party moved swiftly and efficiently, leading the cattle over a route north-ward on the open prairie that skirted the Powder River. After they had traveled nearly thirty miles, far to the northwest of Buffalo, they drove the herd into a shallow length of the river and led them on through the water. Five miles later, Rawlings veered twenty head up a bank and sent Sparks and Eliot swiftly eastward with these cattle.

"You take 'em at least fifteen miles out, then abandon them and come back to the river. You can catch up to us in Recluse Ridge Canyon, where we take our stolen animals."

"We'll be all right," Wild Man Eliot said.

After Sparks and Eliot disappeared with these few head of steers, Rawlings and the others continued driving the huge herd northward. They moved through the river for another ten miles. Then, as the water deepened, the outlaws pointed the stolen cattle up the riverbank and northwest-ward. The outlaw leader left behind Roseberry and Anias, who gathered some brush to try and cover the tracks behind them. Again, Rawlings hoped to hide the spot where he had actually continued overland with the herd. Surely, when or if any pursuers found the mere twenty head and recognized the ruse, they would continue up the river to try to find the real place where the outlaws had left the stream.

The first band of daylight had brightened a ribbon of sky to the east above the Black Hills when the six outlaws drove the herd into the well-obscured Recluse Ridge Canyon, some five miles north of the hamlet of Spotted Horse. Once they moved the animals inside, the rustlers constructed a long, strong fence to keep the steers confined. They had hardly finished when three riders loped toward the canyon. Dude Rawlings recognized one of them as Rene Balfonte, the biggest black-market cattle dealer in the high country. Balfonte was bringing two men with him to examine the herd. By the time the first rays of sunshine emerged over the misty peaks, Balfonte had dismounted and walked up to Rawlings.

"Looks like you did real well, Dude," the black marketeer grinned as he scanned the herd.

"The best; over three hundred of the best," Rawlings said.

"Three hundred twenty-one head to be exact," Jerry Roseberry said.

"They're prime beef," the Dude pointed. "They came off one a the best ranges in Johnson County."

"How far?"

"About fifty miles."

Balfonte nodded. "That means it'll take 'em at least a day to get a lead on these steers. By that time we'll have the brands changed on my range." He cocked his head at his companions, who nodded and then hurried into the canyon. Here they quickly surveyed the herd while making an accurate count. Within five minutes they had returned.

"It's real good stock, Mr. Balfonte," one of his men said, "and we counted three hundred twenty-one head, just like Mr. Rawlings said."

The well-dressed Balfonte nodded, then he ambled to his saddlebag and pulled out a wad of money, before coming back to Rawlings. "You told me the job would bring about three hundred head, so I've got thirty-five hundred dollars in this purse. That should cover the price."

"I'm delighted, Rene." Rawlings grinned.

"Now, you'd best get yourself and your people outta here," Balfonte said. "I don't want any sign a you within twenty-five miles a my range in case some lawmen find these cattle."

"We got no more business here," Rawlings said.

Balfonte nodded and then turned to one of his companions. "Ernie, get the boys. Tell 'em we got to have 'em here in a hurry because we got a big job today."

"Yes sir, Mr. Balfonte."

At about the same moment, Frank Sparks and Clint Eliot loped through the canyon mouth, having completed the job of moving twenty head in a ruse. They quickly joined their fellow rustlers. Sparks leaned from his saddle and grinned at Dude Rawlings.

"Dude, we left a trail that nobody could miss. A posse could be ridin' through that stretch a prairie for a week before they found out what we did."

"Good." Rawlings nodded. He turned to his other companions. "Lets go. We want to be back at our place in the Hole In The Wall country before anybody starts after us." He slipped the purse of money into his saddlebag. "We'll divvy up back at the hideaway."

Rene Balfonte and his hand stood quietly and watched the octet of cattle rustlers lope away from the canyon and then break into a trot. The hand turned to his boss.

"They sure brought us good stock."

But Rene Balfonte scowled. "Trouble is, the Dude will soon enough realize how much this kinda beef is really worth, and he'll be wantin' more money next time."

CHAPTER THREE

When Pete Houston left the cattlemen's association office, he did not go immediately to the sheriff's office for his horse. Instead, he stopped first at the Rawhide Saloon that he found quite crowded even at this noontime hour: drifters, townspeople on lunch hours, and men in Buffalo on business. A piano player banged away on the keyboard, pausing only briefly to sip from a large stein of beer on the piano top. Two bartenders worked feverishly behind the bar and waiters weaved deftly through the crowd to bring them food and drink at the tables.

Along one side of the wall, two housemen ran a roulette wheel and a dice table. However, they had few takers at this time of day, only two customers at the wheel and three at the dice table. Two women in tight-fitting dresses, with heavy mascara on their faces, loitered in a corner, obviously waiting for patrons to take upstairs.

Despite the throng in the saloon, Pete found a table and sat down. He lingered only a few minutes, simply observing those around him, before a waiter came next to him and took his order for beer and a roast beef sandwich. Another five minutes passed before the waiter returned with the food.

"It's real cold, mister," the waiter said of the beer. "We got our own icehouse." When Houston nodded, the man gestured. "Enjoy your sandwich."

As Houston ate, he continued to study others in the saloon, especially the well-dressed man who was dealing poker hands at a nearby table. The man, an obvious card shark, was doing well in the game with three rough-hewn men, apparent miners who had come into town for some diversion. But as the game progressed, Houston could see that one of the miners was growing more irate as he continued to lose. He was soon eyeing the neatly dressed man with more and more resentment. Suddenly, as the gambler dealt a new hand, the miner gripped his wrist, forcing a card at the bottom of the deck to fall from the gambler's thumb to the table. The miner then slapped the dealer's hand, sending the cards flying in a confetti of flat oblongs. The prospector then rose from his chair, leaned over the table, and glared at his fellow card player.

"You no-good son of a bitch," he cried. "You've been cheatin' us!"

The gambler did not speak and the miner suddenly swung viciously, catching the well-dressed man on his narrow face and sending him sprawling to the floor. "I'm gonna kill you, you goddamn bastard!"

The well-dressed man's eyes bulged in horror as the miner reached into his holster and took out his six-gun. However, as he aimed the weapon at the downed gambler, Pete Houston bounded from his chair and lurched to the table, grabbing the angry man's wrist in a tight grip.

"Don't do it!"

The miner turned and glowered at Houston. "Who the hell are you? This ain't no business of yours."

"You'll only end up in jail if you shoot him." Pete cocked his head at the fallen man who was wiping the blood from his jaw.

"He's a no-good cheat," the miner said. "I come in here for an honest poker game. I don't mind losin' if the game is straight, but I ain't givin' away hard-earned money to a goddamn thief."

The other two men at the table did not say anything, nor did they even move. They simply sat immobile and watched Pete Houston and their fellow prospector, while the terrified gambler remained half-sprawled on the floor. Pete looked at the stack of chips on the table in front of the gambler's now-overturned chair. He forced down the miner's gun to the table and he then brushed the chips to the center of the table.

"A snake like that isn't worth it," Pete said.

"A varmint like that deserves to be dead," the angry miner retorted.

"There's all your money." Pete gestured to the middle of the table. "Divide up the chips, cash them in, and get out of here. That man won't complain"—he gestured to the fallen gambler—

"because he knows the law here in Buffalo isn't likely to sympathize with a cheat."

"He's givin' us good advice, Hank," another of the miners at the table said, cocking his head at Houston.

"All right, all right." The standing man nodded. Then he sighed, mitigating some of his fury. Slowly he placed the gun back in his holster before he divided up the chips with his companions, each of whom seemed satisfied. When they finished, one of the men looked at Houston.

"I'm sure glad you didn't let Hank get into real trouble."

"My pleasure," Pete answered.

The third miner now pumped Houston's hand. "I'd like to thank you, too. Hank's got a quick temper. Sometimes he acts before he thinks, although he sure had good cause against that varmint cheatin' us. We got a shack down in the Devil's Peak area where we've been pannin' for silver. Not doin' bad. If you're ever down that way, why, we'd be happy to have you stop in and see us."

Pete Houston frowned. "You're just outside the Hole In The Wall country, isn't that so?"

"You could say that," the miner said, nodding.

"Have you been having trouble with any of those outlaws in there?"

"No, they don't seem to bother us. I guess they're too busy stayin' outta sight from the law since them big companies like Wells Fargo started offerin' rewards. Them thieves and rustlers holed up in there not only have the law chasin' after them, but also every Pinkerton agent and bounty

42

hunter in the territory is lookin' for 'em. If they do need a change, why, they jes' take a quick run into Egleston and then scoot back into the hills. I heard that a bounty hunter took in one of them from that big rustlin' gang only a coupla days ago, when the outlaw came into Egleston just for a cold beer."

Pete Houston did not answer.

"My name is George Caruthers," the man continued. "This is Howie Baker and that hot tempered one is Hank Peters."

Peters, now calm, grinned at Houston. "I guess you did me a favor, mister."

Houston shook his hand. "My name is Pete Houston, and I might surely take up your friend's offer if I'm around the Devil's Peak area." He glanced at each of the trio. "You boys take care of yourselves."

"We'll do that," George Caruthers said.

Houston watched the three men walk off and up to the caged window where they cashed in their chips. He then eyed them as they weaved through the crowd and out the door. Meanwhile, the gambler picked himself up from the floor and slumped into one of the now-empty chairs before he wiped the blood from his face again. He looked at Houston but said nothing. When Pete stared harshly at him, the gambler studied the blood on the back of his hand and then looked at Houston with a grin.

"I suppose I owe you somethin'," the well-dressed man finally spoke.

"You're a damn fool, mister," Pete said, "but I

43

can't say I feel any pity for you. That miner had good reason to kill you."

The gambler extracted a handkerchief from his coat and wiped his jaw as well as the back of his hand. Then he shrugged. "This is my business, just like those miners are in the business a robbin' the earth, and you're in the business a robbin' men's freedom."

The gambler grinned as Pete Houston frowned and stared hard at him. "I recognize you. You're that bounty hunter Houston, and a damn good one. You bring in your man for sure money, the miners desecrate the land for money, and I cheat at cards. We all take advantage a somethin' to make a livin'."

"How do you know about me?"

"I saw you take Colorado McIver in Egleston," the gambler answered. "The word now around Jaycee and Egleston is to keep an eye out for Houston. They say Houston is hard and clever, and he can snare a wanted man better than Ute Indians can snare trout out of a stream."

Pete Houston dropped into one of the other empty chairs at the table and leaned forward. "I didn't know I was so well known."

"They know you, all right," the gambler said, nodding, "and more than one of them would like to get you. I'd guess that the bounty hunters those prospectors were talking about was nobody but you. I must tell you, Mr. Houston, that if you bring in any more of those outlaws from that rustling gang, so that you make it unsafe for them to come out of their Hole In The Wall hiding places, why, they may put a bounty on your head."

"You seem to know an awful lot, mister."

"McClure; Edward McClure," the gambler said, grinning again. "Yes, I know a lot because I get around a lot, and I do more listenin' than talkin'. Outlaws have little else to do but play cards when they aren't robbing safes or rustling cattle. I've been inside the Hole In The Wall country a few times and met some a these people; and they come into Egleston quite often for a chance to play with a real poker player."

"And none of them have caught you cheating and shot you dead?"

"I don't cheat down there. I don't have to." He shrugged. "Them outlaws mostly start drinkin' hard when they come into town and they can hardly think by the time they start playin' poker with me. But even if they're cold sober, most of 'em can't play poker worth a damn."

"I see," Pete said.

"Like I said," McClure continued, "I owe you somethin' for probably savin' my life, and maybe I can do you a favor. I'll be goin' back to Egleston tomorrow, and I heard plenty down there from those who come outta the Hole In The Wall country for diversion. Considerin' that McIver was a rustler, I'd guess he was a member a the Rawlings gang. I got an idea where they are and maybe I can even learn what they plan to do next. Some of 'em do come into town to play cards with me. If you come down to Egleston, look me up and I'll give you any information I can pick up. That'll repay you for savin' my life."

45

"I don't know as I want any information from the likes of you."

Edward McClure sneered. "Don't start preachin' morals, Houston. Your trade is worse than mine. I only cheat men outta their money, and they can always get more. You cheat 'em outta freedom, and maybe even outta their lives."

Pete Houston made no response, and he remained seated as McClure rose from the table. "It was a pleasure meetin' you in person, Houston, and like I say, I'm surely obliged to you. Remember, if you come down to Egleston, look me up. I could have some real good information for you."

"I might do that," Pete answered. He watched the gambler walk away, weaving through the crowd and out of the saloon. When McClure was gone, Pete returned to his own table, but his face soured when he took a heavy gulp of his beer. It was flat. However, he did enjoy his roast beef sandwich. When he finished the meal, he left the table and threaded his way around the saloon patrons before he left the Rawhide. Outside, he took a deep breath, inhaling the fresh air.

Pete Houston was quite tired now, and uncomfortable from the grime that had accumulated on his clothes. He continued up the boardwalk to get his horse from the post in front of the sheriff's office, but he did not stop inside the jailhouse to speak to Angus or anyone else. He loped through the crowded street and veered into 14th Street to the Mercer Hotel, walking the animal through the pathway next to the two-story structure and into the barn at the rear of the hotel. Then, he led

46

his horse into a stall before he loosened his bedroll, emptied his saddlebags, and took out his rifle. He left the horse in the stall, walked through the small courtyard, and entered the hotel through the rear door. When he came into the small lobby the desk clerk greeted him.

"Mr. Houston, glad to see you back. I hope you had a successful venture."

Houston nodded. "Can you draw me a bath? I'd like to clean up a little."

"Sure thing, Mr. Houston. I'll have it ready in about fifteen minutes. Will that be all right?"

"That'll be fine," Houston said. Then he gestured toward the rear of the hotel. "I've got my horse in stall three. Will you have someone unsaddle him and brush him down?"

"We'll also take care of that, Mr. Houston."

The bounty hunter, carrying his gear and rifle, walked up the rickety staircase to the second floor and then down the hall before he stopped at room twenty-three. He fumbled for his key, found it, and opened the door. Inside, he dropped his gear on the floor before he took off his hat and holster and hung them on a rack. Next, he felt the bed before he flopped on it and stretched out. The softness made him feel good, but he knew he could not stay there long. Five minutes later, he hoisted himself to a sitting position and undressed, from his boots to his underwear, until he was stark naked. Then he opened the clothes closet, pulled out a robe, and put it on. Next, he gathered up his clothes and left the room. A few minutes later, he was downstairs in the bathhouse.

Houston found old Charlie already pouring hot water into a tub, and the hotel bathman looked up at the bounty hunter and grinned. "Nice to see you back, Mr. Houston."

Pete nodded and a few minutes later he was sitting in the hot tub. The bath exhilarated him and the warm water soothed his tired muscles. He cleansed himself thoroughly with the soap that Charlie offered him.

"I'll see that your clothes are cleaned," Charlie said, "and I'll polish your boots. You should have them back by late this afternoon."

Again Houston nodded, while he closed his eyes and relaxed in the tub. About ten minutes later, he got out, dried himself off with a towel that the bathman had given him, and then put on his robe.

"I'm going to sleep for a while, Charlie. Wake me up about four o'clock. Will you do that?"

"Sure thing," the bathman said.

Houston then left the bathhouse, walked up the stairs and back into his room. Again he stretched out on the bed, and this time, after the pleasant bath, he quickly fell asleep. Pete slumbered soundly and old Charlie knocked at the door of room twenty-three at four o'clock, tapping the door two or three times without a response. He finally pounded on the door before the bounty hunter awoke.

"Are you up, Mr. Houston?"

"All right, Charlie; thanks."

Pete Houston was still tired when he rose from the bed, but the thought of seeing Jane Clemons recharged his vigor. He took off his robe and, again naked, shaved himself, using the water from a basin. When he finished, he opened the closet and took out a neat suit, tie, and shirt. After laying them on the bed, he opened the dresser drawer to take out clean underwear and socks. After he slipped these on, he dressed neatly and put on a pair of shoes.

By four-thirty he was fully dressed. He combed his hair neatly in front of a mirror and then set his bowler hat on his head. He then took some money from a money box before locking the box and slipping it inside a drawer. He left the room, locking the door after him.

Outside the hotel, Houston walked briskly, and when he reached Gillette Street he found the avenue still crowded. He looked at his pocket watch: 4:50. He would meet the girl right on time. And, in fact, at just about five o'clock he walked into the cattlemen's association office where the girl behind the counter was just putting away the last of some papers before closing up. When she looked up, she gaped and then smiled at the visitor.

"Mr. Houston? Is that you?"

"You told me five o'clock," Pete answered.

"I must say," the girl said, "you look more like one of those rich bankers than a man who spends most of his time chasin' outlaws."

"Would you rather I had come in here wearing dirty trail clothes?"

"Oh no"—she gestured—"but I'll look a little shabby walkin' down the street with you."

"Miss Clemons," Pete grinned, "there's not a

thing about you that's shabby. I'd be right proud to have you walk down the street with me." He searched the room and then turned to the girl again. "Is Big Jim still in his office?"

"He left a few minutes ago and told me to lock up."

"It doesn't matter." Pete shrugged. "It's you I came to see, anyway."

"You'll need to let me freshen up a bit. You don't mind if I do that, do you, Mr. Houston?"

"I'll wait."

The girl ducked into a small room, obviously the toilet room, and she came out a few minutes later. She had washed her face, combed her hair neatly, and straightened her dress. When she smiled, Pete grinned again. Yes, she was surely beautiful and he felt pleased to have her as a companion this evening. Jane Clemons locked a desk drawer and a cabinet drawer before she picked up her handbag and came around from the counter. When she left the building, she also locked the front door and slipped the key into her bag.

"Are you hungry?" Pete asked.

"Starving," the girl answered.

"We can go to the Buffalo Cafe. They serve good meals there."

"I know," Jane Clemons said.

As they walked down the boardwalk, Pete grinned at the girl again. "I suspect you've had plenty of offers to go to dinner."

"I suppose so," the girl answered.

Once seated inside the restuarant, Pete ordered

a steak dinner and Jane Clemons ordered ham. While they waited, Pete looked admiringly at the girl. "You brought some sunshine into that office, that's for sure." The girl only smiled and Pete continued. "You say you've only been there a week. Might I ask what you did before you started working for Big Jim?"

The girl shrugged. "I've always worked in one office or another."

Jane Clemons told Pete Houston that she had originally come from Cheyenne where her father had worked in the bank, and where he had thus become associated with many of the Wyoming ranchers as well as officers in the main branch of the Wyoming Cattlemen's Association at Cheyenne. She herself, after learning basic reading, writing, and arithmetic in a Cheyenne school, had helped out her mother at home in household chores until she had become old enough to take a job in the bank. When she too became acquainted with many of the association ranchers and officers, the association president had offered her a job as a clerk at the association office. She had accepted the position in Cheyenne because the pay was much better than the wages at the bank.

Just after her twentieth birthday, Jane's father had died, some two years after her mother. She had then moved north to live with an aunt in Sheridan, taking a job as an office clerk at the Sheridan branch of the Wyoming Cattlemen's Association. Then, a couple of weeks ago, she was told that the Buffalo office of the association needed a clerk and that Big Jim Simeon would be

51

delighted to hire a woman with her experience. He had offered her top pay of fifteen dollars a week.

"That's pretty high wages for a clerk," Houston said.

"That's why I took the job," Jane Clemons answered. "I've got a small flat at the Durand Boarding House on Thirteenth Street and it suits me fine. I have no problem. Big Jim is real nice to work for, and I've made some new friends here in town. I've already joined the Evangelic Circle at Christ's Church, which I joined, and some of the people there have asked me to join the Auxiliary Circle at the town hall. It didn't take me long, I must say, to become acquainted with a lot of people in Buffalo."

"That's real nice," Pete said.

The girl suddenly reached over the table and touched Houston's hand, and the soft touch sent an electric shock through his muscular frame. Then she looked seriously at him. "Mr. Houston, I worry about a man who's in your kinda dangerous business."

"Everybody has to earn a living," Pete answered. "I chose mine freely and I'm willing to take any risks that go along with this kind of occupation."

"Don't you ever think about settlin' down with a wife and maybe with a few children?"

"I guess every man has."

"Could you have a family and still stay in your kinda profession? It's not only dangerous, but it keeps you away so much a the time."

"I suppose that's why I never thought seriously about getting married." He suddenly looked deeply into the girl's sparkling blue eyes. "I'll say it again, Miss Clemons: you're one of the most beautiful women I've ever seen in a long time. It'd sure be easy to share a lifetime in marriage with someone like you."

"And would you give up your kinda profession to marry and settle down with someone like me?"

Houston did not answer.

The girl sighed and moved her hand away from Houston. "That's what I figured."

Fortunately, the waiter arrived and served the meal to interrupt the awkward moment. For the next several minutes Pete Houston and Jane Clemons ate in relative silence. Then, Pete spoke to the girl again.

"You know, Miss Clemons—"

"Jane, please call me Jane," the girl interrupted.

"All right, Jane"—Pete grinned—"so long as you call me Pete instead of Mr. Houston."

"Sure, Pete." The girl nodded.

"Anyway, Jane, I'm sure you must know that my profession isn't the only one that could be dangerous. Lawmen and Pinkerton agents face danger, and miners face even worse dangers inside those holes deep inside the earth. Cowhands could get hurt or killed in a stampede. A train crew could get maimed in a wreck, or even a blacksmith could get killed by an ornery horse. There's actually no guarantees for any one of us."

"I suppose you've got a point there, Pete, but

53

still—chasin' after dangerous outlaws . . ."

"Those outlaws aren't really dangerous," Pete said. "They're mostly cowards who'd rather run than face a fight, and when they're cornered they just give up without a whimper for the most part. To tell you the truth, it's safer to run down one of those cowardly lawbreakers than to run down a maverick steer. And now that I think of it, as for being away a lot, why, I suspect that I spend more time in Buffalo and in my hotel room than most other people who work outdoors: cowpunchers always on the trail; marshals, deputies, and Pinkerton agents on the highway; drummers who spend their whole lives on the road selling goods; hunters and trappers away for weeks or months at a time. Why, I'd be home so often a wife and family would likely get bored with me," he finished with a grin.

"Pete, you sure got a fancy way of making your occupation seem reasonable."

"Eat your supper," Pete said.

The girl nodded and once more they ate their evening meal in relative silence. When they finished and Pete paid the check, the duo walked along the boardwalk of Gillette Avenue. Dusk had descended over Johnson County now and darkness would soon envelop Buffalo.

"I wish I knew where to take you now," Pete said, "but if you belong to the Evangelic Circle, I'd guess I couldn't take you into one of the saloons."

"Not likely."

"Maybe we could just walk."

"It's a nice evening for that," the girl said.

Pete Houston and Jane Clemons ambled up the street for another hour, occasionally stopping to stare into the windows of shops that were not closed. They halted before the Buffalo Theatre where a sign promised a new play coming next week. They agreed that perhaps they could attend this performance together. Finally, at about seven, they reached the park, kept neatly by the town fathers. Here, they sat on a bench and talked some more. Jane Clemons still tried to persuade Houston that bounty hunting was not a desirable occupation, and Pete again countered: it was a job he liked and a job that paid fairly good money. He did not consider the work particularly dangerous. However, in time, as he saved enough money and lost his fervor for the outdoor life, he might start some kind of small business.

By eight o'clock, they left the park.

"I'm gettin' kinda tired, Pete. Maybe you can walk me home to the Durand Boarding House."

"I'd like that."

They walked slowly, arm in arm now, with Jane Clemons occasionally snuggling close to her escort. Soon, they reached the boardinghouse and came up onto the porch. They stood looking at each other in mutual admiration, and perhaps even with reciprocal passion beaming from their eyes. Houston kissed the girl softly on the lips, and Jane Clemons responded with a kiss of her own but then recoiled.

"I'd like you to come to my flat," she whispered, "I really believe I would. But, I can't do that, Pete."

"I understand," Houston answered. "All I'd like to ask of you is that I can see you again sometime."

"I'd sure look forward to that," Jane Clemons answered. Then she reached up and kissed Houston again. "Good night, Pete." Houston stood on the porch and watched the girl disappear into the house. Then, he sighed and left.

Pete Houston was also tired and he went back to his hotel where he undressed, slipped under the covers, and soon fell into a deep slumber. He needed the sleep badly, and he slept for a full twelve hours before awakening at nine the next morning. Houston was surprised that he had slept so long and so soundly, and he actually felt more bone weary than refreshed. Still, he cleaned up, dressed in simple chino pants and shirt, put on his gunbelt and Stetson hat this time, and went to the Buffalo Cafe for breakfast. He had been there only about fifteen minutes when Big Joe Simeon suddenly came into the place, spotted Houston, hurried to his table, and flopped into a chair across from the bounty hunter.

"Pete, I've been looking all over for you."

"Why, what's the problem?"

"I got a couple of telegrams from Gillette. The Rawlings gang: they rustled over three hundred head from the RX Ranch rangeland on the Powder River. A ranch posse is looking for them now, but it seems the gang did a real good job of hiding their tracks. But guess what?" Simeon said. "Two of the cowpuncher guards said that one of the rustlers was definitely a woman."

"A woman?"

56

"Yes," Simeon nodded vigorously. "She was one of them that tied up the guards at their camp on the riverbank, and those sentinels were sure she was a woman, a mighty pretty one with dark hazel eyes. And the guards identified the other one who tied them up, a man by the name of Clint Eliot, who worked as a puncher on a lot of ranches in Wyoming. Wild Man, they call him. Pete," the association executive said, "this job last night will certainly raise the bounty considerably on those outlaws, who'll no doubt head back to their hideaway in Hole In The Wall. You could earn a real big payday if you brought some of them in."

Pete Houston stroked his chin. He suddenly thought of Edward McClure, who by now might be on his way to Egleston. Yes, perhaps he should call on this gambler. The stakes could be real high now, and McClure could be just the person to give the bounty hunter a good lead.

CHAPTER FOUR

The prospects of earning perhaps twice the bounty as had been offered before for members of the Rawlings gang rustlers surely appealed to Pete Houston, especially since there was now another outlaw identified in the group, Clint "Wild Man" Eliot. But even beyond this, the report that a pretty woman with hazel eyes also ran with the gang had intrigued him. He now felt anxious to ride off again, especially if he could get a lead in Egleston from that gambler.

Houston promised Simeon that he would discuss this new development with him later and Big Jim nodded.

"I'll stop in your office sometime this afternoon."

"Good," Big Joe said. "Maybe I'll have more information by then." He then rose from the table and left the cafe.

After he finished breakfast, Pete stopped at the Wyoming Cattlemen's Bank to deposit $175.00, leaving him with well over $1,500.00 in his account. That left him with more that $50.00 in ready cash, which he considered ample to make the next trek southward, where he would not likely be gone for more than a week. When he finished at the bank, he stopped into one of the local shops to buy another set of riding clothes that he would take with him. As usual, he selected a tan shirt and trousers, his favorite color. Then Houston headed for the sheriff's office where he found Angus looking at some wanted posters. The sheriff grinned when he saw the bounty hunter.

"Pete, what can I do for you this morning?"

"Sheriff, did you know about the rustled herd from the RX Ranch last night?"

Angus squeezed his face. "One of the RX ranch hands left here a little while ago. The poor bastard was riding since five o'clock to bring this information to me. The rider changed horses a couple of times along the way to make better time. Of course,"—he gestured—"we already got a telegram from Gillette to inform us of the robbery."

Houston nodded.

"Relief people from the RX found those guards tied up when they got there early this morning," Angus continued.

"Did this rider mention that a woman, a pretty woman, was with the gang?" Pete asked. "And did they also identify another one of the rustlers as one Clint 'Wild Man' Eliot?"

"How did you know about that?" Angus frowned.

"Big Joe Simeon told me."

The sheriff nodded, then shrugged. "He must've got a telegram too. Anyway, I'm going to wire the Pinkertons in Sheridan for a photo of this Eliot. I'm told the man has a criminal record, so the Pinkertons will most likely have a picture of him in their rogues' gallery. I expect to have the photo of Eliot here in two or three days."

"I'd like to have a photo of the man, too."

"I'd guess that the cattlemen's association will also ask for photos, and you'll probably be able to get one from Big Joe. The one the Pinkertons send me will be used to make up a wanted poster."

"Of course," Pete said.

"Don't go off half-cocked, Pete," Angus said. "We're tryin' to find out where those rustlers will go, and maybe get out a sheriff's posse. Give it a day or two until we know more."

"I can wait," Pete said. "Anyway, like I said yesterday, I'd like to rest up a while." In fact, although Houston did not tell Angus, he wanted to give that gambler McClure time to learn something about the exact whereabouts and movements of Dude Rawlings and his fellow rustlers. Houston guessed that within two or three days McClure would have such information, so he would wait before he sought out the gambler.

When Pete Houston came into the cattlemen's association office about midafternoon, Jane Clemons greeted him with a warm smile. "Mr. Simeon is inside his office, Pete, but I don't think he knows any more now than he did this morning."

"Can I take you to dinner again tonight?" Pete grinned.

"I'm going to the Evangelic Circle tonight," she

answered. "We're meetin' to see how we can raise some money to fix the church roof."

"Too bad."

"Maybe you'd like to come along," Jane said, "join the congregation. Reverend Smith would surely welcome you as he would any others."

"A man in my profession?" Pete huffed. "Besides, I haven't been inside of a church in so long, I'd feel too uncomfortable."

"Don't you believe in God?" the girl asked soberly.

"I believe in Him, all right," Pete answered, "and I must admit, I've prayed to Him many times and still do. But, I guess I've lost touch with any kind of formal religion."

"You can always come back," the girl persisted.

Pete Houston was lost for an immediate reply, but, luckily, Big Joe Simeon suddenly came out of his office to hand some papers to Jane Clemons. He grinned when he saw Houston. "Ah, Pete. Wait for me inside." The bounty hunter nodded and ducked into the office of the association executive as Simeon handed the sheets to Jane. "Will you get these letters in envelopes and mail them out as soon as you can this afternoon?"

"I'll do that, Mr. Simeon."

As Big Joe reentered his office, he gestured Pete to a chair. When the bounty hunter sat down, Simeon walked behind his desk and fumbled through some papers on his desk, scanning three of them before looking at Houston.

"We've got two more telegrams since this morning. That RX Ranch posse hasn't found the trail of that rustled herd. The RX people can only guess that those outlaws ran them through the river for some distance, led the steers to shore again somewhere to the north, and then covered their tracks. It's uncanny how those rustlers could hide the route of three hundred or more steers. The other wire is from the main Wyoming Cattlemen's Association office in Cheyenne. As a result of that robbery last night, they've raised the bounty on the Rawlings gang. They've put a five hundred dollar price on each gang member, and a thousand dollar price on the head of Dude Rawlings himself."

"That's high."

"The association is making up new wanted posters with the revised bounty figure," Simeon continued. "They'll also make up a poster on this Clint 'Wild Man' Eliot. Those posters will probably be distributed by the end of the week. So maybe you'd like to get a fast start after those cattle thieves, and get the jump on a lot of other people."

"I appreciate that, Jim."

"I'm giving you this inside information before we go public because you've always done a good job for us and we owe you something. I'll have some photos of this Eliot by this time tomorrow and you can pick one up."

"I'll do that," Pete said, "and then start out day after tomorrow."

"Good, good," Big Joe Simeon said.

Although Houston did not see Jane Clemons that evening, he did see her the next day and he took her to the Buffalo Cafe for a noon meal. They enjoyed the special, beef stew, with coffee and hot rolls. When he told her that he'd be leaving Buffalo the next day for Egleston, she jerked.

"Pete, you don't intend to go after that gang alone?"

The bounty hunter shrugged.

"Who do you think you are, Hercules?" she asked disdainfully.

"It's not as though I'd walk right into a spider's web where a half-dozen guns could cut me down," Pete said. "I met somebody a couple of days ago, a man who's gone to Egleston and who can give me a lead on the movements of those Rawlings gang members. When I get that information, why, I'll just take them one at a time."

The girl frowned, unconvinced.

"Believe me, Jane," Pete persisted, "I don't intend to get myself in any real danger."

"When did you say you were leavin'?"

"In the morning, right after breakfast. I'll probably be out of Buffalo by eight o'clock and ride straight down the Johnson County Highway and maybe stop at Jaycee for some lunch. I should reach Egleston by midafternoon. I'll see what I can find out there and then go to work day after tomorrow. I shouldn't be gone for more than a few days."

The girl nodded.

The duo said little more to each other as they continued their noon meal, but at the next table, a small, roly-poly man had been listening intently to the conversation. The man, quite inconspicuous, was Dude Rawlings's eyes and ears in Buffalo. He had been hired by the outlaw to keep him informed of all that went on in this town: plans of Sheriff Red Angus, news of any leads the law might have on the Dude's movements and activities, and most recently any information on this bounty hunter Pete Houston. The obese man was Joe Cameron, on whom Rawlings depended.

Cameron had been observing Houston ever since the bounty hunter returned to Buffalo with Colorado McIver. He had seen Houston going about his business and he had seen him with the girl Jane Clemons, and now he had overheard this bounty hunter's plans to start off tomorrow after the Rawlings gang.

Cameron left his table unnoticed, and when he was outside the cafe he hurried to the telegraph office, where he sent a telegram to a cohort in Egleston. By midafternoon, the partner, a man named Nebraska Brake, had hurried out of Egleston and was riding into the Hole In The Wall wilderness to deliver Cameron's information to Dude Rawlings.

The hideout of the rustler gang lay about ten miles northeast of Egleston, deep in the Black Hills. To get there, a rider needed to snake through the canyons, around hills, over streams, and through thick wooded areas. The entire route could be treacherous if someone were lying in ambush to observe and pick off any oncoming rider. In fact, about a mile away from the hideaway was a narrow pass between steep rocks where Rawlings kept one man always on alert.

64

At about four in the afternoon Big Val Henry straightened in his sentinel position and watched the rider come closer. Henry kept his rifle on the ready, but when he clearly recognized the horseman as Nebraska Brake, he relaxed.

Henry watched Brake lope through the narrow pass and then once more rested, peering occasionally at the trail in front of him. After some ten or fifteen minutes more, Brake reached the Rawlings hideaway, a rather ornate log structure that included an uncluttered front porch, a log barn to keep the horses, a neat patch of open ground in front of the edifice, and a clear stream behind the house that separated the structure from a forested slope. Brake brought his horse across the open patch of ground and dismounted before he tethered the animal to a post. The man had started up the front steps when Jerry Roseberry stepped out on the porch and greeted him.

"Nebraska, do you have any news for us?"

"Plenty," the man answered.

"The Dude is inside and anxious to hear it." Roseberry cocked his head.

Within the log structure was a rather comfortable interior: a large living room with a fireplace, soft easy chairs, and two divans. A rack of books, tables, a bear rug on the floor, and even a victrola on an oak stand. Beyond the parlor was a dining room, the kitchen beyond that. Off to the side on the left were four good-sized bedrooms, and an added-on wing of the house included more sleeping quarters.

After his first caper had netted Rawlings

considerable money, the Dude had used most of the loot to construct the embellished structure that seemed so out of place in this Hole In The Wall wilderness. But, like so many other outlaws who hid out in this country, Rawlings wanted to live as well as he could where he needed to spend so much of his time.

Off the kitchen was a good-sized larder that was stocked with ample liquor, bags of beans, flour, sugar and potatoes, canned goods, some large pieces of salted beef and ham, and other food supplies. Rawlings made sure that he would eat and drink well in his hideaway.

Of course, when one had money, as Rawlings had, he could always find those to service him: men to build his house, to sell him furniture, to clear the surrounding land, to bring him needed supplies, and to feed him information.

Dude Rawlings, clad in a neat dark suit, silk shirt, and string tie, rose from a parlor chair and greeted Nebraska Brake. Preacher Rogers, Clint Eliot, and Pedro Anias were also sitting in the parlor. Frank Sparks was out back cutting wood and Laura Renault was in the kitchen preparing an evening meal of beef stew.

"Well, Nebraska?" Rawlings asked.

"Cameron sent me a couple of long wires from Buffalo, in our private code as usual," the visitor said. "I must tell you, Mr. Rawlings, that none a the news is any good."

"Out with it anyway."

"Cameron has been keepin' his eyes wide open up there and he's been askin' a lotta questions."

Brake looked at Clint Eliot. "Wild Man, there's some bad news for you. One a them guards you tied up the other night recognized you. Seems you worked on a ranch with him somewhere, and he knew you up close, even with your face covered." He looked at Rawlings. "The Pinkertons are makin' up new wanted posters on you, the Mex, Sparks, the Preacher, and now Wild Man. An' the cattlemen's association is doublin' the bounty on all of you, with yours goin' to a thousand dollars, Mr. Rawlings. That'll set a lotta hungry people after you."

Surprisingly, Dude Rawlings grinned. "Goddamn, Laura was right. After the RX Ranch caper, they did raise the ante on us. Maybe that bastard Houston will come runnin' after us."

"That was the next thing I was gonna tell you," Nebraska Brake continued. "Cameron has been keepin' a close eye on that bounty hunter in Buffalo, and he heard only today that Houston plans to start after you tomorrow. Seems he'll go right down the country highway, maybe stop for a meal at Jaycee, and then be in Egleston by tomorrow afternoon. I suppose he'll start after you day after tomorrow."

"Is the man loco?" Eliot huffed. "He's gonna ride into this area to get us? We'll kill 'im for sure."

"Maybe he won't need to come in here like a blind man," Brake said. "The worst part is that Cameron overheard Houston say that he knew somebody in Egleston who knows where you fellows are holed up and who knows your movements. If that's true, why, that bounty hunter will choose his own route and time to come in here, and maybe start pickin' you off one at a time. The talk in Buffalo is that this Houston has the patience of a cougar and he'll wait as long as it takes, especially with the kinda money that's on your heads now."

"The son of a bitch!" Rawlings cursed.

Pedro Anias now looked at Brake. "Ain't nobody who can come into a spider's web like that and take eight of us."

"There've been some," Blake said. "You remember that Pinkerton agent, that Springer, who came into the Hole In The Wall country and took them five members a that train robbery gang; and some of 'em were top guns. If Houston is as good as they say he is, why, you never can tell."

"Dude"—Roseberry turned to the outlaw leader—"there's just a chance that Blake is right. God knows, we'll have a slew of men coming after us once those new wanted posters are out. We don't need a man like Houston among them. I don't know how much truth there is about Houston finding someone in Egleston who knows our whereabouts and our movements, but there's no sense in taking chances."

"What do you suggest?" Rawlings asked.

"I say we get Houston before he reaches Egleston," Eliot replied. "He'll have to come through Devil's Pass. He'll be in the open and quite exposed. We can surely have a coupla men in the rocks on both sides to pick 'im off."

"That sounds right if the ambusher knows who

he is."

"You can't miss 'im," Blake said. "He's got a big bay horse that he loves better'n a man likes his wife or children. He wouldn't ride anything else. And he only wears tan-colored ridin' clothes, including his hat, along with a black holster and black boots. They say in Buffalo that whenever he rides out, that's how he dresses. He's expected to reach Jaycee just before noon, and if he stops for a bite, that should put him in Devil's Pass at early afternoon, the time a day when most people aren't on the highway. So, if your men spot such a rider, you'll know it can be nobody but that bounty hunter."

Dude Rawlings grinned. "Nebraska, can you find a coupla men in Egleston who'd be willin' to carry out this ambush for us?"

"Anybody you want," Blake said, shrugging.

"Wait a minute," Pedro Anias suddenly cried. "We don't need any outsiders. Me and Frank, we can do the job. We can both handle rifles pretty well, and I know that Frank would sure love to get that Houston. Frank's been moonin' ever since that bounty hunter took in Colorado, and he'd do anything he could to finish off Houston."

Dude looked at Roseberry. "What do you think, Cap?"

Roseberry nodded. "Pedro and Frank can probably do the job as well as anyone. Besides, the fewer people we have involved, the better. But," he said, "they should take him alive if possible."

Dude Rawlings scowled. "What are you talkin' about, Cap? The bounty hunter has to be killed."

69

"I don't like killings," Roseberry said.

"Sometimes there ain't no choice." Rawlings persisted.

Jerry Roseberry did not answer.

Dude Rawlings turned to Blake. "You did well, Nebraska, although the news you brought us ain't good. But, at least we know where we stand." He reached into his pocket and took out a roll of bills, handing the man two twenties. "One of them is for you and you can wire the other twenty to Cameron in Buffalo. I'm givin' you bonuses, a little extra this time, because you been doin' a good job. Keep it up. We need to be informed about everything."

Blake grinned as he took the money. "It's a pleasure workin' for you."

Frank Sparks was elated when asked to join Anias in a bushwhacking job against Pete Houston. He and the Mexican spent the rest of the day and early evening in readying themselves to leave in the morning at first light. Both men were eager, but Laura Renault warned them not to be overconfident.

"We've heard how good he is," the girl said, "and he's smart enough to figure out that somebody'll be looking for him if he comes after us."

"We ain't gonna give 'im a chance to take us, Laura, I can promise you that," Frank Sparks said.

"Just don't lose your heads in your enthusiasm."

"Niña,"—Anias grinned—"I know how to kill a man from ambush. In Mexico we did this many times. We will give this bounty hunter no chance at all to get suspicious before he is a dead man."

70

"I'm only tellin' you to be careful," Laura said. "Like I said, he's smart enough to guess that some-body will try to get him, and he'll be lookin' out for bushwhackers like a hawk lookin' for prey."

And in fact, some 40 miles away, in Buffalo, Pete Houston did indeed consider the possibility of an ambush on his way to Egleston. The bounty hunter had certainly suspected that Dude Raw-lings and his gang members were probably irate because he had taken in Colorado McIver for reward money. Pete also suspected that Dude Rawlings had people everywhere and that they informed him on what was going on. And perhaps, as soon as he left Buffalo in the morning, some informant might get word to the outlaw that Houston was on the way south. Pete was also smart enough to realize that ambushers would pick out an excellent hiding place to trap him.

In the evening, Pete again took Jane Clemons to dinner at the Buffalo Cafe, and he again walked with her arm in arm along the planked sidewalks abutting mired Gillette Avenue. They once more sat in the park for a while before Pete walked hand in hand with her to the boardinghouse. On the front porch, in the evening darkness, Jane Clemons held his hands and looked fervently into his dark eyes.

"You will be careful, won't you, Pete?"

Houston responded by kissing her lightly on the lips. The kiss prompted Jane to jerk and then to press herself closer to him and throw her arms around his neck. "I want you so bad, Pete. I just don't want anything to happen to you."

71

Pete kissed her again and he then pressed himself close to the girl before running his hand over her back and then around the back of her neck.

"It's still early, Jane," he whispered.

But the girl suddenly recoiled. "No, Pete, no. It ain't right. I want you bad, but it ain't right."

Pete Houston held her shoulders and pushed her gently away from him before he looked fervently into her sparkling blue eyes. "Meeting you has been one of the best things that ever happened to me, Jane. Knowing you want to see me again is enough reason to make sure I'm real careful on the trail. I want you too, Jane, want you bad, but I admire you too much to force myself on you."

Jane Clemons pursed her lips, almost bursting into tears. She threw her arms around him again and kissed him hard on the lips, but then she retreated, squeezed his hand, and half-smiled. "Good night, Pete. I'll pray you come back to me." Then, she suddenly bounded away from him, into the boardinghouse, closing the door after herself.

Pete Houston stood alone on the porch for a moment and then heaved a deep sigh. He left the Durand Boarding House and walked to his hotel. He would need some sound sleep tonight, for he had a long day tomorrow and perhaps an even longer one the day after tomorrow.

Pete rose early the next morning and he quickly packed his gear before he came down the steps and stopped at the hotel desk. "Can you saddle my horse and tie this gear on him? I'm going out for some breakfast and I'd like the mount ready by the time I come back. I'll be gone for a few days."

"Sure thing, Mr. Houston." The desk clerk smiled. "Your horse and gear will be ready by the time you get back."

Pete left the gear in the middle of the lobby and then walked to the Buffalo Cafe where, despite the crowd, he was waited on relatively soon. He ordered a big meal of eggs, ham, toasted bread, and home fries. He had no idea when he might eat again, so he wanted a full stomach before leaving Buffalo. He scanned the crowded cafe, hoping to see Jane Clemons here, but he knew better than to expect anything like that. He was half-tempted to call on her at the boardinghouse or even at the association office before he left, but he dismissed the idea.

By eight o'clock, Pete was atop his big bay and loping out of Buffalo. Soon enough he was moving over the open road. He rode for nearly four hours and finally reached the hamlet of Jaycee at about noon. He had met no danger on the road thus far, but the bounty hunter did not expect any until he got south of this village. At the small eating place, he got a quick snack that included a sandwich, pie, and coffee. Then he continued south, but now he studied carefully the high tors and forest-studded terrain on both sides of him.

As he approached a bend in the road he suddenly stopped. Up ahead was Devil's Pass and Pete suspected that here was where someone would try to bushwhack him. He would need to expose himself totally before starting through the

73

snaking length of road below the rocks. He decided instead to leave the highway before reaching a point where ambushers might see him coming. He veered his horse to the left and moved carefully through a jumble of rocks, upward over the dangerous terrain until he reached a point that was above some of the potential hiding places about Devil's Pass.

Pete Houston had guessed right.

Pedro Anias and Frank Sparks had been waiting in ambush for the past three hours behind some boulders above the winding segment of the Johnson County Highway. They had grown impatient while they waited for the supposedly unsuspecting Pete Houston to come through the pass. As the minutes passed during the early afternoon, a tinge of panic had gripped them. Perhaps Blake's information was wrong. Perhaps Houston was not coming south today at all.

Houston himself, meanwhile, finally dismounted and tied his horse to a scrub brush. Then he moved quietly through the rocks, somewhat irked, because he had no idea where to look. But then the neigh of a horse alerted him and he headed in that direction. He crouched down, peering carefully over each new boulder in front of him before continuing on. Finally, when he looked over one rock, he saw a man crouching behind a large stone with the barrel of his rifle aimed downward. And as he scanned the area about him more closely, he could make out the dim shape of another man also with a rifle, that weapon also aimed on the curving road below.

Houston had spotted the waiting ambushers, Pedro Anias and Frank Sparks, with Anias on the near side and Sparks on the far side. The two men had positioned themselves well, and no unsuspecting traveler passing over the open stretch of highway to the north could likely escape their view. Such a traveler would not likely escape a barrage of crossfire from the two rifles on either side as the rider passed through here.

Pete stood erect and aimed his own Winchester at Pedro Anias, who was below him. "Hey, you!" Pete shouted. "What are you doing down there?"

The sudden cry from above startled the rustler, and when Anias turned, he looked up at the inquirer in horror: tan shirt, tan trousers and hat, black gunbelt and black boots. The man above him was obviously the notorious bounty hunter Pete Houston. The Mexican's assumed victim had instead trapped Anias himself.

The rustler bushwhacker panicked, whirled, and fired his rifle wildly at Houston. The shot missed before Houston aimed his own gun and fired, winging the Mexican in the right shoulder and drawing blood. The terrified ambusher then scrambled away, stampeding in shock until he reached his horse. He mounted quickly and hurried down the slope as fast as he could without endangering himself or his animal.

Frank Sparks had jerked in surprised when he heard the two shots and by the time he could digest this he saw his cohort fleeing frantically. Frank stared in surprise at the Mexican's quick exodus from his hiding place. But then the rustler caught a glimpse of the figure in the high rocks and he no longer hesitated. He realized that their prey had become the hunter. Sparks too scampered away from his hiding place, mounted his horse, and clodded as swiftly as he could, hell-bent to reach the highway. He came onto the road only moments after Pedro Anias had reached the road.

Pete Houston came down from his high perch for a better view of the highway and he got a good look at the pair of would-be bushwhackers. He noted the color of their horses and the color of their attire. He smiled grimly as the two men galloped swiftly southward. The bounty hunter nodded to himself. These men were no doubt heading for Egleston. Houston firmly implanted the description of the two men and their horses in his mind. When the bounty hunter reached Egleston, he would find the duo and make them talk.

The would-be ambushers would have a lot of explaining to do.

CHAPTER FIVE

Egleston was a rather small hamlet on the Salt River, southeast of the Hole In The Wall country. The town, a former mining community, consisted of a single main street where every other business place was either a gambling saloon or a bordello, several of which doubled as hotels. However, Egleston did also have livery stables, blacksmith shops, and stores. The town's police force consisted of a mere village chief and two patrolmen, none of whom knew much about law enforcement. But, the businesspeople here only wanted police to keep the peace and nothing more.

Egleston supposedly served as a way station for stage passengers or freight wagons along the lengthy highway between Casper to the south and Sheridan to the north. However, like so many other remote towns in the west, this place catered primarily to outlaws. The shops in town sold mostly riding gear and weapons, the general stores sold salted meats, jerky, canned goods, flour, and coffee, the kind of staples that one could store for a long time in the many Hole In The

Wall hideouts.

The two barbers in town also acted as dentists and pharmacists, while a single doctor, once disbarred because of illegal activities, cared for any sick or injured. Doc Hubbard spent most of his time in extracting bullets from wounded outlaws who had been in running fights with the law. Yet, despite Wyoming law that required a report of any gunshot wound, Doc Hubbard filed very few such documents, and when he did, such reports always concluded that the gunshot had been an accident.

All of the saloons served food as well as drink, with prices nearly double the usual cost as found in other Wyoming saloons. The bordellos also charged double the going rate for a woman, and sometimes triple for the prostitute if the woman had gained a reputation for giving a patron a better-than-average thrill. The most shapely and pleasurable bed partners in town most likely worked for Mabel Evans, who paid her girls well, but who demanded cleanliness and good behavior from customers.

"No filthy trail hog is ever goin' to bed with one a my girls," she once said.

Mable maintained a bathhouse, where she insisted that potential patrons cleanse themselves thoroughly, with no lingering body odor, before taking one of her girls to bed.

The bulk of Egleston's spenders were men from the wild country hideouts who often got an itch for diversion and who felt reliably safe in town. These wanted men were welcome anywhere so long as they could pay and so long as they behaved. Ironically, a gentlemen's agreement prevailed among these outlaws from the Hole In The Wall country: they themselves would deal with any miscreants whose conduct might jeopardize their welcome in the town.

Of course, since gambling was a major pastime for visitors, card sharks abounded in most of the saloons. Such men inevitably beat their opponents and they were allowed to operate in most of the places so long as they paid a percentage to the saloon keeper. Rarely did a visiting outlaw come away winner at one of the gaming tables. Thus, for a man like Edward McClure, Egleston offered a bonanza. And, since outlaws tend to trust anyone in town, such professional gamblers usually learned plenty about wanted men who hid themselves in the Hole In The Wall country. The gamblers generally knew who was holed up, where they hid out, the nature of their alleged crimes, the kind of money they had, and the bounty on their heads, if any.

Thus, McClure had spoken the truth when he told Pete Houston that the gambler might have some useful information for the bounty hunter if Pete came to Egleston.

Surprisingly, when Frank Sparks and Pedro Anias scampered away from Houston after their misfired ambush attempt, they did not scoot back to their Hole In The Wall hideout as any sane men might have done. Instead, they stopped in Egleston to buy some diversion before returning to their elaborate log hideaway. Perhaps Anias and

Sparks were naive enough to believe that the bounty hunter would not come after them.

By the middle of the afternoon the outlaws had come into the Salt River Saloon, where they stepped up to the bar for some cold beer. Like other places, this saloon maintained its own icehouse to keep their beverages cool. The duo ordered and drank several big glasses of cold beer with an ecstatic relish, invigorating themselves after they had come hell-bent from the ambush site under a hot sun. They quickly consumed five or six glasses of lager, sating their thirsts, before they scanned the saloon and saw the well-dressed Edward McClure playing solitaire at a table.

Sparks nudged his companion. "Look at the dude. Maybe he'd like to play a little poker."

"Dummy." Anias scowled. "He ain't no dude, Frank. He's a card shark. Anyway, maybe we better go back."

"I ain't got no desire to go back to the hideout right now," Sparks said. "Quenchin' my thirst with this beer has put new life in me and it's only a start. I also intend to get a good bath, a nice juicy steak, and then a soft bed with one a Mabel's girls. Tomorrow will be soon enough to go back to our hideout."

"I don't know if it's safe to stay here," the Mexican said. "Look what happened to Colorado."

"He was stupid," Sparks answered. "He didn't keep his eyes open and he let the bounty hunter take 'im. But then, Colorado didn't have the brains of a jackass. Anyway, there's two of us and we can look out for each other." He grinned at his companion. "Jesus, Pedro, ain't you got an itch for a woman like me? You must have, if you're any kinda man."

The Mexican returned the grin.

"And wouldn't you like a nice steak with heaps a potatoes and hot bread?"

"Maybe you're right," Anias nodded.

"But we needn't do those things right now. Why don't we go over to that dude and see if we can play a little cards?" When the Mexican shrugged, the two men left the bar and approached the table.

"Good afternoon, sir," Sparks said. "It can't be much fun playin' solitaire. How about a little stud with my friend and me?"

McClure kept a casual appearance as he studied the two men. He recognized Frank Sparks at once as a member of the Rawlings gang, as he clearly remembered his face from a wanted poster. He did not recognize Anias, but he suspected that the Mexican was probably one of the Rawlings gang members who had not yet been identified. He studied the Mexican carefully, noting his round, dark face, straggly dark hair, and bull-like frame. He would absorb the description well in case McClure ever had need to remember the man.

"Why not?" The gambler shrugged.

"You don't deal off the bottom, do you?" Sparks asked, tapping his holster. "It wouldn't be healthy to do that."

"I play a square game," McClure answered.

The two outlaws sat down and soon absorbed themselves in a stud poker game, with only a moderate ante. The pot rarely grew beyond three or four dollars, since they played for a mere quarter opening. But the two outlaws were in the game only to kill a little time and not to make money—or lose money. As for McClure, he had nothing to do at the moment, so even a few dollars' profit on this dull afternoon suited him fine.

Anias and Sparks had little skill and McClure might just as well have been playing with sheer novices. So, as the game continued for the next hour, the gambler allowed the two rustlers to win an occasional hand, but he himself took most of the pots, building himself a fifteen- or twenty-dollar profit. The gambler had no need whatever to cheat, and he even made certain that their losses were low enough to keep them relatively content.

As often happened with other outlaws who drank heavily and then decided to play poker, the senses of these two rustlers had become somewhat dulled by their heavy beer consumption. Not only did they play a poor game, but they were inclined to talk openly, and Edward McClure deftly extracted considerable information out of them.

Without realizing it, Anias and Sparks revealed some damaging details on the Rawlings gang. They admitted their membership in the gang, they expounded on their ornate log hide out in the Hole In The Wall country, they boasted of their recent RX Ranch caper and how they had herded the cattle to a black marketer in the Spotted Horse country, hiding the trail of the stolen cattle by running them through the river,

82

up a bank, and then covering the tracks. They also admitted they had tried to ambush a bounty hunter today, and then mentioned how they would soon carry out a new rustling operation.

The two men also said they intended to remain in Egleston until tomorrow. They would get a good meal after this game, clean themselves up, and spend a night with a prostitute at Mabel Evans's bordello.

"She's got the best," Frank Sparks slurred. "She charges too much maybe, but no man ever came away from there without bein' satisfied."

McClure only grinned.

"You might want to spent a night there yourself, mister," Sparks continued. "You've earned enough from us to pay for such a night at Mabel's place and even have enough left over for your supper and breakfast."

"I'll give it some thought." McClure grinned.

After an hour at the table, during which time the outlaws had lost about twenty dollars between them, Sparks and Anias quit the game. They would have a couple of more beers, get themselves cleaned up, have a good meal, and then retire to Mabel Evans's bordello.

The sun was still quite high in the sky an hour later when Pete Houston loped into Egleston. Few people on the street or in front of the facades of their businesses even paused to look. Men were always riding in and out of town and few of the permanent residents here paid much attention to them unless they wore lawmen badges or U.S. Army cavalry uniforms. Anyone else who came into Egleston was not likely to cause trouble.

Houston studied the mercantile places on both sides of the street and then frowned. He counted six saloons, and he knew that Edward McClure could be inside any one of them if the gambler had come to Egleston at all. Or, McClure could be in one of the bordellos along the street or even in a rooming house, or perhaps in some friend's private residence. However, Pete was sure that many people in town probably knew McClure; and perhaps one of them might tell Houston where to find the gambler.

When the bounty hunter saw the sign over a small building, Egleston Police, he decided to try here. Pete knew full well that the so-called lawmen here were hardly honest, but he hoped to get information from them. Pete dismounted and tethered his horse before he slapped away some of the dust on his trousers and shirt before he walked into the small jailhouse. A young, slender-built man wearing a policeman's uniform looked up at him.

"Can I help you?"

"I hope you can. Is your police chief here?"

"No, Chief DeLisle ain't here."

"Well, maybe you can help me. I'm looking for a man by the name of Edward McClure. He's a gambler by trade, and I suspect he works one of the saloons here in town."

The policeman stroked his chin and then peered hard at the visitor. "Why do you want to see him, mister? You know we can't just give out information to anybody who asks for it, even if we have such information."

"I've got some personal business with him," Pete said.

The slim officer behind the desk studied Houston and the low-slung black gunbelt around his waist. "If your business is violence, mister, we don't tolerate that kinda business in this town. We don't want no gun shootin' nor fightin' in Egleston. We keep the town peaceful."

Houston leaned over the desk. "Look, kid, you tell me where I can find Edward McClure."

The police officer did not answer; he rolled his tongue around his lips.

"Your face is like an open book," Houston continued. "It tells me you know McClure and you know where I can find him. I can promise you, I mean him no harm. I got business with him. Now, just answer me and I'll be on my way." He leaned even closer to the youth and scowled. "You wouldn't want any violence to start right here, would you?"

The youth trembled momentarily and licked his lips again. "Might I ask who wants to see Mr. McClure?"

"Houston; Pete Houston. He's expecting me, I assure you."

The young police officer's eyes widened. He knew the reputation of this bounty hunter and he wanted no trouble with him. "No need to get upset, Mr. Houston. All right, I'll tell you. You'll probably find Mr. McClure at the Salt River Saloon. That's where he plays cards when he's in town. If he ain't there, he's likely at the Egleston

Boarding House where he rooms."

"I'm obliged, Officer."

"But I've got to warn you, Mr. Houston. If you hurt anybody here in town, you'll be in a lotta trouble."

"You needn't worry about that."

The village officer sat stiffly and watched Pete Houston leave the jailhouse. Then he pursed his lips, worried. If anything happened between that bounty hunter and Ed McClure, the chief would take it out on him for telling Houston where to find the gambler.

Pete mounted his bay and loped up the street until he saw the sign—Salt River Saloon. He again alit, tethered his horse, and walked inside. The place had few customers, since crowds did not start coming in until after dark. So, Houston had no trouble spotting the small, thin, well-dressed Edward McClure. The gambler was again sitting alone at a table and playing solitaire. Houston ambled to the table and flopped into a chair across from the man, who only looked up, said nothing, and continued his solo card game. The gambler had shown no emotion whatever, neither greeting nor frown, grin nor scowl. Houston also said nothing, but sat silently and watched McClure play his game. Finally, the gambler looked up at the bounty hunter.

"I guessed you'd come lookin' for me, especially after they raised the bounty on that Rawlings gang."

"You told me to look you up," Houston said.

"So I did." The gambler nodded. Then he grinned. "You know, I usually have an askin' price for Pinkerton men and bounty hunters who want information from me. And I must tell you, the kind of information you hope to get is worth much more than usual." Houston said nothing and McClure continued. "Of course, there ain't no kinda money that's worth my life, and that's what I owe you—my life. I may be a lotta things, but I ain't no welcher."

"Then, you can give me some information on the Rawlings gang, is that right?"

McClure nodded again. "I've been kind of expectin' you, so I drew a map." He extracted the slip from his pocket, scanned the area around him, and then put the map on a table. "Here's how to find Rawlings's place inside Hole In The Wall. Take this trail, over the Powder River about ten miles north a here, follow the trail past Cantor's Peak for about five miles to a big patch a forest, here. Go straight through the woods and then you'll need to go through this pass. On the other side is a patch a open ground, and across the creek is the Rawlings hideout on a knoll, a big log building." He leaned closer to Houston. "To tell the truth, I doubt if you can go through that pass, because Rawlings keeps a sentry in the rocks above the trail and nobody comes through there unless Rawlings wants him to come through."

"I'd guess that's so," Pete said.

"It ain't none a my business," McClure said, "but I sure as hell wouldn't go in there. You're much more likely to get a pine box instead of bounty money, especially since them rustlers got it in for you."

"Whatever I do is something I'll have to decide for myself," Houston said. He took the map, folded it, and slipped it into his shirt pocket.

"I do have some sure money for you, though." The gambler grinned. "Frank Sparks and one of his partners, a Mexican, left me less than an hour ago. They were playin' cards with me. I'd guess the Mex is also somebody in Rawlings's gang. They said they was gonna get a bath, have a steak dinner, and then go to Mabel Evans's place to get a bed and girl."

"That is some good news," Houston said, nodding.

"They can't play poker worth a damn, and I suspect they can't handle guns any better," the gambler continued. "Why don't you jest settle for them and then get yourself a sure thousand dollars? You can wait out the rest a them. Sooner or later they'll all get bored and come into the open."

Pete Houston rose from his chair. "I'm real grateful to you, Mr. McClure. You've sure made my trip to Egleston worthwhile."

McClure suddenly gripped Pete's wrist. "Houston, this settles my debt with you. I hope you understand that if you come to me again, why, you'll have to pay the price for any information, just like everybody else."

Houston did not answer. He simply looked down at his wrist and waited until McClure released his grip. Then, Pete walked away quickly. McClure watched the bounty hunter leave the saloon before he reverted to his game of solitaire. He looked up at the wall clock: 5:35. He suddenly scooped up his cards and replaced them in his pack box, because he decided he was hungry and would get some supper. Then he'd clean up at his boardinghouse and come back here to fleece some of those who came into the saloon this evening.

But, as McClure rose from his chair, he frowned, irritated with himself. He should have cleaned out those two rustlers this afternoon. He was sure the bounty hunter would catch up to Frank Sparks and Pedro Anias, and after Houston did so, the pair of outlaws would no longer have need of any money.

Gambler Ed McClure had certainly guessed right, for Pete Houston wasted no time as he hurried up the street toward the Egleston Restaurant. He wore a determined look on his face. He peered through the big front window of the eating place, but saw no one he recognized. Still, he went inside and walked up to the cashier.

"Pardon me, miss," Pete said, "I'm lookin' for a couple of men who came here for dinner. They told me to meet them here. One of them was kind of tall, thin, and light hair, and the other was dark and burly, a Mexican." He then described their dress as he remembered from his short encounter on the trail.

"Yes, a couple of men like that just left here," the cashier said. "I guess they got tired of waiting for you. They had some big steaks, but I don't know where they might have gone."

"I thank you anyway, miss," Houston said.

When the bounty hunter left, he knew right where to go—Mabel Evans's bordello. Even at this early hour, the two men had probably gone there to satisfy a sexual lust. Within ten minutes he had reached the two-story building and he walked inside. In the foyer, the obese white-haired Mabel Evans studied him and then smiled.

"You're sure handsome enough, mister, and I daresay I know a lotta women who might pay you to go to bed with them. However, you'll have to clean yourself up if you want one of my girls. You can get a bath out back, right through that door at the end of the hallway."

Houston studied the five young, shapely, pretty women sitting in chairs. The girls eyed the visitor with a mixture of curiosity and admiration, but they said nothing. "Is that your stock?" he asked the madam.

"Yes sir, five beauties, ain't they?" Mabel Evans grinned. "The two on the end have been called for, but you can have any one of the other three."

"I'm not here for any girl," Pete said. He then glared at the madam. "Two men just came in here. One was tall and thin with light hair, and the other was a burly Mexican. I'd guess they're the ones who've hired out your two girls, is that right?"

Mabel Evans glowered at Pete. "Who the hell are you? I ain't gonna give you any information on patrons who come in here. Now you get outta here before I call the law."

But Pete Houston looked at the door at the end of the hallway and then at the five girls. That meant that there was no one yet upstairs, so the two outlaws were no doubt out back cleaning up. He brushed past the madam and started toward the rear, but Mabel Evans grabbed his arm.

"You can't go back there."

However, Pete shoved the madam again, hard this time, and almost knocked her to the floor. He took out his six-shooter, made sure it was cocked, and continued to the end of the hallway. When he opened the door he squeezed his face from the cloud of steam that greeted him, vapor from the hot tub water. He squinted through the thin mist and saw two men scrubbing themselves inside the tubs. He recognized both of them as the men who had tried to bushwhack him on the trail. He especially noted Frank Sparks. A Chinaman stood against a wall of the room, apparently ready to offer assistance to the bathers.

Houston approached the Chinaman, and gestured with his gun. The bathhouse attendant knew exactly what Pete meant and the Chinaman darted out of the room. The bounty hunter then approached the tubs and brandished his weapon between the two outlaws.

"All right, boys, out of there and get dressed."

Both men stared in surprise before they stiffened in horror. Through the thin hovering mist they noted the tan attire, black gunbelt, and black boots. The intruder was the dreaded bounty hunter Pete Houston. The two men exchanged glances but made no moves. "I said to get out of those tubs and get dressed," Houston threatened. "It makes no difference to me whether I take you in alive or take you in dead."

"D-don't get excited, mister," Frank Sparks said, raising his arms. "I'll come out, just like you say."

"Me, too," Anias said, also raising his arms.

Then, dripping wet, the two outlaws got out of their tubs and walked to a rack for their clothes. The Mexican, however, tried to yank his gun out of his hanging holster, hoping he could cut down Houston through the steamy mist. But Anias made a fatal mistake. He had barely extracted the weapon before Pete unleashed two quick shots that slammed the Mexican against the wall before he collapsed to the floor in a growing pool of his own blood.

Still, the unexpected incident had momentarily drawn Pete Houston's attention and Frank Sparks, totally naked, darted out the rear door. Houston only glanced at the dead, bloodied Pedro Anias and he then bounded himself out of the rear door. He easily followed the path of the fleeing Sparks, who left a trail of dripping, soapy water behind him.

Dusk had not yet descended over Egleston when Houston came through an alley, then a gangway, and then into the town's main street. Here, he saw the nude Sparks running frantically and Pete dashed after the outlaw.

"Sparks, stop right there! Don't make me kill you!"

92

But the rustler ignored the cry and continued up the street with Pete in hot pursuit. Now, ogling spectators about town gaped in awe at the naked man bounding over the avenue and the armed man chasing after him. They were too startled to do anything else but stare, not even moving when Houston fired two shots that popped out small chunks of dirt about the rustler's bare feet.

"I won't miss next time," Houston cried again.

Frank Sparks glanced back at the oncoming Houston and he then turned, almost running into a loping horse and rider. He swerved away, slipped and fell, and then tumbled out of the way. On the ground he muddied himself in a mix of his nude wet body and the loose dust on the street. Before he could rise again, Pete Houston stood over him and aimed his gun at the outlaw's head.

"On your feet!"

"D-don't shoot, Houston," Sparks stammered. "I w-won't give you any more trouble, I promise."

By the time Sparks was standing again, the town police chief, DeLisle, was in the street and scolding Houston. "Hey, mister, who the hell do you think you are, causing this kinda ruckus in my town? I've a mind to run you in. You leave that man alone. If he's done anything wrong, I'll handle it."

Pete Houston glared at the chief. "You penny-ante outlaw protector," he scolded DeLisle. "Go about your business. This man is wanted and I'm taking him in."

"You're one a them stinkin' bounty hunters," the lawman huffed. "I said I'll handle this. I'm the law here."

"Mister," Houston said, "if you interfere with me, I'll have the U.S. Army, the Johnson County Sheriff's Department, and the Wyoming Cattlemen's Association coming into this town. Would you like to answer to them?"

The police chief retreated and stroked his neck nervously.

"Now you get the hell out of my way and let me get on with my job."

"A-are you sure this man's wanted?" the chief asked meekly.

"You and I both know he's wanted." Houston scowled. "Harboring a man like him is bad enough, but preventing his arrest is even worse. Shall I go back to Buffalo and tell Sheriff Angus and Big Joe Simeon that you wouldn't let me take this man in?"

"No, no," DeLisle said quickly. He then stepped aside as Houston shoved the naked, mud-spattered Frank Sparks before him, forcing him all the way back through the alley and into the rear door of the Evans Bordello bathhouse. Here, he found Mabel Evans and the Chinaman gaping at the bloodied body of Pedro Anias, while some of her girls peered in horror from beyond the door. The madam glowered at Pete Houston.

"You no-good son of a bitch!" she cursed, "Causin' all this trouble in my place. You got my bathhouse fulla blood, you left a dead man here, and you've scared hell outta my girls. Do you know what that'll do to my business? I'm gonna call Chief DeLisle and have you arrested."

Houston ignored the ranting madam and turned to the Chinaman. "Get some clothes on that body there." He gestured. Then he shoved the naked Frank Sparks toward the wall. "Get dressed. We've got a long way to go. Where are your horses?"

"Out back," Sparks answered meekly as he started to dress.

"You ain't listened to a word I said, you no-good bastard," Mabel Evans raved on. "As soon as I get the chief in here, you're goin' to be sorry you was born. You'll be in jail."

"Shut up, lady!" Houston barked. "I'm telling you the same thing I told your Chief DeLisle. You cause me any trouble and I'll have the entire cattlemen's association down here. Do you want that?"

Mabel Evans retreated as she suddenly clammed up. Houston watched and waited until Sparks had dressed and the Chinaman had put some clothes on the corpse. Then he gestured to the bathhouse attendant. "Get that body on his horse." The Chinaman bowed meekly and then dragged the dead man out of the bathhouse. Pete took a wad of bills and peeled off a ten that he handed to Mabel Evans. "Here, this will more than cover the cost of cleaning up in this damn place."

"You'll be sorry, bounty hunter, you'll be sorry," the madam said slowly, deliberately. However, she took the ten-dollar bill.

"Let's go." Houston shoved Frank Sparks still again. "We've got a long way to go and I want to start right now."

"You mean we're leavin' town tonight? Now? On the trail in the dark? Why can't we wait 'til mornin'?"

"Because if I stayed in this town with you tonight, I could be a dead man before daylight." He shoved the rustler again. "Move!"

CHAPTER SIX

People along the main street of Egleston, law breakers, visitors, and permanent residents, watched somberly as Pete Houston loped up the avenue with his burdens. They stared silently at the captured Frank Sparks, whose hands were bound to the saddlehorn and whose legs were tied to the saddle stirrups. Then they looked at the third horse and the body of the slain Pedro Anias. He had been hastily clothed by the Chinaman and now lay draped over the animal's back.

In the approaching darkness, Pete watched both sides of the street. He spotted Chief DeLisle and one of his policemen, who merely frowned in irritation at the small caravan. The obese Mabel Evans, standing in front of her bordello, watched the procession with a scowl, while two of her prostitutes merely ogled at the spectacle. Others on the boardwalks abutting the street, including gambler Edward McClure, peered with a mixture of awe and uneasiness, but also made no comments. McClure was surprised by Houston's quick success, but the others, patrons and entrepreneurs alike, recognized the threat reflected by the scene in the street. Men like Houston could make this town unsafe for visitors. Outlaws might not come here anymore and businesspeople would lose a lucrative trade.

The bounty hunter ignored the onlookers, and he was soon into the open countryside and moving north.

Among those who had seen the three-horse parade was Nebraska Brake, the eyes and ears in Egleston for Dude Rawlings. However, with the growing darkness and the treacherous terrain through the Hole In The Wall country, he decided to wait until morning to inform the Dude of this news. When Houston finally disappeared into the distance, Brake shrugged and reentered the Salt River Saloon along with others who had been drawn into the street.

Houston himself decided to ride as long as he could during the dark hours of early evening, determined to traverse the dangerous, possible-ambush areas along the Johnson County Highway as far as Jaycee. Near this town he would find a cozy brake where he could camp for the night. Occasionally, the bounty hunter craned his neck to look at his burdens, the bound Sparks behind him and the slain Anias bringing up the rear. Sparks himself rode quietly and glumly, anguished by his unexpected capture and distressed by the prospect of a prison term. He knew full well that once they had locked him in one of Sheriff Red Angus's cells at Buffalo no one was likely to free him.

98

Houston loped over the trail for more than two hours until he reached the open stretch of plains south of Jaycee. Gone now were the high, rocky tors and the snaking sections of highway that constituted the most dangerous part of the route. Houston soon reached a patch of trees through which he caught glimpses of crimson sparkles on the now-darkened surface of the Powder River. He veered his three horses off the highway and into the brake until he reached a small clearing on the bank of the river.

Here, Pete dismounted and looked at Sparks. "We'll camp here tonight."

Frank Sparks only glowered at the bounty hunter as Houston laced the reins of the outlaw's horse around a tree before Pete unloosened the ropes that held the rustler's hands and legs. "Okay, get down."

Sparks complied, but he still said nothing.

"We've got to get your partner down and stretch him out for the night. You'll have to give me a hand."

Once more the rustler complied, but he still remained silent. The duo hoisted the body off the horse and laid the corpse on the ground before Houston covered Anias with a blanket. Then he sat Sparks against a tree and bound him to the trunk, leaving his hands free. Next, Pete unsaddled the three horses and tied them to an improvised tether line between two trees so the animals could rest comfortably for the night. The outlaw sat and watched as Houston now gathered kindling and firewood to build a fire. Sparks also

99

looked on silently as Pete built an improvised grate with stone before he boiled water for coffee and heated up beans and jerky in a pan.

"We'll only have a bite," Pete said. "You can't be too hungry after that big steak you had in Egleston earlier today ..."

Frank Sparks glowered at Houston.

"But you might be up to the coffee," Pete continued.

Sparks still said nothing. He watched Houston stoke his fire, brew coffee, and cook the beans and jerky. Soon, Pete poured two cups of coffee and put some hot beans and jerky into two plates. He extended one cup and plate to Sparks, who hesitated for a moment but then accepted the offer. Sparks only picked at the food, for he was not very hungry. However, he gulped the coffee. Houston, on the other hand, ate his meal ravenously, as he had not eaten since the lunch snack in Jaycee almost nine hours ago. He also drank his coffee with relish.

After Houston had cleaned his own plate of food, he offered Sparks more, but the outlaw declined although he did have more coffee. Houston then emptied the pan of its remaining beans and jerky onto his own plate since hunger still lingered inside him. When he finished, he relaxed with his cup. Sparks studied his captor as the bounty hunter sipped his coffee. The outlaw then frowned curiously when he saw Pete Houston extract a pad and pencil from his pocket and begin to write. He stared for several minutes and then he finally spoke.

"You know, Houston, you made a big mistake takin' me and him." He cocked his head toward the covered corpse.

But Houston continued to write.

"When Rawlings hears about this, why, your life won't be worth a plugged nickel. You may get me behind bars, but you're gonna be dead."

Houston finally looked up. "That dead man—is he Pedro Anias?"

"How do I know?" Sparks shrugged disdainfully. "He was jes' takin' a bath, same as me."

"Sparks, I haven't got time to play games. You two rode together, you tried to bushwhack me at Devil's Peak together, you both played cards at the Salt River, and ate steaks at the same table. Then the both of you went into that whorehouse together. Now, what's his name?"

"I don't know," Sparks insisted.

"I've got to have his name for this," he brandished the pad.

"What're you writin' there, anyway?"

"Your confession that you belong to the Rawlings gang and that the dead man, whose name you'll need to give me, was also a member of the gang."

"You must be crazy," Sparks huffed with a sneering grin. "Do you expect me to give you that kind of information?"

Pete Houston rose full to his feet and looked down at his prisoner. "Sparks, I don't need this confession to prove that you're both members of the Rawlings gang. Your pictures have been on wanted posters for some time, and I suspect that

101

by the time we reach Buffalo tomorrow, those new posters will be out and you'll be worth five hundred dollars to me. To be honest, I'd rather have a thousand than five hundred."

"You ain't gettin' nothin' from me," Sparks huffed again. "I told you, I don't know who the dead man is."

"Suit yourself." Houston shrugged. "If that dead man isn't worth any money to me, then I may as well dump him into the river. As for you, I'll get my five hundred whether I take you in dead or alive. I can kill you right here and put your body under that blanket while I throw that other fellow in the river. If I have to settle for five hundred, why should I waste my time keeping an eye on you tonight and tomorrow? You'll be dead and I can get a good night's sleep."

"Y-you can't do t-that," Sparks stuttered fearfully. T-they saw you t-take me outta Egleston. All them people s-seen you."

"You tried to escape," Houston answered nonchalantly. "Who's going to care, since you're only an outlaw—which most people have no use for, especially those influential members of the Wyoming Cattlemen's Association." He leaned close to his captive and grinned.

"All right, all right." Sparks gestured. "His name is Anias, Pedro Anias. He's a wetback that came north from Mexico a coupla years ago. He's been on three or four rustlin' capers with us, including the one from the RX Ranch."

Pete nodded and resumed his writing. The prisoner watched in fearful silence for the next several minutes and then stiffened as Houston handed him the pad. "There's three sheets there; you sign all of them and I'll witness them."

"I can hardly read at all," Sparks said, "and I can hardly sign my name."

"It doesn't matter," Pete said. "It only says that you admit being a part of the Rawlings gang that rustled that herd from the RX Ranch. It also says that this dead man, this Pedro Anias, was also a part of the gang; that he also participated in the RX Ranch thing, and that this Anias is an illegal alien from Mexico."

Frank Sparks nodded, took the pad and pencil, and slowly signed his name to the three sheets of paper. Houston looked at the signatures, nodded and then signed his own name to the sheets as a witness.

"I appreciate your cooperation, Sparks." The bounty hunter grinned. "Now I'm going to clean these cups and other things at the river before we curl up for the night. I really ought to tie your hands, but I won't do that. However, I must warn you—I'm a light sleeper and my six-gun will be with me. If I hear a sound, I'll shoot first and ask questions later."

"I won't give you no trouble," Sparks promised.

And, in fact, Frank Sparks behaved himself throughout the night. He fell asleep in his sitting position even before Pete did. The bounty hunter lay under his blanket, looking at the campfire that slowly diminished as the night wore on. The fire had been reduced to glowing embers by the time Houston himself fell asleep.

Peeping birds and bands of daylight flickering through the trees awoke Pete the next morning. He blinked his eyes, tossed aside his blanket, and looked to his right. The bound Frank Sparks was still sitting against the tree, still asleep. Houston grinned to himself, rose to his feet, and again gathered kindling and wood. Once more he built a fire and boiled coffee while frying jerky and beans in a pan. The aroma of coffee and meat awoke Frank Sparks.

"I'll bet you're hungry this morning," Pete said.

"Real hungry."

"I cooked a little more beans and jerky, but I'm real sorry I don't have some nice hot rolls to go with it."

"Whatever you've got will do," the outlaw said.

For the next half-hour the two men ate their food and drank their coffee, with Frank Sparks still tied to the tree trunk. Then, Houston once more cleaned and washed the utensils in the river before stashing them in a saddlebag. He doused the campfire with water before he threw loose dirt over the smoking embers to make certain that no sparks remained.

Pete next resaddled the horses and untied his prisoner before he and Sparks took the now quite stiff and cold body of Pedro Anias and hoisted the corpse over the saddle. They had to press hard to bend Anias so he could lay in a balanced position over the animal's back. Pete then ordered Sparks atop his own saddle before the bounty hunter again tied the prisoner's hands to the saddle and

104

his legs to the stirrups.

"We should reach Buffalo by noon," Pete said. "You'll get your next meal in the jailhouse."

"Ain't we stoppin' at Jaycee? It ain't but a couple more miles up the road and we could get us some real good eggs and ham and hot toast.

"Do you think I'm crazy, Sparks?" Houston grinned. "By now your boss Rawlings could have a half-dozen guns waiting for me between here and Jaycee. In fact, we're not going up the highway at all. There's a trail about a half-mile up that we can take around Jaycee and bring us out only a few miles south of Buffalo. It's a little rough and it might take a little longer, but it'll be a lot safer."

"You're pretty smart, ain't you?" Sparks huffed.

"That's how I stay alive, mister," Houston answered as he tied the reins of the two other horses to his own horse.

After Pete hoisted himself into his own saddle, he whipped his mount slightly before he led the three horses out of the brake and onto the main highway again. The bounty hunter blinked from the morning sun that had now emerged from the east. Then he looked at his prisoner and the dead man before loping up the highway. He remained alert, continually studying the terrain ahead or the patches of forests around him. Soon, he reached a narrow lane running off the road and he veered left into a quiet, obscure trail. Soon, he was deep into the forest and he turned to Sparks.

"It's an old trail, an Indian trail, but it'll suit us fine."

"Sure," Frank Sparks grumbled in disgust. If Rawlings had indeed set up an ambush to the north to take Houston and rescue Sparks, such efforts would be futile. This bounty hunter was one of the cagiest men that Frank Sparks had ever known.

At first light on the day after Houston had taken Pedro Anias and Frank Sparks, the informer Nebraska Brake galloped out of Egleston. He rode swiftly into the Hole In The Wall country but then slowed down and moved gingerly over the more hazardous portions of the trail that ran through the forests. He took care while loping over jumbles of rock in the craggy clearings as well. Still, he made good time, for he had reached the snaking part of the trail that led to Rawlings's place even before the Dude had sent out his morning sentinel for the day. By ten o'clock, Brake had crossed the stream and loped into the area of open ground in front of the ornate log structure.

By the time Brake had dismounted and tethered his horse, two men had come out of the front door, Dude Rawlings and Ralph "Preacher" Rogers. Even at this early hour, the Dude was decked out in neat, clean attire: a blue suit, silk shirt, ascot tie, and shiny shoes. He had combed his hair and shaved his face cleanly. Rogers, although quite neat himself in his clean chino pants and cotton shirt, looked shabby alongside the Dude. The two men had come onto the porch with aimed guns, for they were surprised to see someone loping flagrantly up to their house. They relaxed when they recognized the man as Brake, but then ogled in surprise at this morning visit by their Egleston informant.

Brake grinned when he came onto the porch. "I guess I'm lucky you fellows don't shoot first and then check things out."

"Nebraska," Rogers said, "What the hell are you doin' here so early? You must've left Egleston before daylight."

"We weren't expectin' you today," the Dude said.

"Do you have any hot coffee?" the visitor asked.

"Come inside." Rawlings cocked his head.

In the parlor, Nebraska Brake sat in a chair, while Rogers sat in another. Rawlings dropped onto a divan and then shouted toward the kitchen. "Laura! Will you bring some coffee out here? We got a visitor—Nebraska Brake. You might bring us some a them rolls, too, if you still have any left."

"I'll heat them up," the girl's voice echoed from the kitchen.

"All right, Nebraska"—Rawlings gestured—"what the hell brought you out here so early and in such a hurry?"

The visitor's face suddenly sobered. "More bad news, Mr. Rawlings. You lost Sparks and the Mexican."

"What?" Rogers gasped. "You mean that bounty hunter wasn't killed by them two?"

"Sparks and Anias was done in themselves,"

107

Nebraska said.

"Goddamn," the Dude huffed. "They said they had a perfect spot around Devil's Peak to get that Houston. How could they have failed and got themselves done in?"

"It wasn't at Devil's Peak," Brake said. "To start with, Sparks and the Mexican never got that Houston on the trail. I don't know what happened out there; whether they missed the bounty hunter or Houston took a different trail or what. All's I know is, your men came into Egleston in the afternoon and that bounty hunter came into town a little later. Your boys was havin' a little time for themselves, drinkin' beer, playin' a little poker, havin' a meal, and then goin' to Mabel's place. Next thing, that Houston got Sparks and Anias at the whorehouse while they was takin' a bath. He killed Anias and cowed Sparks."

"Son of a bitch!" the Dude said.

"Jes' before dark, Houston left town with Sparks tied to his horse and the Mex draped over his own horse."

"Jesus," Rawlings cried, "didn't that Chief DeLisle do anything about it? Didn't he and his policemen stop Houston? What the hell are we supportin' them fellows for?"

"I think it was the other way around," Brake said. "The bounty hunter made DeLisle back off, as near as I could find out. He must've threatened to bring a sheriff's posse or some cattlemen's association regulators into Egleston, and DeLisle must've figured it was better to let Houston take them two than to risk somethin' like that."

108

"What were them two doin' in Egleston, any way?" the Preacher now spoke in a huff. "If they missed Houston on the trail, they shoulda come right back to the place here."

Then, both Jerry Roseberry and Laura Renault came into the parlor. Roseberry was quite neat in a clean shirt and trousers. Laura, in a housedress, laid a tray of coffee, rolls, cream, sugar, and cups on a table. Both of them listened in shock as Nebraska Brake repeated the woeful tale of what had happened to Frank Sparks and Pedro Anias.

"I'd guess that bounty hunter is about back in Buffalo by now," Brake said, "and he'll soon be a thousand dollars richer."

"The bastard!" the Dude cursed. "That son of a bitch is makin' more money than we are." He looked at Roseberry. "What do you think, Cap?"

Roseberry stroked his chin and then looked at Brake. "If Houston came into Egleston sometime after our boys and he caught them so soon, how did he know they were in town and that they'd be at that bordello? He caught them stark naked, literally stark naked."

"I don't know." Brake shrugged.

"Yeh, how?" Dude Rawlings asked.

"Somebody in that town *told* Houston where to find Anias and Sparks," Roseberry said emphatically. "That bounty hunter had an informant just like we have. I suspect that's how Houston got Colorado as well. All we hear about this Houston leads me to believe that he never goes off half-cocked like so many others do. He knows what he's doing. He knows where to go and he knows where he'll likely find what he wants to find."

"The bastard!" the Dude cursed Houston again.

"Damn it." The Preacher scowled. "Cap'n"—he looked at Roseberry—"are you sayin' that if any of us leave this place and go to Egleston or Jaycee for a little fun, that bounty hunter will find out about it?"

"That's my guess." Roseberry nodded. "The way he nabbed those others so easily is too coincidental."

"I'll admit it ain't bad here," the Preacher said, but all of us like a little change now and then. Are you sayin', Cap'n, that we can't never go into Egleston anymore?"

Jerry Roseberry only shrugged.

"We lost three men now," the Preacher said, "and that's bad enough, but things could get a lot worse if that bounty hunter has an informant. He might know how to find our place here."

"Maybe," Roseberry answered.

"Ah, hell," the Dude huffed, "he couldn't take all of us in here."

"Unless he came in here with a big posse," Rawlings said. "And if he does know his way here, he could take some detours to avoid our sentry."

"What'll we do?" Rogers asked Rawlings.

Dude Rawlings watched Laura pour the coffee and he stared intently at the creases of her breasts along the top of her dress. Laura saw the hard look but she ignored Rawlings. The Dude then stroked his chin in obvious thought. She was beautiful and shapely and any man would give anything to have her. When Laura straightened, the Dude turned to Brake.

"This Houston . . . does he like women?"

Brake grinned. "I don't know of any man who don't like women. I suspect he gets his lays in a house like everybody else who's got the price, and the way that bounty hunter is goin', he's got money to buy the best."

"I bet he'd never find a woman like Laura here." The Dude grinned at the girl.

Laura frowned.

"Yes sir, even a man like Houston would melt if he thought he could have Laura. No matter how smart he is, his brain would go to sleep."

"What are you talkin' about, Dude?" Laura frowned again.

"I'm talkin' about using you to get that dirty bounty hunter," the Dude said. "If you was to cozy up to him, why, you could surely get him into a trap for us."

"You want me to take up with that bounty hunter?" the girl gasped. "You must be crazy."

"That's ridiculous, Dude," Roseberry suddenly spoke up. "We can't use Laura for bait like we'd use a lamb to trap a wolf. I'm against it. We just can't do that."

Dude Rawlings half-grinned at Roseberry. He knew well enough that the ex-army captain had a fervent desire for Laura Renault. He was almost obsessed with her, but he had remarkably restrained himself. The Dude also knew that if Laura herself ever warmed up to anyone in the gang, she would select the handsome Cap'n. In fact, Roseberry had often shown a tinge of anger if the

Dude or any of the others in his gang got too close to the girl. However, so far as Rawlings knew, there was nothing between the Cap'n and Laura, who still remained aloof from him and the others.

The Dude now looked hard at Roseberry. "Cap, we're talkin' here about our freedom and our livelihood. We've got to do whatever we have to so's we can protect ourselves."

"I can't say I like the idea one bit," Laura now spoke. "Why should I cozy up to someone who's our sworn enemy?"

"To get rid of 'im, that's why," the Dude said.

"It just isn't a good idea," Roseberry persisted. "Why, Laura could get herself killed if she tried to do what you suggest, Dude. That bounty hunter is too smart and too cunning. And even if she wasn't killed, Laura could at least end up behind bars. That Houston seems to have nothing on his mind but money. "No"—he shook his head vigorously—"I'm against it; totally against it."

The Dude ignored Roseberry's tirade and looked at Nebraska Brake. "Didn't you tell us that them RX Ranch cowhands said a woman was with us, a pretty woman with dark hazel eyes?"

"Yes." The visitor nodded.

"There you are." Roseberry pointed to Rawlings. "That Houston would guess right away that Laura's probably the woman who's running with us."

"Exactly." Rawlings smiled. "That's just what we'd like that bounty hunter to do."

The others in the room frowned.

"Don't you see?" Rawlings grinned. "Laura

112

could go into Egleston or Buffalo and find Houston, and tell 'im she's run out on us because she didn't like something. Maybe she could say we overworked her, or wouldn't give her a big enough share, or that one or more of us tried to ravage 'er. She's now disgusted with us, angry with us, and wants to get even with us. So, she'll lead him to us, so's we can take 'im."

The others exchanged glances.

"You can do it, Laura," the Dude insisted. "You can warm up to him, get him so hot he won't even be able to think anymore. In two or three days, he'll do whatever you want, especially if you satisfy him."

"There's no better way to leash a man into doin' what you want than to go to bed with him." The Preacher grinned.

"Absolutely not!" Laura cried.

"No, no, Dude," Roseberry shouted, "that's the worst thing I ever heard."

But the Dude grinned at the girl. "You must've gone to bed with a man before, Laura; somebody as pretty as you."

"Whether or not I went to bed with anybody is none a your damn business." Laura scowled. "I told you, I'll pick and choose for myself."

"Laura"—the Dude pointed, his face suddenly hardening—"we're in trouble with that bounty hunter, as you heard. We lost three people already and we could lose more if we don't do somethin' about him. The best way is through you. Maybe you won't need to sleep with 'im, only make it look like you might. That alone could be enough to

113

meddle 'im so's you can lead him into a trap. And if you do so, why, we'll give you a bonus."

"I'm willin' to give up some a my share." Preacher Rogers grinned.

Neither Laura Renault nor Jerry Roseberry answered now. They only looked at each other, then at Rawlings, and finally at the Preacher. However ugly the suggestion, they inwardly suspected that Dude Rawlings was right. It was obvious now: they would need to get Pete Houston, and apparently they could not do this by having bushwhackers lurking behind rocks. Houston was too smart, too suspicious, and too careful. They would have to use a ruse that had succeeded since the dawn of history—seduction by a pretty woman.

CHAPTER SEVEN

Pete Houston's decision to take a detour had been unnecesary. By the time Dude Rawlings had learned of the incident in Egleston, the bounty hunter was already approaching Buffalo at midmorning. For the entire trek, Frank Sparks had sat glumly in his saddle, fully aware that only an eventual prison term awaited him. And worse, under duress, he had confessed that the slain Pedro Anias had also been a member of the Rawlings gang.

At the Buffalo jail, after locking Sparks in a cell, Sheriff Angus read the signed confession of Frank Sparks and then looked at the jailed outlaw, while Pete himself stood quietly.

"Did you sign this?" Angus asked the rustler.

"Yes," Sparks answered softly.

"You're tellin' us that this dead man out there was also a member a the rustler gang; Pedro Anias. Is that right?"

Frank Sparks first glowered at Houston and then looked at Angus before pointing to the bounty hunter. "He made me sign it; threatened to kill me if I didn't. Why, I can hardly sign my own name, let alone read. I didn't know what that man wrote on them sheets."

"Didn't he read it to you?" Angus asked. "Didn't he tell you it said you were part of the Rawlings gang as was this dead man Pedro Anias? And didn't Houston tell you the paper also said that you and this Pedro Anias were in on the RX Ranch caper?"

"Yes, he told me all that"—Sparks nodded—"but I couldn't read it myself. And like I said, he threatened to kill me if I didn't sign them sheets."

"Is that right, Pete?" Angus asked Houston.

"That's what he says." Pete shrugged.

"It's the truth," Frank Sparks cried. "I told him, I didn't even know the dead man. He was only takin' a bath in that hotel, same as me."

"Then, how did you know his name was Pedro Anias?"

"I guess he musta told me while we was in them tubs," Sparks said. "But, I'm tellin' you, Sheriff, if you try to use them papers in a court a law, I'll insist I only signed 'em because that bounty hunter threatened to kill me. What else could I do when I was bound helpless to a tree?"

Sheriff Angus scowled. "You bastard, Sparks! That confession will hold up in any court because the Mexican's picture is also on a wanted poster. We got plenty a witnesses on both of you, and the cattlemen's association has offered a reward on you and at least three others." He turned to Houston. "Pete, I'll give you a voucher for Sparks as well as the dead man if he's truly Anias."

116

"I understand," Pete said.

Houston stood erect while Sheriff Angus left the office to look at the dead man draped over the horse outside. He came back a few minutes later. "The face on that corpse sure matches the photo on the association's wanted poster." Angus then walked behind his desk, opened a desk drawer, pulled out a pad, and filled out two blanks: Name, Frank Sparks; captured, Egleston; captor, Peter J. Houston; time, six P.M., Thursday, October 6, 1882. Then the second one. Name, Pedro Anias; captured, Egleston; captor, Peter J. Houston; time, six P.M., Thursday, October 6, 1882. He then handed both slips to Pete.

The bounty hunter took the vouchers.

"Don't worry about the dead man out there." Angus gestured. "I'll take care of 'im."

Houston nodded and then left the sheriff's office. Within ten minutes he had tethered his horse in front of the Buffalo cattlemen's association branch office and walked into the building. Behind the counter, Jane Clemons looked up and smiled in near ecstasy. She rushed around the counter, threw her arms around him, and kissed him fervently. But then she quickly retreated, embarrassed.

"I'm sorry, Pete."

Houston grinned. "It's mighty nice to have that kind of welcome after a man has been on the trail."

"It's just that I'm so glad to see you," the girl said. But then she frowned. "But you only left here yesterday mornin'. How come you're back so soon?

117

You couldn't have finished your business this soon."

"I was lucky enough to get two of those rustlers right off," Pete said, "and I thought I'd bring them in before I went out again."

"Out again? When?" she asked anxiously.

"Not right away," Pete said, "maybe in two or three days." He cocked his head. "Is Big Joe inside?"

"Yes."

When Houston knocked at the private door, the bellowing voice of Joe Simeon echoed from inside. "Yes?"

"It's me, Pete Houston. Can I come in?"

"Sure, sure." When Pete entered the room, the association executive rose from his chair, leaned over the desk, and shook the visitor's hand vigorously. "Goddamn, you're back in a hurry. What happened?"

Pete explained: the attempted ambush on the trail, the confrontation in the bathhouse of that Egleston bordello, the need to kill one of the would-be bushwhackers, and the return of Frank Sparks and the body of Pedro Anias. "Sparks signed a confession, admitting that he and Anias were both members of the Rawlings gang," Pete said. "Once behind bars, though, Sparks claimed he signed the confession under duress, but Sheriff Angus checked the dead man's appearance with the wanted poster and agreed that the dead man was Anias."

Joe Simeon looked at the vouchers and nodded. "If Sheriff Angus verified those two men as members of the Rawlings gang, that's good enough for me."

Pete nodded, but then Big Joe frowned. "We don't have that kind of money in here right now, but I'll send a draft to the bank and have them transfer a thousand dollars from the association account to your own account. The money should be available to you by sometime tomorrow. Is that all right?"

"That'll be fine, Joe."

When Pete Houston finished his business inside, he left the office and stopped at the counter to speak to the girl. "Jane, I'm going to clean up and then rest a little bit this afternoon. But I'd sure like to see you a little later. Can I pick you up at five and take you to dinner?"

"I'd like that, Pete; I'd like that real well."

"Then, I'll see you at five."

When Houston left the association office, he walked to the nearby Rawhide Saloon for a sandwich and some cold beer. The place appeared relatively quiet with only a few patrons about, including two men who watched Houston settle himself at a table at the far wall. They were quite shabbily dressed, with mops of unkempt hair and unshaven, rough faces. The duo quickly downed their glasses of beer and ordered two more which they sipped slowly while Houston ordered from a waiter. After the bounty hunter was served his roast beef sandwich and pitcher of beer, the two men at the bar looked at each other and then quickly drank their second beers. One of them wiped his lips with the cuff of his shirt and the

119

other man gave a hitch to his trousers. Then, after a gesture from the man who had wiped his lips, they walked to Pete Houston's table and just stood there looking at him.

The bounty hunter had just taken a bite from his sandwich when he noticed the duo glaring at him.

"Don't you remember us?" One of them grinned. When the bounty hunter frowned, the visitor leaned close to Houston with a sadistic look in his eyes. He then gestured toward his companion. "This is Snake Dawson and I'm Hank Beaudoin. You're the man who stole our horses and gear and left us high and dry on the trail. Don't you remember?"

"Oh yes, the friends of Colorado McIver."

We wasn't friends a his," Snake Dawson now spoke. "We was only innocent riders on the trail, and you almost killed us before you stole from us. All we wanted to know was how far to Jaycee."

"No, it was Egleston," Houston corrected him. "Your memory isn't very good."

"It's good enough to remember what you done to us," Dawson pointed out.

"Well, as I told you then," Pete said, "you could stop at the sheriff's office and reclaim your horses and guns, because that's where I left them. And while you're at it, you can also press charges against me if you have the mind to. Now, if you don't mind, I'm having my lunch."

Houston had started to take another bite from his sandwich when Beaudoin gripped his wrist and slammed his forearm on the table, jolting the half-eaten sandwich from Pete's hand. The bounty hunter looked at the man's grip for a second and then at the man before he rose from his chair.

"Didn't you boys have enough trouble with me on the trail? Are you looking for more?"

Snake Dawson sneered at Pete. "We aim to teach you a lesson so's you don't bother other innocent people on the highway." Then, before Houston could act, Hank Beaudoin grabbed his arms and hooked them behind his back, and Dawson sent a strong fist into Pete's abdomen, knocking the breath out of him and doubling him over in pain. Then Snake threw a solid uppercut to Pete's chin, snapping his head backward before Houston fell to the floor. He had barely moved when Hank Beaudoin kicked him in the ribs and the bounty hunter jerked from a sudden pang of pain.

Now, as Snake Dawson approached Houston to also kick him, Pete grabbed his foot, twisted it, and sent Dawson sprawling to the floor. Then, he rolled quickly as Hank Beaudoin tried to kick him again, and this second man's foot swung through a void that threw him off balance. By the time Beaudoin steadied himself, Pete had bounded to his feet and glared at his assailant.

"You're crazy, mister" Pete said. "You and your friend are both loco." However, Pete could hear the second assailant rising to his feet, so he quickly retreated to the wall while the two men came toward him with sadistic grins on their faces.

"You're gonna pay for what you did to us, bounty hunter," the Snake said. "We're gonna give you a beatin' you'll never forget." As the Snake came toward him, Pete Houston suddenly swung his leg, carefully and accurately, and caught the man in the crotch. The Snake stopped suddenly and gasped in pain before he doubled over, held his crotch, and staggered away. But Houston kicked him again in the same area and the man howled in agony before he whirled drunkenly and involuntarily from the excruciating pain.

Now Pete looked at Hank Beaudoin, who shifted his glance nervously between his tormented companion and the bounty hunter. He went for his gun, but before he reached it, Pete had already extracted his own six-shooter from his holster and pointed the weapon at the man.

"Take your gun out nice and easy and throw it across the room." The now-rattled Hank Beaudoin blanched as he slowly lifted his weapon and threw it away. The six-gun skidded across the floor almost to the other side of the saloon. Then, Pete Houston put his own gun on the table and came toward Beaudoin, who now retreated, while his companion still staggered about dizzily in pain.

By now, those in the Rawhide Saloon, including the bartender and the two prostitutes, were watching the drama intently. They had seen the first action where the duo had floored Houston, then the next round where the bounty hunter had left one attacker in a helpless position, and then round three where Houston had forced the second attacker to throw away his gun. They now waited for the next, and most likely the final, round.

Hank Beaudoin glanced at the spectators and knew his pride was now at stake. He stopped, waited for Houston to come near him, and then swung viciously at his opponent. However, Pete deftly sidestepped the punch and countered with a left of his own to Beaudoin's stomach. The man gasped, and before he straightened, he caught a hard right to the jaw that bounced him against a table, which upended, sending Beaudoin sprawling to the floor.

As the man shook his head to rid himself of his dizziness, Pete reached down, grabbed his shirt, and hauled him to his feet. Then Pete slammed him with a right, opening a cut on his face; a left opened a cut on Beaudoin's chin and spun him around; then another right bounced the man against the wall before he sank to the floor in a sitting position.

Houston now turned to the still-groaning and doubled-over Snake Dawson. He grabbed the man and pushed him against the wall. "Now, you listen, you bastard. If you or your friend ever try that again, you'll be dead men. Do you understand that?"

Snake Dawson nodded weakly.

But then, Houston sent a vicious knee punch into the man's crotch again and Dawson screamed in agony. Houston ignored him and kneed him twice more in the genitals before the Snake collapsed painfully to the floor in near-unconsciouness.

Houston glared at him.

"You won't be able to visit any whorehouses for a while." He then turned and walked back to his table, sat down, and calmly finished his lunch.

At promptly five o'clock, Pete Houston arrived at the Buffalo cattlemen's association office. He had gone to his hotel after the incident at the Rawhide Saloon, taken a warm bath, sent his clothes to the laundry, and then taken an afternoon nap. By four-thirty he had shaved and dressed himself neatly in his suit, shirt, tie, and bowler hat. Now he was leaning over the counter and smiling at Jane Clemons, but the girl answered with a sober look. Pete then turned as Big Joe Simeon suddenly came out of the office.

"Pete," the executive said, "we heard what happened at the Rawhide this afternoon. Jesus, you might have been killed."

Pete shrugged. "They were just a couple of drifters who were looking for trouble and they found more than they could handle."

"But men like that . . ." Simeon shook his head. "They might come looking for you again."

"I don't think so," Pete said. Then he looked at the solemn-faced Jane. "Believe me, it was nothing to get excited about. Besides, I didn't start it. I was minding my own business."

"I suspect you were, Pete," the girl said softly, "but just the same we were worried about you."

"Don't fret about me," Houston said, looking first at the girl and then at Simeon. "If that's the worst thing that happens to me, a couple of men trying to beat me up, why, I'll be a fortunate man indeed."

"All right, Pete." Big Joe nodded. Then he looked at the girl. "You will lock up, Jane?"

"Yes, Mr. Simeon." Jane and Pete watched Simeon leave the building and then the girl looked at Houston. "Are you sure you're up to takin' me to dinner?"

"I'd like nothing better, unless you don't want to go out with me."

She suddenly gripped Pete's hand. "I'm willing to go anywhere with you, Pete, anywhere. I was just worried about you, that's all." Then she forced a smile. "You sure look handsome, Pete. I'll be the envy of every girl in town, walkin' up the street with you."

The duo left the association office just after five and then walked arm in arm slowly up Gillette Avenue. Again they paused before some of the now-closed shops while Jane window-shopped. Finally, they ducked into the Buffalo Cafe. Here, Jane ordered the beef stew and Pete ordered a steak. They did not say much to each other during the meal. Pete was too busy eating, for he was hungry, and Jane Clemons was perhaps worrying too much about her companion, with whom she was now badly in love.

When they left the cafe, they once again walked to the park, sat on a bench, stared up at the first stars popping out of the deepening darkness, and talked in soft tones. Again Jane expressed her fear at the bounty hunter's profession, and once more Pete tried to convince her that his occupation was no more dangerous than any other outside job.

Then, a little after eight o'clock, Pete and Jane again walked slowly up Gillette Avenue, turned into deserted 13th Street, and ambled slowly toward the Durand Boarding House. They walked up the porch steps and stood there alone, while Pete gripped the girl's hands.

Jane Clemons stared about and then looked at Pete. "It's really quiet in this neighborhood at this time a night. That's why I like it here. Nothin' ever wakes you up from your sleep."

"It isn't quite the same at my hotel—but it's quiet enough, I guess, because I sleep there pretty well." He peered into the girl's eyes. "It was sure nice seeing you again, even though it's only been two days."

"I missed you too, Pete," the girl said. "I'm afraid I care for you more than might be good for me. I just have this hankerin' for you."

Pete Houston pulled her close to him and she threw her arms around his neck while he kissed her hard. She almost gasped, but then she pressed herself closer and Pete ran a hand over her back, then along her side, and finally to the front of her dress. He moved his hand slowly and touched her breast. She jerked slightly, but held him even more fervently before Pete pressed his hand harder on her breast.

"I want you so bad, Pete," she whispered. "I never in my life wanted someone so bad as I want you."

Houston did not answer. He only squeezed her breast, and she shivered slightly before she moved back.

"Pete, come upstairs with me," she whispered. "Come inside and stay with me tonight. Will you do that, Pete?"

"I can't think of anything I'd rather do more." But then he pushed her slightly away from him. "Jane, are you sure you want to do this? Are you sure you want to spend the night with me? I don't want you to feel sorry or guilty."

"How about you, Pete? Will you feel guilty? Will you think it's wrong?"

"I don't know if it's wrong or not," Houston answered. "I only know that I want you more than anything else in the world." This time he kissed her gently on the lips and she laid her head on his shoulder.

"Come upstairs with me, Pete," she whispered still again.

Pete Houston did not answer this time. He hooked his arm around hers and then opened the front door. Quietly, the duo walked up the dim-lit staircase, down the second-floor hallway, and into the girl's apartment. Jane Clemons locked the door behind her.

By early morning the next day, Laura Renault had boarded the stage at Jaycee. She had ridden into the hamlet alone. As she left the Hole In The Wall hideout, Big Val Henry had given her a parting bit of encouragement. "You'll get that bounty hunter for us, Laura, I know you will. There ain't a prettier woman in Wyoming Territory and he can't help but give in to you."

At Jaycee, she had left her horse in the stable and walked to the stage station. She still wore her riding clothes, somewhat dusty from the early ride out of the Hole In The Wall country. However, the attire of black riding skirt, checkered shirt, buckskin jacket, and black boots did not hide her shapely figure. She wore a flat loaf tambourine sombrero with a laced chin string and she carried a tanned leather bag, while her suitcase was atop the stage. She had used just enough makeup on her face to enhance the sparkle in her hazel eyes and the smoothness of her creamy, oval face.

When Laura dropped on her seat inside the stage, the others aboard eyed her with mixed reactions, though all with deep interest. The woman aboard almost glared, obviously jealous of this beautiful co-passenger sharing this coach with her. A small child, six or seven, the apparent daughter of the woman, peered hard at Laura Renault, perhaps wondering why her mother was not as beautiful as this fellow passenger. A third passenger, a middle-aged man in a business suit, ogled in obvious lust at the girl, no doubt wishing he could have Laura as a mistress. The fourth passenger, a buckskin-clad hunter, stared in admiration, for he had probably not seen so comely a woman in a long time.

The quintet aboard the stage said little or nothing to each other during the three-hour ride to Buffalo, and when they reached the town, Laura Renault alit. The stage driver carefully brought down her suitcase and turned to her.

"Where are you going, miss?"

"The Mercer Hotel."

"That's on Fourteenth Street," the driver said. Then he turned to an attendant at the stage depot. "See that this young woman and that passenger—" he gestured toward the man in the business suit— "get to the Mercer Hotel."

"I'll see that both them and their baggage get there, Jim," the attendant told the stage driver.

The man in the business suit was ecstatic when he learned that this comely woman was going to the same hotel as he was. When the attendant sat them on the seat of the buckboard and started for the hotel, the man turned to Laura Renault.

"Miss, it seems we're going to the same lodgings. Perhaps I could take you to dinner."

Laura Renault eyed the man coldly. "Mister, I got business in Buffalo, and I'll be too busy to go anywhere with you or anyone else. You was just a passenger on the same stage as me, and I think we should let it go at that."

"I was only trying to be friendly, miss."

"Well, I ain't," Laura answered brusquely. "I hope I make myself clear."

The rebuffed businessman slumped in his seat and said nothing more.

Inside the Mercer Hotel, the desk clerk stared at the beautiful Laura Renault, obviously impressed by her good looks and fine figure, despite her riding clothes. He almost trembled as he signed her in and gave her room twenty-seven on the second floor. "I ain't got no help here,

129

ma'am, but when I'm finished here, I'll be glad to take your bag upstairs myself."

"I can carry it," the girl answered as she took the key. "Now, can you draw me a bath?"

The clerk pursed his lips. "Ma'am, we only have Charlie to attend to people in the bathhouse. We ain't never had a woman in there before."

"Just tell this Charlie to draw my bath and leave my necessaries there," Laura answered in a somewhat snobbish tone. "When I get there, why, he can just leave the room until I'm finished."

"Yes, ma'am—er, miss"—he looked at the register—"Miss Renault."

The girl then handed the man a twenty-dollar bill. "This should cover my stay here for a week or so and take care of other incidentals like a bath."

"I guess it will, Miss Renault." The clerk grinned.

Laura Renault carried her suitcase and bag up the stairs and down the hall to room twenty-seven. She opened the door, went inside, dropped her bags, and walked to the window to stare out at quiet 14th Street. She turned and felt the soft bed, dropped on it in a sitting position, and then sighed. She only sat for a couple of minutes, and then unpacked her gear and put her clothes into one dresser drawer. She undressed and threw her attire on the bed before she slipped on a robe and slippers. She next gathered up the clothing from the bed and left her room. She saw the arrow pointing left, to the rear staircase, and the sign: Bath House.

The girl hurried through the length of the

hallway and down the back stairs to the bath-house, where clouds of steam greeted her as she opened the door. As she came deeper into the room, Chinaman Charlie ogled at the pretty young woman, somewhat awed by the unusual appearance of a woman seeking a bath. Under the robe was a naked, shapely female body, and the thought aroused a lust in him that he managed to restrain.

"Are you the attendant?" Laura asked.

"Yes, Missie." Charlie nodded vigorously.

"Is everything here? Soap, towel, comb?"

"All ready, missie," Charlie said. "The water is clean and hot."

"Fine," Laura said. She then handed the pile of clothes to the Chinaman. "Have these cleaned and ironed for me and bring them to my room, twenty-seven. I may have to use them in the morning. How soon can I get them back?"

"This afternoon," Charlie said. He then took each item and placed them into a basket. He had no problems with the skirt, blouse, and jacket, but he felt embarrassed when he tossed in the stockings, petticoat, bloomers, and bodice sash.

"Will you clean my boots?" Laura asked.

"Yes, missie."

"Now you can leave." The girl gestured. "Can I lock this door?"

Charlie nodded as he picked up the basket of clothes and left the room. Laura then locked the door, took off her robe, and finally settled into the hot tub. She closed her eyes in near ecstasy, allowing the warm water to loosen her muscles and soothe her bones. For a full five minutes she only sat in placid comfort, and she then scrubbed herself thoroughly with the soap and washcloth. After fifteen minutes, she left the tub, dried off, put on her robe, and slipped on her slippers.

She walked to the mirror and combed her hair until the dark flowing locks lay in straight, shiny strands. Then she unlocked the door. No one seemed about, but Charlie had been loitering in the hall, and when he saw the girl, he rushed to her and handed her the polished boots. She smiled at him and he watched her go up the back stairs. Then, Charlie hurried into the bathhouse to clean it up for the next customer.

In her room, Laura Renault dressed, putting on clean underclothes, a neat white blouse, clean tan wool skirt, large bow tie, and tan wool jacket. She slipped on her black boots that Chinaman Charlie had just polished and she then used just enough mascara and powder to enhance her face. Finally, she set her tambourine hat on her head. When she finished, she left the room, locked the door, and went downstairs to the front desk.

"Pardon me," Laura said, "but do you have a Mr. Peter Houston stayin' here?"

The clerk jerked in surprise for a moment, but then recovered. "Why, yes. He's in room twenty-three, but to tell you the truth"—he grinned sheepishly—"I don't think he stayed in his room last night. I'm told he came in briefly this morning to change his clothes and then went out."

"Has he left town?"

"No," the clerk said, "he took no traveling bags

with him, and his horse is still in the hotel stable, so he must be in town. He wouldn't go anywhere without that big bay. I can't say where he is right now."

"I see."

"He might come back, though," the clerk continued. "But if you have to see him right away, I'd suggest you try the cattlemen's association office. Big Joe Simeon might know where he is because he does a lotta business with Mr. Houston. Just go down to the end of Fourteenth, turn on Gillette, left, and the association office is about a block up the street."

Of course, Laura thought. Houston would be close to this Simeon since the bounty hunter did most of his work for the cattlemen's association and got most of his paydays from them. Houston had no doubt been there yesterday to collect a bounty on Sparks and Anias. Laura could only guess that perhaps Houston had spent the night in some local bordello. Still, she would find this Simeon and try to locate Houston.

As Laura walked up the street at this near-noontime hour, pedestrians, shopkeepers, and customers on the boardwalks all stared at the unusually pretty woman in her sharp attire. She strode brazenly, straight and haughty, and simply ignored those who ogled at her. The onlookers, in turn, said nothing. They had rarely seen in Buffalo such a striking woman with such an aura of egotism. When two somewhat drunken men saw her, they blocked her path.

"My, what a pretty girl," one of them said,

grinning. "Can we buy you a drink?"

Laura glared at them, reached into her bag, and took out a derringer that she aimed at the two men. "You have five seconds to get outta my way. And who's gonna fault a woman for killin' a coupla molesters?"

The two men stared at the gun, sidestepped around the girl, and hurried away. Laura watched them for a moment and then continued on until she reached the Buffalo office of the cattlemen's association. She walked inside where Jane Clemons looked up and gaped at the visitor. Jane couldn't remember ever having seen such a beautiful woman who was so stylishly dressed. She felt an instant pang of jealousy, but she composed herself quickly.

"Can I help you?"

"I'd just like a little information," Laura said. "I'm looking for Mr. Peter Houston, and I understand he does considerable business with this office. I thought perhaps that you or Mr. Simeon could tell me where I could find him."

"You're lookin' for Pete?"

"Pete?" Laura asked in surprise.

Jane lowered her head sheepishly. "I'm sorry— Mr. Houston."

"I checked at his hotel where I checked in myself this morning," Laura Renault continued, "but they tell me he didn't stay there last night, although he's still in town."

Jane Clemons pursed her lips and her face reddened slightly, offering the visitor a clue. Laura Renault smiled, almost certain that this girl behind the counter had been the reason that Pete Houston had not slept in his hotel room last night. Of course! A man like Pete Houston— someone with his adeptness and strength and cunning . . . He wouldn't need to visit a bordello to find a woman. Laura guessed that Houston was good looking, too.

"I—I don't know where he is," Jane Clemons stammered, "and Mr. Simeon is out to lunch. Anyway, he ain't seen Pete—er, Mr. Houston— since yesterday."

"And how about you, miss?" Laura asked with a slight grin. "Have you seen Mr. Houston this morning?"

Jane pursed her lips.

"Well?" Laura persisted.

"I understood he was goin' to the bank and then to the stable to have some work done on his horse and saddle. Maybe he had some other business as well." She looked at the clock. "It's noontime. He might have gone to the Buffalo Cafe or the Rawhide Saloon for lunch."

"I'm grateful, miss," the visitor said.

As she started to leave, Jane Clemons suddenly leaned over the counter. "Wait!" When Laura stopped and turned, Jane spoke again. "Are you a friend a Mr. Houston? How long have you known 'im?"

"I never met the man," Laura smiled. "I don't know him at all. However, I have need of his services. He is a bounty hunter, ain't he?"

"Yes," Jane answered.

"How will I know him, miss?"

Jane Clemons shrugged. "Just ask anybody in them two places. They'll know."

Again Laura thanked Jane Clemons, and then left the office. Jane felt a little relieved. This stunning woman in her natty dress only wanted to see Pete on business. But then, a tinge of panic gripped the girl. Would Pete be overwhelmed by this comely girl?

Laura first stopped at the Buffalo Cafe, now jammed with lunch customers. The cashier told her that Houston rarely stopped there for lunch. He generally went to the Rawhide Saloon because he apparently liked cold beer with his meal and they did not serve beer in the cafe.

Laura Renault continued up the street until she reached the Rawhide Saloon. She then, without inhibitions, went inside through the swinging doors. About a dozen customers were in the place at this hour. A few were at the bar and others at the tables. They stopped and stared in fascination at the girl, alone, coming into their midst. Females rarely came there, even with an escort, much less by themselves. The two prostitutes tarrying in the corner, the men at the dice table and the roulette wheel, the bartender, and the waiter also stopped and ogled in surprise at the girl.

Laura ignored them and walked up to the counter. "Bartender, can you tell me if Mr. Peter Houston is in here?"

The bartender gaped.

"Well, is he here?" she asked irritably.

"Yes, ma'am," the bartender answered.

136

"That's him at the small table over there by the wall; the man eatin' the ham sandwich and drinkin' from that pitcher a beer."

"I'm obliged," Laura said. She then weaved through the saloon, ignoring the multiple pairs of eyes following her. When she reached the table, Pete Houston was just downing a glass of beer. "My, my, they didn't tell me you were so handsome along with your other features."

The bounty hunter looked up and gaped when he saw the beautiful girl standing next to his table. He stared at her intently: her smooth dark hair, her clean oval face, the sparkling eyes, the trim figure, and the neat clothes. He could not even speak. Laura smiled and then dropped into a chair opposite him.

"You don't mind if I join you, do you, Mr. Houston?"

But Pete only stared.

"I was lookin' for you because I'm offerin' you a chance to make some real big money."

Houston's eyes widened, but he did not speak. He only took another bite from his sandwich.

"You are a bounty hunter, ain't you?"

Pete nodded.

"Then I got a proposition for you that you won't be able to resist."

Houston still did not speak. He poured himself another glass of beer and downed it quickly in several big gulps.

CHAPTER EIGHT

Many of those in the Rawhide Saloon continued to look at the woman who had boldly entered the place without an escort. They were more surprised when she had simply forced herself on the man at the small table eating his lunch. None of them said anything, but as they went about their business, they could not help glancing at the girl. When Laura Renault returned the stares to those in the saloon, the patrons turned their eyes away from her. Then, she smiled again at Pete Houston, who was now filled with curiosity.

"You'd think that none of you men have ever seen a woman before."

"Not in here, alone," Pete finally spoke.

"What about them?" Laura cocked her head toward the two harlots loitering in a small corner of the room.

"They work here." Houston shrugged. "It's normal to find them in this place. But you, a woman by herself, coming into a saloon . . . no one expects that, so they can't help wondering."

"There's no law against it, is there?"

"No, but it usually isn't done."

"Look, Mr. Houston," Laura said pointedly, "I didn't come in here to drink and gamble and look for a prostitute like mosta the men in here. I came to find you. I was told that you'd be havin' a noon meal in this place, as is your usual custom. So, that's why I'm here."

Pete Houston gestured. "I stay at the Mercer Hotel. Everybody knows that."

The girl leaned closer to the bounty hunter and smiled again. "You didn't sleep in your room last night, ain't that right? And you only went to the hotel this morning to change your clothes. Were you wanderin' around last night like a stray cat gettin' himself in trouble? Is that what you did? Maybe with that pretty filly at the cattlemen's association office?"

Pete Houston's eyes widened in surprise.

"It ain't no affair a mine"—the girl gestured—"I want to see you on business. I want to give you a chance to make some real money, like I said."

"Big money?" Pete huffed. "Why would you want to help me, a total stranger, to make big money?"

"Because I want a percentage a the bounty, say, one third," she answered.

Pete Houston stroked his chin. "I'm listening."

"It ain't no secret that you're after the Rawlings gang. Everybody in the Wyoming Territory knows it, and they know you've already brought in some a them rustlers. Now, that's a fact, ain't it, Mr. Houston?"

"Yes," Pete conceded.

"We all know them new posters came out today," Laura continued. "A thousand dollars for Dude Rawlings himself and five hundred for the others. I can help you to get all of 'em."

"What do you know about the Rawlings gang?"

The girl glanced first at the others in the saloon and then leaned even closer to Houston. "Take a good look at me, Mr. Houston—at my eyes."

Pete stared hard at the girl; his jaw tightened. Her eyes were a sparkling hazel color, the same color reported by those RX Ranch guards who had been tied and gagged at the riverbank campsite. "You're the one," he whispered. "You're the woman running with those outlaws."

"Not anymore," Laura said in a near whisper of her own. "I'm finished with 'em and I just want to see all of 'em dead or behind bars. There's the Dude and four of 'em left. They're worth three thousand dollars dead or alive. If I help you to take 'em, I want a thousand from that bounty money."

Pete Houston leaned over the table and grinned at the girl. "Thirty-five hundred if I take you in as well."

"Don't make them kinds a jokes." Laura scowled angrily. "Anyway, you can't prove that I'm one a them. Anything I said at this table is in confidence, and I'd just deny everything if you tried to do that. Besides, who'd show sympathy for a bounty hunter like you over the word of an innocent young woman like me?"

"You've got a point, miss—er . . . what is your name, anyway?"

"Just call me Mary Smith. You don't need to

know anything more, only what I can do for you so's we can both earn some money."

"How do I know I can trust you? And even if you do have those hazel-colored eyes, how do I know for sure that you're the one who was running with those outlaws?"

"You'll just have to trust me," Laura said. "I ran out on them because some a them was tryin' to get too close to me, and a few times I had to fight them off from tryin' to ravage me, especially after they had considerable whiskey in 'em. Besides, I never got my fair share a the money, and they worked me like a slave to cook their meals, keep their house, and wash their clothes. It wasn't right."

Houston took another swig of his beer.

"Then I thought a you," Laura said. "I heard how good you were, how you handled Colorado, and then Sparks and Anias, who tried to ambush you."

Houston's dark eyes widened in surprise. "How did you know about that ambush attempt?"

"Mister, I was at the hideout when they planned it. The Dude was gonna hire out a couple a professionals, but Anias and Sparks said they could do the job just as well. They sure botched it up, didn't they?"

"I must tell you, Mary Smith," Houston said. "I know where the Rawlings hideout is in the Hole In The Wall country."

"But not how to reach the place safely," the girl countered, "or how to surprise 'em so's you can take 'em one at a time. I know their routine, what

141

they might be doin' every hour a the day. I know where the Dude keeps his sentries, and I know how you can sneak up behind the sentry and take 'im. I know about the relief man, so's you can take him too. I know how you can surprise the rest of 'em, so's you can get them without danger to yourself. Do you understand what I'm sayin', Mr. Houston?"

"I'm still listening."

"Well, then," the girl said, "if I can help you to round up the whole gang, wouldn't it be worth givin' me a third a the bounty money?"

"There is one thing that bothers me," Pete said. "How did you you leave the Hole In The Wall alone and manage to come up here to Buffalo?"

Laura Renault shrugged. "I often go into Jaycee or Egleston to buy food and bring it back. Neither the Dude nor the rest a them was suspicious when I needed to go into town to get emergency supplies. I told 'em I was low on coffee, sugar, and bread, and these things might not hold out until our regular grub man brought new supplies. Since I handle the cookin' and such, they wasn't gonna think nothin' wrong with my goin' into town. I just left my horse at a stable in Jaycee and took the first stage into Buffalo."

Houston stroked his chin again. "You said you brought a traveling bag and clothes with you. How did you manage to do that without suspicion?"

"I managed," she said. "I was able to pack 'em on my horse without them knowin' it. When I got here and checked into the Mercer Hotel, I took a good bath and then dressed in clean clothes."

"I see," Houston said. Her story sounded pretty convincing to the bounty hunter. "Suppose we start out tomorrow. Is that all right?"

"First thing in the mornin'," Laura said. "Like I said, I'm checked into the same hotel as you are. I got my ridin' clothes bein' cleaned now and they'll be ready this afternoon. However, I will need a horse."

"I can arrange that."

The girl rose from her chair. "Then, if you don't mind, I'm goin' back to the hotel. I want to rest a bit this afternoon. I've had a long day already, since I was up before daylight this mornin'."

"Wait." Houston gripped her hand. "Can I see you before morning?"

Laura Renault smiled. "That wouldn't set too well with that filly in the cattlemen's association office, would it?" When Pete did not answer, the girl gestured. "I'm tempted, Mr. Houston, because you're sure a handsome man. A girl would be lucky to have you. But, I don't think so. Our association is strictly business, at least right now. Besides, startin' tomorrow, we'll be together every minute for at least a coupla days."

Pete Houston nodded and watched the shapely girl leave the saloon. A dozen pairs of eyes followed the girl out of the Rawhide.

Laura Renault, however, did not return immediately to her hotel. Instead, she walked up Gillette Avenue and turned into narrow 12th Street, continued on for a block, and stopped before a small clapboard one-story cottage. The structure sagged from age and neglect, and its siding had corroded from lack of care. She recognized the house as the domicile of Joe Cameron. She stepped gingerly up the rickety wooden steps to the equally warped, rotting floor of the porch. Then she knocked at the door.

The squat, obese Joe Cameron, clad in simple trousers and undershirt, opened the door. He stared at the pretty woman standing there, but he rightly guessed that she was probably Laura Renault, whom he had been expecting. Still, he said nothing as he watched the girl take a lead medallion out of her bag and show it to Cameron. Then he nodded.

"Come inside," he said.

Within the dingy and squalid parlor, Cameron offered the girl a seat in a tattered armchair. When the girl sat down, he spoke again. "Now, did you see Houston?"

"I showed you my medallion, mister, where's yours?"

The man grinned. "Of course." He reached into a cabinet and took out a brass medallion. Laura looked and nodded.

"All right, Mr. Cameron, now we can talk."

"As I was sayin', did you see the bounty hunter?"

"Yes. It's all taken care of," the girl said. "We'll be leavin' Buffalo together at first light in the mornin' and we'll probably reach Jaycee before noon. We'll probably stop for lunch there and then we'll ride into the Hole In The Wall country. She took out a piece of paper on which was drawn a simple map. "Here's the Dude's watch point—" she tapped the map with her finger. "We usually have a sentry there in the rocks, just above this curvin' section of the trail. I intend to take Houston in this direction—" she ran her finger over another portion of the map. "We'll come up from behind here to take whoever is on sentry duty, most likely Big Val. Then, we'll wait for his relief. But I'll keep that bounty hunter here"—she moved her finger again—"so that Dude and someone else can arrive behind us and take us. Do you understand?"

"I think so," Cameron said.

"You can't think so," Laura cried sharply. "You've got to be certain. This Houston is as sly and wise as an old mountain lion, and we can't have no mistakes. The Dude has to be sure he comes up in the right direction, at the right time, and to the right place."

"I'll study the map real well," Cameron said.

"When me and that bounty hunter take the sentry, I'll tell 'im that the relief man is comin' at four o'clock in the afternoon and that we'll need to sit patiently and wait. But the Dude should come up there about three, when Houston won't be expectin' anyone. That'll make it easier to take the bounty hunter."

"I'll get off a telegram right away to Nebraska," Cameron said, "and he'll be out to your place in a couple of hours."

"Good," Laura said, rising from the chair.

"Wait, Miss Renault," the man said, suddenly grinning at her while a tinge of lust beamed from his eyes. "No need to run right off." He studied her shapely figure and then grinned again. "Why, I could give you a little drink and we could sit here for a while, maybe get to know each other better; get friendly. After all, we both work for the Dude."

Laura Renault smirked. "Mister, I finished my business here and I'll be on my way."

"Now wait; no need to be so impatient." He gripped the girl's wrist and she glowered at him before she pulled her arm away.

"Let me tell you somethin'. No man puts a hand on me without my wantin' him to," she said coldly.

"Like I said, I only want us to be friends."

"If you want a woman, why, this town is full a whores, and Dude pays you enough so you can afford one," Laura said. She then reached into her bag and pulled out her derringer and aimed it at the surprised Cameron. "I'm on my way out, mister, and to be honest, it wouldn't bother me in the least to blow your brains out right here. The only thing that stops me is the fact that you need to send a telegram. However, if it came down to the telegram or me bein' ravaged by the likes a you, why, I'd just as soon kill you."

"I—I didn't mean no harm," Cameron stammered.

"Give me a half-hour to leave here and go back to my hotel. Then you can head for the telegraph office. And you better not make any mistakes, or I swear I'll come back and kill you."

"Sure, Miss Renault, sure," Cameron said quickly. "I suggest that you go up the street and circle around into Fourteenth Street to go back to your hotel. That way, you can avoid Gillette where that bounty hunter might see you."

"That advice is the only good advice you've given me," Laura said.

Laura left the cottage and walked quickly down 12th Street. Joe Cameron stood on the porch, stroking his bearded chin as he watched her depart. Then he grinned to himself. The girl could be a wildcat when she got riled up, and she was colder than Simon Legree. He guessed that she probably treated all men with contempt and he also suspected that perhaps she was a troublsome member of the Rawlings gang. Still, it looked like she'd succeed against that sly bounty hunter where ambushes had failed. Without a doubt, she was pretty enough to decieve Pete Houston.

Houston himself, meanwhile, had gone to the cattlemen's association building after his meeting and meal at the Rawhide Saloon. Jane Clemons met him with a hint of uncertainty and she greeted Pete soberly.

"I thought I'd get a friendly smile." Houston grinned.

"Pete, there was a real pretty woman in here some time ago; said she was lookin' for you. I told her you might have gone to lunch at the cafe or at the Rawhide. Who is she, Pete? Did she find you?"

"Yes, she found me," Pete answered, "but you shouldn't worry about her. My meeting with her was strictly business. She offered to give me some vital information on how to find and capture the Rawlings gang, but she wanted a share of any bounty money in return."

"But who is she, Pete?" Jane asked again.

"A girl named Mary Smith whom I've never seen before," Pete said. "She's from Egleston and she's learned a lot about the movements of those outlaws. She gave me a good plan on how to take them without any danger. We'll be leaving together the first thing in the morning."

"Leavin' together!" Jane gasped. "But you don't even know her. How do you know she's not in with them rustlers and that she might lead you into a trap?"

"I don't know for sure," Pete admitted, "but it's a chance I'll have to take." He did not tell Jane that the girl had been one of the gang members or that she was staying at the same hotel as he was. "I swear, Jane, I'll be back in a couple of days. This girl doesn't mean anything to me; it's only business."

But Jane Clemons pursed her lips, pouting. A tinge of jealousy gripped her. The visitor had been beautiful, and Jane could not bear the idea of Pete going off with the woman for two or three days. Yet, Jane Clemons had resigned herself to the fact that Pete Houston was determined to continue his profession as a bounty hunter, and she would no longer try to change his mind.

Pete leaned over the counter. "Can I see you this evening?"

But Jane Clemons looked coldly at Houston. "I'll be busy at the Evangelical Circle tonight," she answered. "Maybe when you come back." At the moment, Jane's umbrage prompted her to react frigidly.

"I'm sorry, Jane," Pete said, "I'd have sure liked to be with you tonight. But please believe me, this woman means nothing to me. It's only you I'm interested in. Nothing pleases me more than to be in your company. I swear, as soon as this business is finished, I'll probably never see Mary Smith again."

"All right, Pete," Jane said, but her coolness still simmered.

"I'll see you when I get back." Houston leaned over the counter and kissed the girl, but Jane offered no response, although she did not stop him. She stood rigid and watched Pete Houston leave the office.

Daylight had barely emerged above the Black Hills to the east when Pete Houston and Laura Renault loped up Gillette Avenue and out of town. Houston had spent a rather boring time since yesterday, after leaving Jane Clemons at the cattlemen's association office. He had returned to his hotel, but he had not found Laura, whom the clerk said had gone out to do some shopping. He had not seen her until the early evening when he called on her at her hotel room, only two doors down from his own, to tell her that he had hired a horse for her use in the morning. She had not invited him into her room, and she had declined an invitation to dinner, still maintaining her strictly business attitude. Nor had Houston seen Jane Clemons, who apparently remained aloof because of Pete's decision to go off with Laura

Renault, even if only on a business venture.

Laura herself had meandered about town for a couple of hours yesterday afternoon after her visit with Joe Cameron. She had visited some of the shops and had purchased a blouse and a blanket for use on the trail. She had spent the remainder of her time in her hotel room, except to order some dinner that Chinaman Charlie had brought to her. And, save for the visit by Houston, she had not seen anyone again until she'd met Pete this morning to begin the ride into the Hole In The Wall country.

Full daylight had arrived by the time Houston and the girl came five miles south of Buffalo. Laura had said little to her companion, but she occasionally stared at him with a tinge of admiration. He was certainly a well-built, rugged man, with a handsome face, clean brown eyes, and neat dark hair. He was also tidy in appearance with his clean riding clothes, shiny boots, and shaven face. He had obviously spruced himself this morning before leaving the hotel.

Pete also glanced now and then at the girl, and each time he did so, he felt a new tingle. She was indeed beautiful, with her creamy oval face, smooth locks of dark hair, and the lustrous hazel eyes that could enchant anyone. And even in her riding britches, loose blouse, and buckskin jacket, he could easily see her shapely figure. She too was clean and neat, also obviously having preened herself before leaving Buffalo.

They had come about halfway down the Johnson County Highway when the girl finally smiled at Pete. "I must say, Mr. Houston, if I have to be on the trail with a man, I can't think of a more handsome companion than you."

Pete Houston grinned.

"I've heard you were strong, and clever as a cougar, and also quite well educated."

"I've been through full elementary school."

"And now I find you're also comely," the girl continued. "Somehow, it don't seem fair that one man should have so much goin' for 'im."

"And what about yourself, Mary Smith?" Pete asked. "How can one woman have so much beauty? I must tell you that I don't remember the last time I've been in the company of a woman as pretty as you. What I don't understand, though, is why you got tied up with those rustlers."

"Money, Mr. Houston, money."

"But I'd have to guess that half the rich men in Johnson County would have given you any kind of luxury you wanted."

"Only if I went to bed with them," the girl said. "Them with any money are already married, and that's all they wanted from me."

"Would that have been so bad? There must have been some men that you might have wanted in bed with you."

"No, I ain't found that man yet," she said. Then Laura smiled at her companion. "But I must confess, Mr. Houston, I'm sure tempted to take up with you."

Again, Pete Houston only grinned.

By late morning the duo had reached Jaycee and stopped at a small cafe for a noon meal. Pete ordered a roast beef sandwich, some vegetable soup, and coffee, while the girl ordered a ham sandwich and coffee. Here, the girl ate slowly, obviously procrastinating, as she occasionally looked at the clock on the wall. She did not want to start into the Hole-In-The-Wall country much before noon because she knew that Dude Rawlings needed time to set his trap.

And in fact, even as the duo sat in the Jaycee cafe, Rawlings completed plans at his ornate log hideout. He had seen Nebraska Brake late yesterday, after the man had received telegram instructions from Joe Cameron in Buffalo. The Dude had then begun preparations to snare Houston the next day. Now, he was repeating final instructions to his men.

"You understand what you need to do, don't you, Big Val?" Rawlings asked.

The burly outlaw nodded. "I'm to take my usual sentinel position in the rocks and not look behind me at all. Laura and the bounty hunter will sneak up on me and take me. And if Houston asks, I'm to say that my relief will come at four o'clock. I suspect he'll probably tie me up at that clump a scrub brush below the rock and wait for my relief. That's all I need to do, ain't it?"

"Yes," Dude Rawlings said. He turned to Jerry Roseberry. "We'll leave here about two-thirty and just walk to them rocky cougar trails and come up behind Laura and Houston as quietly as we can. We can't make any noise at all 'cause that snake can hear anything. Laura will see to it that him and her sit and face west, with Big Val tied in

152

front of 'em. She might even cozy up to the bounty hunter to keep his attention."

"I'm ready," Roseberry said. He was quite happy that Laura had made her deal with Houston so quickly, eliminating the necessity of spending too much time with Houston. However, the ex-army captain did wonder if perhaps Laura had spent the evening with the bounty hunter last night.

"What about me and the Preacher?" Clint Eliot now spoke.

"You boys just say put here," Rawlings said. "If we ain't back in an hour, why, the two of you better come out lookin' for us."

"All right." Eliot nodded.

The Dude then turned to Henry. "Get movin', Big Val."

"I'm on my way," the big man answered.

At just about noontime, Pete Houston and Laura Renault finally left the cafe in Jaycee and he turned and grinned at her. "I must say, you sure are a slow eater."

"I guess that's one a my faults," the girl answered.

After they boarded their horses, they loped out of town and then moved southward for about another five miles until the girl reared up. "This is the trail that leads to our place. We're only goin' in about two miles and then I'll take you over a cougar trail, so's we can come up behind the Dude's sentry. He's probably there by now, and he'll stay put until somebody relieves him about four o'clock."

Pete Houston nodded.

Now the pair of riders loped carefully over the trail that led into the Hole In The Wall country. They moved slowly, with Houston occasionally looking at the girl with obvious infatuation. Laura caught the looks and returned reciprocal ones of admiration. However, she now began to feel an inward pain. She liked this man and she was taking him into a trap, perhaps even to his death. The idea suddenly brought a feeling of nausea inside her and she was sorry she had agreed to this caper. But it was too late now. She hid her feelings nicely and smiled at Houston.

"Believe me, Mr. Houston, you can trust me."

"All right, Mary Smith."

But suddenly the girl blurted, "Laura, Laura Renault. That's my real name. Seein' as how you trust me, I should do the same. When this is over," she said, continuing her ruse, "maybe we can have a little time for ourselves."

"Maybe," Pete answered.

They continued on and soon they once more veered off the trail, riding slowly and cautiously over some rough, upward paths that had once been used by Indians and were now used by mountain cats or deer. Laura led the way, trotting warily until they finally reached a brake of scrub brush. Here, she dismounted and gestured to Houston. The bounty hunter also dismounted and led his horse toward the girl.

"We'll tether the animals here," she whispered.

"The sentry is alone up in them rocks, no more'n a hundred yards or so. You can take 'im easy."

Pete nodded and extracted his rifle from his saddle scabbard. Then he followed the girl as both of them clambered slowly up through some jagged, rocky terrain. The girl slipped and Pete caught her, holding her close in the process. He did not let her go at once and Laura made no effort to loosen herself from his grip. For a moment they stared into each other's eyes. But then Houston released her.

"Be careful," he whispered.

Laura Renault smiled. "If I'm not, maybe I'll be lucky enough to have you catch me and hold me again."

"Let's keep going," Pete said.

Once again the pair continued slowly and cautiously through the harsh terrain, stepping lightly to make no noise as they approached a rocky area at the top of a peak. Then, the girl stopped Houston, came close to him, and spoke in an almost-inaudible voice. "The sentry will be right behind them rocks, and crouchin' down, lookin' down at the trail."

"Go back to the brake,"Pete said.

The girl nodded, crouched down, and watched Houston continue on. Pete finally peeked from behind a boulder and saw Big Val Henry in a sitting position with his rifle barrel resting on a rock in front of him, while the outlaw himself peered nonchalantly at the trail below him. As planned, Henry made certain that he looked away from Houston's approach area. The bounty hunter rose full to his feet and aimed his rifle.

"All right, mister, you're covered."

Big Val turned to face the barrel of Houston's gun and he started in apparent surprise. "God-damn, who are you?"

"Move away from that rock, and don't go for your Winchester or you'll be a dead man."

"Hey"—Henry grinned—"I ain't crazy enough to get myself killed." He rose to his feet and raised his arms. Pete came forward and peered over the rock at the excellent view of the trail below. Yes indeed, from this spot, nobody could come through the Hole In The Wall country unless someone wanted the rider to do so.

A moment later, Houston led the man down the ragged slope and all the way back to the brake of scrub brush where Laura Renault was standing by the horses. Big Val was shocked at the sight of the girl. "Laura! What the hell are you doin' here? Did you betray us like this? Let a god-damn bounty hunter take us? I'll be a son of a bitch!" Henry was playing his role well.

Laura did not answer and Pete sat the man down, while the girl held her derringer on him. Houston then tied Big Val securely to a small tree.

"What are you doin' this for?" Henry asked the girl.

Laura did not answer, but Pete gestured to Henry. "What time does your relief man get here?"

"None a your damn business."

Houston recocked his rifle. "All right," Val relented. "Clint Eliot is my relief. He'll be here

156

about four o'clock and he'll be comin' up that trail." The big man cocked his head to his left.

"You're mighty cooperative," Houston said.

"I heard what you done to Anias. I don't want that no matter what. So long as I'm alive, I'll still have a chance. As for you, Laura," he sneered at the girl, "you're a no-good bitch, givin' us away like this. Ain't we always treated you fair? Why the hell would you do this to us?" Big Val continued his acting role in an exemplary manner.

"You men was usin' me more like a slave than anything else," Laura answered sharply, "and it was only a matter a time before one a you animals ravaged me. Don't you think I could see the lust in the eyes a all a you every time you looked at me?"

"The Dude will kill you for sure," Henry said.

"No he won't," Laura sneered, "because we'll get him too."

A moment later, Pete Houston and Laura Renault sat against a rock and faced the bound Big Val, who soon fell asleep in his sitting position. The girl looked at her companion. "We done all right so far, ain't we, Mr. Houston? We'll just need to be patient and wait for the relief man to come up that trail. Then, we'll need more patience, because the Dude and the others will come out lookin' for them when Big Val don't come back to the hideout."

"I've got to admit," Pete said, grinning, "you did everything you said you would, and I couldn't be more pleased."

The girl smiled and snuggled close to Houston,

and as she did, her warm body sent a thrill through his muscular frame. He looked at the girl again and once more a tinge of lust gripped him. But when Laura stared back into Pete's eyes, he saw more than a reflection of mutual desire. He saw what seemed almost like a tinge of regret, almost remorse, and he could not understand it.

The girl suddenly moved away from Houston and the bounty hunter believed for a moment that perhaps she was afraid to get too familiar with him. However, just as suddenly, she moved close to him again and smiled once more, but Houston thought it was a forced smile and he was puzzled. What Pete didn't realize, of course, was that the girl needed to hold his total attention as long as possible.

"I like bein' next to you, Mr. Houston," Laura said. "You're the first real man I ever met."

The flattery indeed kept Houston off guard and he felt a new excitement when the girl twirled his shirt with her warm fingers and ran a soft hand down his arm. She then snuggled close as Houston put his arm around her. The bounty hunter had taken the bait completely and he was utterly unprepared for what happened next.

Suddenly, from above the rock against which Pete and Laura sat, the point of a rifle touched the back of Houston's head. "Don't move, bounty hunter; not one movement, or you're dead."

Pete Houston froze and then gaped at Laura Renault, who now extracted Pete's six-shooter from his holster and picked up the rifle lying against the rock next to him. She rose to her feet and looked at him, an obvious agony visible in her eyes. As she moved back, Dude Rawlings came around the rock with an aimed six-shooter and grinned smugly.

"Well, bounty hunter, now it's you who's in trouble."

A few seconds later, Jerry Roseberry came around the rock with his rifle and pointed his weapon also at Houston.

"We ought to kill this bastard right here," Dude said.

"No," Roseberry pointed out, "that wouldn't be smart. I suspect this man had enough sense to tell somebody he was coming in here, and we don't want any murder charges hanging over us. We'll just hold him a prisoner for a while until we can figure out what to do with him."

Dude Rawlings nodded, and then looked at the girl. "Laura, I got to hand it to you. I don't know of anybody in Wyomin' who could've lured this smart bounty hunter into a trap like you did. Like I said, there'll be a bonus for you."

Laura Renault did not answer, but Pete Houston stared intently at the girl. Yet, he was more infuriated with himself than with Laura Renault. He should have known better, and now he had made a mistake that could cost him his life.

CHAPTER NINE

Within an hour, the outlaws had taken Pete Houston to the ornate log house in the depths of the Hole In The Wall country. Now, having untied Houston from his horse, the Dude prodded him up the steps of the porch and into the parlor of the house. Rawlings then shoved Houston into a parlor chair before he grinned.

"You wanted to see this place, bounty hunter, and now you're here. How do you like it?"

"Nice, very nice," Pete said, looking about the living room.

The Dude leaned down closer to Houston. "Enjoy it while you can, 'cause you ain't gonna be here much longer; nor will you get a chance to tell others how to reach this place."

Pete did not answer, as Clint Eliot and Preacher Rogers suddenly came into the parlor. Both men were clad in simple trousers, checked shirts, and boots. They wore no hats, but did carry their gunbelts around their waists. Eliot studied the prisoner, staring with a mixture of anger and curiosity in his eyes. He looked at Pete for a full half-minute before he turned to the outlaw leader.

"Dude, what are we gonna do with him?"

"I'm for killin' him right now," Rawlings answered, "but Cap don't think that's a good idea."

Eliot scowled at Roseberry. "Goddamn, Cap, you know what this bounty hunter did to us. He killed one of our partners and jailed two others. He don't deserve to live. He's nothin' but trouble. We gotta kill 'im. Ain't that why we set this trap for 'im? He's too smart to have alive—we can't have that."

"You're right about one thing, Eliot," Roseberry said. "He's smart. Whether he believed Laura or not before coming after us, I have to think that he told somebody he was comin' here, maybe Sheriff Angus or that Simeon of the cattlemen's association. If he doesn't come back to Buffalo, why, they'll know we killed him. They may want us for cattle rustling, but they don't work too hard at looking for us. However, murder is something else."

"Well, what the hell do you think we can do with the bastard—turn 'im loose!" Eliot cried angrily.

"No," Roseberry admitted, "but we'll have to plan some way to make sure he can no longer interfere with us in our operations."

As Roseberry spoke, Pete Houston and Laura Renault exchanged glances. The mutual infatuation between them had returned, but a hint of disappointment came from Houston's brown eyes, while a tinge of regret radiated from Laura

161

Renault's hazel ones. No doubt the girl now felt remorse for her action in leading the bounty hunter into this trap. The others in the room had not caught the exchange of looks, except for Jerry Roseberry. He now suspected that Laura felt something for Houston and he did not appreciate this. Roseberry said nothing, however, and he turned away when Dude Rawlings spoke to him again.

"Look," the outlaw leader said, "for the time bein', the best thing to do is to keep this bounty hunter locked up. We got a big job tonight and the sooner we get started the better. Them cattle ain't gonna wait for us, and Balfonte is anxious for a new herd. Anyway, the word from Buffalo is that the price a beef has gone up. So, I think we can get more than ten dollars a head."

"But we're short-handed," Preacher Rogers now spoke. "Who's gonna stay behind and watch this man?" He gestured toward Houston.

"Not me." Big Val Henry suddenly grinned. "I want to go after them steers." He looked at Eliot. "Maybe Wild Man will stay with 'im."

"No," Roseberry said. "He's likely to kill this prisoner."

"I ain't that dumb, Cap'n," Eliot protested. "I heard what you said about Houston maybe tellin' somebody he came out here. Still, I don't want to stay behind, either," he said, looking at Rawlings.

"Well, don't leave me here," Preacher Rogers said. Then he pointed to the girl. "Hey, Laura brought him here, and maybe she can keep an eye on 'im."

162

The girl's eyes widened, but she did not respond.

"No, no." Roseberry shook his head vigorously. "We can't leave him here with Laura. That would be too dangerous."

"Not if he's good and locked up," Dude Rawlings suddenly spoke.

"Sure." Eliot nodded.

"True, Laura's been a help to us on these capers," Rawlings said, "but we'll all have to admit that if we need to leave somebody behind, that ought to be Laura. Besides, if the bounty hunter's locked up, why, he wouldn't even need a guard."

"Sure." Eliot nodded. "I'll board up that window in the Mexican's room and there won't be no way he can get out, especially if we also lock and bolt that heavy bedroom door."

"Well, Laura?" Rawlings asked.

The girl only shrugged.

"No," Roseberry still protested. "She's only a woman, and if he did get out, he'd easily overpower her."

"Now, how the hell can he do that if he's sealed tight in that bedroom?" Wild Man Eliot gestured acidly. "Why, you could leave a puppy dog behind to watch over 'im with no trouble."

Jerry Roseberry did not answer this time. He only pursed his lips. He remembered the mutual, doting glances between Laura Renault and Pete Houston, and he felt more than mere irritation. Not only did he dislike the idea of the girl feeling anything for the bounty hunter, but this very feeling could lead to an escape, if Houston convinced the girl to free him. Still, how could he tell the others that he harbored such suspicions? They would only laugh at him, or accuse him of jealousy. After all, hadn't the girl done a first-rate job in leading the bounty hunter into a trap? Did Rawlings now expect this same girl to free Houston after she had worked so hard and so deftly to bring him here?

The ex-army captain groped for another argument to dissuade Rawlings and the others from leaving Laura behind with the bounty hunter. However, he could think of nothing. He would have to hope for the best. Still, he promised himself, he would take the girl aside before he left this evening and he would warn her of his suspicions; remind her that he would personally kill her and the bounty hunter if she allowed Pete Houston to escape.

Dude Rawlings again looked at the girl. "Well, Laura, do you mind stayin' behind tonight?"

"If that's what you want," Laura answered.

Rawlings then pointed at Houston. "That'll be somethin', won't it, bounty hunter? You bein' held prisoner by a woman? It must hurt your pride."

"What difference does it make?" Pete shrugged.

Rawlings looked at Eliot. "All right, Wild Man, get some a them thick planks to board up the window. Then check the door to make sure the hinges on the door are tight. Then make sure the bolt lock is all right. Take Big Val to help you out."

"Sure, Dude, sure," Henry said.

Rawlings looked at Houston. "We'll feed you

before we go and then leave you some bread and water while you're in that room all night. That way, Laura won't have no need to even come near you while you're locked up. We'll be back sometime tomorrow and then we'll decide what to do with you."

Pete did not answer and Rawlings turned to the girl. "Laura, I hate to ask you this since you already did so much in bringin' in this bounty hunter. But, could you start cookin' up some beef stew for us? I know it don't seem fair, but we'd like to be off with full bellies. Besides, we'll need to fill up the prisoner too, so's he won't get hungry until we get back."

"I'll get started," Laura said.

"Don't worry," the Dude said to the girl, "you're gonna get a bonus from all of us for bringin' in this man, and you'll get an equal share from the money we get for that herd we take tonight. That ought to make you feel a little better for doin' all this work for us."

Laura Renault nodded, glanced at Houston, and then left for the kitchen.

Preacher Rogers now sat in the parlor, holding a six-shooter on Pete Houston, while Rawlings and Roseberry left the house to ready the horses for tonight's caper. Big Val and Wild Man, meanwhile, hurried out of the rear door and gathered up several two-by-eight planks from the lumber shed, along with hammers and nails. They hurried to the ell wing of the log structure, and within a half-hour they had nailed the heavy planks across the window of the small bedroom that had been formerly occupied by Pedro Anias. They did a thorough job so that Houston could not escape.

When the two men finished outdoors, they next came inside and checked the heavy plank door of the small bedroom, making certain the hinges were screwed on tightly so that the prisoner could not break down the door. They then examined both the key lock and the bolt lock which were both snug and tight.

When the two men reported that the room was secure, Preacher Rogers led Pete Houston into the bedroom. "We'll let you out to eat with us," he told Pete before he shoved the bounty hunter into the room, locked the door with a key, and then slammed the bolt lock into place.

For the next two hours, while Houston sat quietly on the bed in the small bedroom, and while Laura Renault prepared the beef stew, the five outlaws sat in the parlor to finalize their plan for tonight's job. They intended to run off about three hundred head from the Branden Ranch, about sixteen miles south of Buffalo. Again, the steers would be near the Powder River, and there would be the usual four sentinels watching the animals. But this time, Jerry Roseberry and Big Val Henry drew the job of taking both horseback guards, and they would need to subdue them one at a time, since they no longer had Anias or Sparks to help them. Preacher Rogers would again remain with the horses and bring them into the open on a signal from Dude Rawlings.

Meanwhile, Dude Rawlings and Wild Man

Clint Eliot would take the campsite guards alone, which meant two on two. However, since the outlaws would have the element of surprise, the Dude believed they would have no problem. As usual, the Dude had already cased the herd and the usual locations of the four nighttime sentinels.

When they finished in the parlor, the five men left the house and ambled to the barn. Here, they readied their mounts, feeding them, brushing them down, checking the shoes, and then saddling the animals. Next, they rolled up their bedrolls, putting inside each a blanket, hardtack biscuits, and beef jerky. Rawlings slipped some coffee, tin cups, and a pot in his own roll, in the event they got a chance to brew some coffee in the morning. The quintet also checked their weapons and lassos, slipping loaded rifles into their scabbards, coiling their ropes neatly, and loading their six-guns. They certainly had no intention of killing anyone, but they needed to be prepared.

When they left the barn, Rawlings squinted into the darkening sky. "Laura ought to have that stew just about ready by now and we should be off by nightfall."

"I'm as hungry as a wolf." Big Val Henry grinned.

Once inside the house again, they found the girl already setting plates, cups, and silverware on the oblong table in the dining room. As the five outlaws began seating themselves, the Dude gestured to Rogers. "Preacher, bring that bounty hunter out here now. Maybe we sure need to kill him, but we ain't gonna starve 'im to death."

The Preacher nodded and hurried to the ell section of the house where he unbolted the door and brought out Houston at gunpoint. "Time to eat, bounty hunter, but don't try nothin'. Any one of us would be happy to find an excuse to kill you."

Pete Houston looked at the gun and then quietly walked ahead of Rogers, through the corridor and into the dining room. Dude Rawlings grinned at the prisoner. "Sit down and eat. You might not get anything else until this time tomorrow."

After Houston had seated himself, Laura returned to the dining room with a huge cauldron of beef stew. She placed it in the center of the table and then left. A moment later, she came back with a loaded plate of hot rolls and a big pot of coffee. By the time she sat down herself, next to Rawlings, the others were already plucking rolls from the platter and ladling heaps of stew onto their plates. However, neither the girl nor Houston had moved, and Dude Rawlings grabbed Pete's plate.

"Like I said, we don't aim to starve you." He then filled the plate and laid it in front of Houston. Rawlings then took Laura's plate, filled it with stew, and placed it in front of her. "You can't go without eatin', either."

For the next fifteen minutes the seven diners at the table ate their meals. Dude, Big Val, Preacher, Wild Man, and Roseberry ate ravenously, but Pete Houston ate slowly, while the girl only picked at her food. Pete, of course, faced an uncertain future that had obviously lessened his appetite, despite his hunger. The girl now wrestled with her conscience and the agony had erased her own appetite. Still, when the Dude glanced at one or the other of them, they quickly resumed eating. By dark, the meal had ended. Rawlings looked at Rogers.

"Preacher, take the bounty hunter back and bolt the door as well as lock it with the key after he's inside. And you, Laura"—he gestured to the girl—"go with the Preacher. Get a good piece a bread an' a pitcher a water to leave with the prisoner. He might get hungry or thirsty before we get back tomorrow." Laura nodded and followed the two men.

Within a few minutes, Pete Houston was again confined to the small bedroom, this time with a half a loaf of bread and a full pitcher of water on the small dresser. As he sat on the bed, he heard Rogers first lock the heavy door with a key and then slam shut the bolt lock.

"He won't get outta there." Rogers grinned to Laura. "Hell, you can hardly open that door when it ain't locked, much less when it's locked and bolted." Then Rogers grinned and shouted through the heavy plank door, "Hey, bounty hunter, that's a real soft bed in there. You're luckier than we are. You can sleep but we'll be out on the trail all night."

When Rogers returned to the dining area, he found Laura Renault already clearing the table, bringing the platter, cauldron, pot, and plates back to the kitchen. Roseberry was helping her. The others, meanwhile, had returned to the parlor, and Rogers went into the living room to join them.

"Well?" Rawlings asked Rogers.

"All taken care of." The Preacher grinned. "There ain't no way that bounty hunter can get outta that bedroom. Why, Laura won't need to watch him at all."

"That's good." The Dude nodded.

In the kitchen, as Laura began washing plates, Jerry Roseberry suddenly moved next to her and gripped her wrist. The girl jerked but then glared at him. "I thought I made myself clear. No man touches me 'less I want 'im to. You're a fine man, Cap, and I got to admit that if I had a mind to take up with any of you, why, it'd likely be you. Still, I ain't encouragin' anyone right now and I don't like bein' touched."

"I'm not denying that I'd certainly be grateful to have you, Laura," Roseberry said, "and you know that I've honored your privacy and wishes more than anyone else in this band. I just want to talk to you."

"Well, you don't need to grab my wrist to do that," Laura said, pulling her arm away. What's on your mind?"

"That bounty hunter."

"What about him?" the girl huffed. "I brought him in for you and he's safely locked up in that bedroom. It ain't my say as to what to do with 'im next. You got the influence with the Dude, not me. So, I'd say that you and the Dude can take it from here. My only job tonight is to keep an eye on 'im, but it don't look like that'll be necessary, seein' as how you all but sealed Houston in that room."

Roseberry leaned close to the girl. "I want to be sure that he stays locked in that room."

"What do you mean?"

"I mean," Roseberry said slowly, "that I didn't like the way you were looking at him in the parlor, and the way he was looking back at you. Perhaps the others didn't notice, but I certainly did. It almost seemed like you two have an infatuation for each other."

"You're crazy, Cap," the girl sneered. "He don't mean nothin' to me. You seem to have a craw in your throat anytime anyone looks at me. If I had a thing for that bounty hunter, do you think I'd have brought him here to get caught like some unsuspectin' cougar?"

"You were with him for some time before you brought him here," Roseberry said. "Something could have developed between you two while you were close and alone together for so long."

"He don't mean nothin' to me, I'm tellin' you," Laura insisted.

"I just want to make sure," Roseberry said. "I need to warn you, Laura, no matter how much I think of you, Houston better be in that bedroom when we get back. If he isn't, we could only assume that you turned him loose, and we'd need to do something harsh to you."

"Cap'n"—Laura grinned—"if he ain't in that room when you get back tomorrow, it won't be my fault. That bounty hunter is smarter than all of you put together. I'll make regular checks on him for the next twelve or sixteen hours, but he might get outta there anyway. If you don't like what I'm tellin' you, then I'd suggest you tell the Dude to leave somebody else here tonight."

Jerry Roseberry did not answer. He moved away from the girl, turned, and stalked out of the kitchen.

By dark, Laura had cleaned the supper plates, the cooking utensils, and the kitchen itself. Now, with a .45 by her side, she sat in the parlor next to a lamp and began to read. She occasionally glanced up at one or another of the rustlers as they left the room and headed for the stable. When Roseberry came through, he only glanced at the girl before he left. Finally, Dude Rawlings showed up and stopped to speak to the girl.

"I see you have that gun loaded and ready. That's good. You just relax this evening, but you should go back there every few hours to make sure he's still in that bedroom. You will do that, won't you, Laura?"

"That's what I intended to do," she answered.

"Good, good," Rawlings said, nodding.

When Laura heard the sound of horses a few minutes later, she rose from the divan and walked to the porch. Here, she only stood and stared, watching Dude Rawlings and his four companions whirl their mounts and trot away from the house, across the open stretch of ground, through the narrow stream, and then into the dark depths of woodlands. She pursed her lips, returned to the parlor, glanced at the loaded six-gun on the stand next to her, sat down, and then picked up her book again.

*　　*　　*

Dude Rawlings and his rustlers rode for more than four hours, walking their horses carefully through the woods and over the rocky terrain beyond the depths of the forest. They then trotted up the Johnson County Highway, detouring off the main road whenever they saw a lighted farm or ranch house, or when they spotted any nighttime rider on the open road. They loped onto the trail south of Jaycee and skirted the town before emerging north of the hamlet. Rawlings had maintained an unusual caution, because he did not want anyone to see him or his four cohorts.

Shortly before midnight, the quintet came over a rise and trotted slowly to a patch of trees. Four of them dismounted, with Ralph "Preacher" Rogers taking the reins and mustering the horses into a packed group. From atop his mount, Rogers watched the others crouch forward until they were out of sight. Rawlings and his companions moved forward on foot until they reached a spot with a clear view. As with all nighttime herds, the steers stood immobile, dormant, while one rider walked his horse in a shuttle on the left, and a second rider rode on the right. The outlaws also saw two men near a campfire on the other side of the herd, loitering in the camp near the riverbank.

The Dude whispered to Roseberry and Henry. "Give me and Wild Man fifteen minutes. Then move on the rider to the left. You'll need to be real careful and quiet, because you don't want that other rider to see or hear you before you can reach him too."

"We know what to do," Roseberry said.

A moment later, the foursome split up, with Rawlings and Eliot moving stealthily around the herd to the riverbank so they could come up behind the two relief guards in the camp. Roseberry waited until the duo were out of sight and he then motioned to Big Val Henry.

"Let's go."

The ex-army captain and the burly Henry crawled quietly toward the man on horseback near the western perimeter of the herd. Soon enough, they reached their quarry, and Roseberry looped the man with his lasso and yanked him from his horse. The man had barely hit the ground before Big Val pistol-whipped him into unconsciousness. Then, Henry gagged him, while Roseberry bound his hands behind his back and tied the sentinel's legs.

They had completed this chore quickly and quietly, and now moved toward the other end of the herd where they successfully reached the second mounted rider undetected. Once more, Roseberry lassoed his victim from his horse before Big Val struck the downed rider with the butt of his six-gun. The two men bound their prey and left him wiggling helplessly on the ground. The pair of outlaws then stood upright to wait a signal from Rawlings.

The Dude and Wild Man, meanwhile, had just about reached the camp area from the riverbank and were clambering toward the camp with aimed six-shooters. However, Eliot stepped on some twigs, and in the near silence the crackles sounded like popping firecrackers. The two relief sentries rose full to their feet and stared into the riverbank darkness, while they reached for their holstered guns. But Wild Man Eliot fired several quick shots from his own Colt and dropped both men, who died instantly and lay contorted in pools of their own blood. Rawlings glared at Eliot.

"You dumb son of a bitch! Why did you kill 'em? Why?"

"I couldn't help it," Eliot said. "Them two men went for their guns."

"Goddamn it," Rawlings cursed, "now we're in real trouble. They told me you couldn't be trusted. With them two men layin' dead there, we'll have the whole Wyoming Territory out lookin' for us. Only the Good Lord knows what kinda bounty they'll put on our heads now."

"It's like I said, Dude," Eliot defended himself, "they was goin' for their guns. I didn't have no choice but to shoot 'em."

The Dude sighed. "Well, there ain't no sense a-cryin' over what's been done." He then gathered up some brush, rolled it into a long improvised kindling rod, and lit the end from the fire. He then waved the torch.

Rogers, Roseberry, and Henry had heard the several quick shots and all of them had stiffened with curious uncertainty. Why the shooting? Who had fired at whom? Had this caper gone awry? However, the trio were somewhat relieved when they saw the waving torch from the campsite. Whatever had happened, the shooting had apparently not affected the Dude's part in this plan.

Preacher Rogers quickly loped away from the

small grove of trees and hurried into the open with the horses. He then weaved through the herd of cattle and soon reached the campsite, where he first saw Rawlings and Eliot standing erect and then the two men lying dead.

"What happened, Dude?" Rogers asked.

"Where are the others?" Rawlings asked.

"I don't know." The Preacher shrugged. "I'd guess they saw your signal, too, and they ought to be here soon."

Rogers had barely finished speaking when Jerry Roseberry and Val Henry walked into the campsite. They first looked at their three companions and the horses. Then they ogled at the two dead men on the ground.

"My God!" Roseberry hissed. "What happened?"

"I had to kill 'em," Eliot said. "I had no choice. They drew on us."

"Jesus, Wild Man," Big Val grumbled, "couldn't you come up behind 'em without them hearin' you?"

"There ain't no sense dallyin' over this," the Dude said. "What's done is done. We'll need to move that herd fast and get as much money as we can from Balfonte. Mount up."

Within the next several minutes the five men were aboard their horses and spooking the three hundred head of cattle, veering them northward and moving them in a swift trot. The outlaws continued their pace for more than two hours until they once more reached a shallow stretch of the Powder River. Here, they drove the cattle into the stream, struck north for more than ten miles, and brought them up on the east bank of the river.

The outlaws took the huge herd some two miles northwest of the river and then Rawlings turned to Eliot and Henry. "Okay, go back and cover our tracks and then you can catch up to us. We won't be too far ahead."

"Don't worry, Dude," Eliot said, "There ain't no way any posse'll find out which way we took them steers."

Rawlings did not answer. He watched his two men gallop off before he gestured to Roseberry and Rogers. "Let's keep these steers movin'."

The three rustlers had driven the herd about another twenty miles when Clint Eliot and Val Henry caught up to them. "Everything's done, Dude," Eliot said. "Nobody'll know what direction we followed."

"Keep 'em movin'." Rawlings gestured. "We got about another hour to go before we reach that Spotted Horse canyon. Balfonte is bound to be waitin' for us there, and I'll insist on at least fifteen dollars a head."

"Fifteen dollars!" Roseberry cried. "That's fifty percent more than last time. Suppose Balfonte won't pay us that kind of money?"

"Then, goddamn it, I'll drive this herd right back to the Powder River and stampede 'em south. It'll be fifteen dollars a head or nothin'."

Roseberry did not answer for nearly another hour as they continued northward with the herd. Finally, the ex-army captain looked at Rawlings. "Dude, what happened back there?"

"You heard; Eliot killed them two."

"I always knew he was too trigger-happy."

"He claims they drew on us."

"Did they?" Roseberry asked.

"I don't know," Rawlings said, shaking his head. "Everything happened so fast. But I know that Wyoming ain't gonna be safe for us no more, not even Egleston. Them people there ain't gonna shelter nobody who's wanted for murder, no matter how much money we got."

"They don't know that we killed them."

"They'll suspect us, and that's enough," Rawlings said. "No, we'll need to get outta Wyoming Territory and work somewhere else. Maybe we'll even break up the band. That's why we need all we can get outta Balfonte."

"What about the bounty hunter? Have you figured what to do with him?"

"I don't have to figure no more," Rawlings said. "We'll just kill Houston. What difference does it make, now that we left two dead men back at the Branden Ranch campsite? As soon as we get back, we'll kill that goddamn Houston, split the money, and leave the territory."

"What about Laura?"

"What about her?" Rawlings scowled. "She'll need to get out, too. She can take up with you if she wants. I don't give a damn what she does."

Roseberry did not answer. He liked the idea—Laura going off with him. However, a sudden panic struck him. Suppose she was gone when he got back? Suppose she had freed that bounty hunter and run off with him?

CHAPTER TEN

Jerry Roseberry had reason to feel uneasy. Back at the log hideout, Laura Renault had sat on the divan in the parlor for about an hour after the five riders had left the house. She had remained there reading in the dead quiet, but her mind had too often drifted from the pages of the book and into the ell wing of the house where the prisoner was confined. Finally, she had risen from the divan, put down the book, and walked through the house to the wing. She stopped before the locked door and pressed her ear against the heavy portal. However, only a silence came from beyond.

Inside the room, Pete Houston had stretched out on the bed with his arms behind his head. He had taken off his shirt and boots and he lay clad only in his trousers and underwear. Houston had also struck the lamp, keeping the wick low so that only a dim light radiated through the chamber and cast shadows on the wall. Occasionally he stared at the door, but he knew he could never open it. And when he squinted at the window, the night outside seemed even darker because of the

179

heavy planks against the panes.

Pete had resigned himself. At least he was not dead, and so long as he was alive and strong, he had a chance, no matter how slim. During this isolation, his mind whirled, trying to hatch a plan for escape from these outlaws tomorrow. When they came back, they would take him out of his room and do something or take him somewhere. That's when he would need to act.

But then Pete heard a soft knock on the plank door and he bolted upright to a sitting position on the bed. He said nothing, but stiffened when the knocks came again. Finally, he heard the low, soft voice of Laura Renault.

"Mr. Houston, are you all right in there?"

Pete did not answer.

"Mr. Houston," Laura called again. "Are you all right. Is there anything I can do for you?"

Pete rose from the bed, his mind whirling again. She cared! The wench who had led him into this trap really cared. Why else would she come to the door of his prison only an hour after the others had left? He would need to encourage her, charm her, melt her, as she had done to him. He must lure her into allowing him to escape as she had lured him into making himself a prisoner. He stepped softly to the door.

"Is that you out there, Miss Renault?"

"Yes."

"And you're alone in the house?"

"They're all gone; none a them will be back until at least midday tomorrow."

"Yes, I guess everything is all right in here,"

Pete said, "but I'd sure like to sit with you for a while."

"But I ain't supposed to open the door."

"Are you afraid of me?" Houston asked.

"It ain't that, but they'd kill me for sure if I ever let you out."

"Then, why did you come back here?" Pete said. "You know there isn't any way for me to get out of here."

"I just wanted to make sure you was all right."

"What do you care?" Pete huffed.

"It's just that I'm kinda down, knowin' what I done to you. I feel real bad about it."

"You did what you had to do," Pete answered. "I was a serious threat to you, and you can be proud of the way you handled me."

"But I feel bad about it," Laura said again, "and to tell the truth, I'm surprised that you let me fool you like that."

"It's because I couldn't think anymore once you warmed up to me," Pete said. "You're so damn beautiful, you could talk anybody into anything. You know something, Miss Renault, the thing I miss right now is not seeing you: your pretty face and those sparkling eyes. I almost think this was worth it just to spend a little time with you."

The girl remained immobile and silent and Houston continued: "Just riding with you, being next to you . . . I never thought I'd see the day I'd have such company. And then there was that short spell in the rocks, sitting next to you and having you close to me. I do believe it was one of the most enjoyable things that ever happened to me. And like I said, that's what I miss most, just sitting next to you and looking into those enchanting eyes. If I could only do that, why, it wouldn't matter what happened to me tomorrow."

When Pete stopped his flattery, he still got no answer from the girl. However, suddenly, he heard the insertion of a key in the door, a click, and then the thump of the rod as the bar came back from the bolt. Seconds later, the heavy plank door squealed and swung open. The girl stood there and stared at Pete Houston.

"You can take a good look at me, Mr. Houston; you can look at my face and into my eyes." Pete grinned and started out the door. However, he stopped when he saw Laura point the six-shooter at him. "But don't come too close."

"Then, maybe you'd like to come inside?" Pete grinned.

Again, Laura Renault did not answer. She only stood rigidly and eyed the bounty hunter avidly. She did not know if the man had merely cajoled her or if he really spoke his true mind. However, she did know that the figure just inside the door was a real man—strong, straight, and handsome.

"Do you want to come in?" Pete asked again, softly this time.

"I—I c-can't," Laura stammered, wavering as she brandished the gun. Pete almost went for the weapon but then thought better of it. Instead, he grinned at the girl again. "It doesn't matter. If I can just stand here for a minute or two and just look at you, why, that would be enough. Then you can lock the door again and I'll just go back to my bed." Houston now stared into her sparkling hazel eyes, and he could see the hardness slowly changing to desire. He took a step forward and the girl did not raise the weapon. So he moved even further and he was soon out of the room and into the hallway. But still she made no move to raise the weapon, and in fact, she even retreated slightly.

The bounty hunter came closer to her and looked avidly into the girl's eyes. She returned an equally fervent stare. She had lost her harshness and lost her snobbishness. Gone was her aura of self-confidence and gone was her air of vanity. She had suddenly become filled with desire for the man standing before her. She offered no resistance as Pete put his hands on her shoulders. Nor did she resist when he moved one hand to the nape of her neck, and then stroked her hair.

With the other hand, Pete Houston now pulled the girl close to him and kissed her on the lips. A tremorous spark ran through her shapely body, and suddenly the six-gun dropped to the floor. She then threw her arms around his neck and pressed her body close to the bounty hunter as she returned a fervent kiss of her own.

Pete Houston pushed the girl slightly away from him and looked into her eyes again. They burned with passion now and she had obviously become a helpless victim. However, strangely, Houston did not take advantage as he had planned. He did not shove her away, beat her, or pick up the gun to expedite his escape. No, for in him too had come an aroused passion, a dizzying lust. If Laura Renault had become vulnerable, Pete himself now wallowed in an excited ardor.

Pete kissed Laura again and then ran his hand over her body, stopping at her chest and squeezing one of her breasts. The girl jerked but then moaned in ecstasy and pushed herself even closer to him.

"Do you want to come into my room?" he whispered.

"Please, take me inside."

"We don't even have to close the door," Pete said with a half-grin. "There isn't anybody in the big place but us."

"Please," she answered soberly before she again threw her arms around him and kissed him hard on the lips, stopping finally only to catch her breath.

Soon, the duo were on the bed, entwined in naked ecstasy in the small, darkened room. Only the squeal of the rickety old bed interrupted the silence.

They lay there for almost two hours together and finally, his lust satisfied, Pete rose to his feet and began to dress. The girl simply lay on the bed, watching him. Occasionally, he looked down at her and grinned. When he had put on his underwear and trousers, Laura rose to her feet and came close to him, pressing her nude body next to him and kissing him. He returned the kiss but then pushed her gently away from him.

"What are you gonna do, Mr. Houston?" She smiled.

"Get out of here."

"There ain't no need for that."

"You can't be serious," Pete answered. "They plan to kill me, you know that. I want to be long gone before they have a chance to do that."

"I told you, they can't be back here 'til at least noon tomorrow."

"I can't be sure of that," Pete said.

"Yes, you can," the girl said. "Why, just about now they're movin' that herd along the Powder River and they won't even reach their canyon until daylight. Then it'll take 'em at least another four or five hours to get back here. You can be sure I'm tellin' the truth 'cause I rode with Rawlings and the others on these capers."

"Maybe," Pete conceded.

"Besides," Laura continued, "if you try to leave here in the middle a the night, you'll likely lame your horse on some of them holes and rocks you can't see in the dark. Then you wouldn't have no way a gettin' outta here." She moved close to him again and whispered, "Let's go back to bed, Mr. Houston. We can leave together at first light. I'll cook you some breakfast so's you can have a full belly before we do go." When Pete hesitated, Laura gripped the edge of his underwear. "You can believe me, Mr. Houston."

"I suppose I'll have to"—Pete grinned—"even though you're the one who got me here in the first place."

"I promise, I'll get you safely outta here, too."

"I'll have to admit," Pete said, "I can't think of any better place to be than on that bed with you."

The first hint of daylight between the heavy

planks on the window awoke Pete Houston. He blinked and then turned quickly, suddenly remembering that Laura Renault had shared this bed with him all night. However, she was not next to him—and for a moment panic gripped him. But then he saw the bedroom door open and he smelled the aroma of coffee. Pete hoisted himself from the bed, slipped into his underwear, and then put on his trousers. He left the room and walked up the hallway to the kitchen where he saw Laura slicing bread for toast and cracking eggs before dropping them into a pan.

When the girl saw Pete, she smiled, "I'll have breakfast ready pretty soon. I was gonna wake you up as soon as it was ready."

When Pete came next to her, he frowned. She was already clad in riding clothes: shirt, skirt, and boots, with her tambourine hat and buckskin jacket lying on the end of the table. On a counter next to the cast-iron stove lay the six-gun. Pete was tempted to grab it again, but restrained himself.

Within a few minutes, Laura Renault had set a heaping plate of scrambled eggs and slabs of toast in front of him. She had also set the coffeepot on the table, while she served herself only a small portion of eggs and one thin slice of toast. The duo said little to each other as they ate, and when they finished, she gestured to Pete. "You'd better get dressed."

"It won't take me long," Pete answered. He hurried to the small bedroom to put on his shirt, his boots, and his Stetson hat. By the time he came back to the kitchen, Laura was ready to go, with jacket and hat on, along with a gunbelt around her slim waist. She handed a second gunbelt to Houston. "You better put this on."

Pete looked about the kitchen. The girl had not removed or cleaned a single thing from the table and he grinned at her. "Are we going to leave everything just like this?"

Laura shrugged. "Rawlings and his boys can take care a them when they get back. I sure spent enough time cookin' and cleanin' for 'em, and now they can do for themselves."

"Wait." Pete suddenly gripped the girl's wrists. "Laura, are you sure you want to do this? Help me escape? They'll know exactly what happened when they return. They'll surely be looking for you to take their revenge."

Laura Renault did not pull away from Pete's grip. Instead, she looked down and rubbed his hand before she looked up at him. "You know, at first I thought I was lyin' when I said all them nice things about you, but now I know they was true. And I must say, when I was sittin' with you up in them rocks, and lookin' at you, and knowin' I was snarin' you into a trap, I knew I was makin' the biggest mistake a my life. I ain't sorry one bit for turnin' you loose, nor in goin' to bed with you."

"I hope not," Pete said.

"Anyway, these men made a female slave outta me," Laura continued. "Me doin' all the cookin' and cleanin' and washin', while they just lolled about this big place doin' nothin'. I ain't ever had

187

one extra nickel for all this extra work, so leavin'
'em high and dry and lettin' you escape would
serve 'em right—all of 'em. But you needn't worry
about me: I was able to take care a myself when
these men had lust in their eyes, and I can take
care a myself if they come after me."

Pete did not answer.

Within five minutes, they had saddled two
horses, Pete's big bay and the pinto he had rented
for Laura. Then they loped out of the barn and
into the open. They crossed the small stream and
soon ducked into the dense forest beyond. They
would ride for most of the morning, all the way to
Buffalo, except for a stop in Jaycee to pick up
Laura's horse. They would be long gone by the
time the rustlers returned to their hideout in the
Hole In The Wall.

At about the same early morning hour, Dude
Rawlings and his fellow rustlers were herding
more than three hundred head of stolen cattle into
the familiar canyon outside the hamlet of Spotted
Horse, northeast of Buffalo. As usual, Rene
Balfonte and two men were waiting there for the
outlaws. The black marketeer watched the riders
move their cattle before they dismounted and
again set up a barricade to keep the steers penned
inside. When Rawlings approached his buyer,
Balfonte gestured.

"How many head do you have?"

"At least three hundred," Rawlings said, "and
they're prime stock. They come from one a the

best spreads on the Powder River."

"What spread?"

"You know I won't tell you that," the Dude said, "but you can probably guess for yourself when you study the brands."

Balfonte nodded and then gestured to his companions. The two hands scooted quickly into the herd of cattle. "It'll take a while for my men to count and examine that herd," Balfonte said, "but I got some coffee and hot rolls that you and your boys might enjoy. I know you've been out all night."

"That's a nice offer, Mr. Balfonte." Eliot grinned.

For the next fifteen or twenty minutes the five rustlers sat on logs, drank hot coffee, and ate soft rolls. The repast was satisfying after the long, hard night. Finally, the two men came back and looked at Balfonte.

"The Dude is right, Mr. Balfonte," one of them said. "They're prime stock and we counted three hundred and ten head."

The black marketeer nodded and then reached into a leather pouch. "That means I owe you three thousand dollars, but I'll make it an even thirty-two hundred."

"No, you won't," Rawlings said. "I know what them steers are bringing now, over thirty dollars a head. I want fifteen a head and not a penny less."

"Now wait a minute," Balfonte said. "The price has always been ten dollars."

"That was before a steer was worth thirty dollars"—the Dude gestured—"and this is prime beef that might bring you more than thirty dollars. No"—he shook his head—"I can't let them go for under fifteen."

Balfonte leaned forward and grinned. "What are you gonna do if I won't pay it? You can't take 'em back where you got 'em. There ain't nobody there who'll buy 'em. Why, you'd have to drive 'em clear out to eastern Wyoming to sell 'em and that would keep you on the trail for a week, while them steers sunk to skin and bones. I suggest you take the ten dollars a head, Dude, and maybe we can negotiate a higher price the next time."

"It's fifteen dollars a head," Dude persisted. "In fact, I want an even five thousand for the entire herd."

"My God, you keep uppin' the price." Balfonte grinned. "That's mighty brash for a man who ain't got nowhere to go with them steers."

"Rene," Rawlings said slowly, "if you don't come up with five thousand dollars, I'm takin' them steers outta that canyon. I'll drive 'em back to the Powder River and just turn 'em loose. We won't make a dime, true, but you ain't gonna get rich off of us, either. You're gonna miss out on a chance to make a five-thousand-dollar profit, maybe more. And you know as well as I do, you won't have no trouble at all sellin' prize stock like that."

Balfonte shook his head. "I can't do that."

Rawlings rose to his feet. "That's your privilege, Rene." He turned to his men. "Okay, boys, let's mount up. We got a long ride this morning with them steers."

"W-what do you mean, Dude?" Big Val asked anxiously.

"I mean we're takin' them steers outta the canyon and drivin' 'em south. I don't give a damn if we have to scatter 'em all through the Black Hills country. That's what I'll do before I'll let that herd go for under five thousand."

"Goddamn, Dude," Balfonte said, "I do believe you'd really do that."

"Yes, I'll do that."

"All right, all right," the black marketeer said. "I'll give you five thousand." He opened his money pouch and counted out $5,000. "The only reason I'm doin' this, Dude, is 'cause we've been doin' business together for some time and you always brought me prime stuff."

"I don't give a damn what your reasons are," the Dude said. "So long as you pay me."

Within fifteen minutes, Rawlings and the others had remounted and the Dude looked down at Balfonte. "I must tell you, if the price a beef goes up some more, why, I'll expect an even higher price for the next herd."

"We'll see," Balfonte answered. Then he and his men watched the five rustlers move off. He turned to his men. "Get the boys with the brandin' irons. We got a lotta work this morning."

"Sure, Mr. Balfonte."

As the five outlaws rode southward, Clint Eliot rode up to the side of Rawlings. "Goddamn, Dude, I didn't think you could do it. You bluffed that dealer real well and he paid off."

"I wasn't bluffin'," the Dude answered soberly.

Eliot's face suddenly changed as a shocked look replaced the grin on his countenance. As the five men rode on, they said little more to each other until they reached the Powder River some two hours later. Then, Jerry Roseberry suggested they stop and water the horses. As they loitered in their saddles, with the animals drinking from the river, Roseberry looked at Rawlings.

"Dude, I've been thinking about that bounty hunter."

"Like I said, Cap, there ain't no sense a-worryin' now; they'll soon enough blame us for killin' them two guards at the Branden Ranch campsite and it ain't gonna make no difference if we add a dead bounty hunter. If they catch us, they can only hang us once."

"But they can't be sure we killed those guards," Roseberry said. "They could never convict us of murder on the basis of suspicion. They need to produce eyewitnesses and other evidence. No one can definitely say that we rustled that herd last night and that one of us shot those cowpunchers. On the other hand, I'd bet money that Sheriff Angus, some people from the cattlemen's association, and somebody else knows that Houston came into the Hole In The Wall country to find us. I'm sure they'd also know that Houston left Buffalo with Laura, who was bringing him there. The law would have a good case of circumstantial evidence if they found Houston murdered."

Dude Rawlings did not answer but only pondered Roseberry's comments. He finally agreed that his companion made sense and he pointed to the ex-army captain. "Cap, what do you suggest we do with that bounty hunter? You know we can't let 'im live."

"We'll threaten him enough to run him out of the territory," Roseberry said.

"No," Dude insisted, "he's got to die; maybe an accident like fallin' off his horse."

"Sheriff Angus would never believe that." Roseberry shook his head. "Houston is too good and too cautious to allow anything like that to happen to him."

Then the Dude's eyes brightened. "I know, we'll get 'im into a gunfight, and him and the other man can get killed when they draw on each other."

"Gunfight? Draw?" Roseberry gaped. "How do you expect to do that? And just who would be willing to give up his life for us? The idea is ridiculous."

"Not if we plan it right," Rawlings said.

Roseberry shook his head. "No one would be foolish enough to get himself killed for us."

"I had in mind Nebraska Brake," Rawlings said. "He'd be just the man to use on somethin' like this."

"Nebraska Brake?" The ex-army captain frowned.

The Dude nodded. "Look, everybody in Egleston suspects that Brake is the man who's been keepin' us informed. And as you say, Cap, somebody in Buffalo knows that Laura left there with the bounty hunter to take 'im into the rough country to find us. It's logical that she might take Houston to Nebraska to find out where we're hidin' out. Brake is the man who knows what we do and where we go. Suppose Brake wouldn't tell Houston nothin'? Or Houston threatened Nebraska and they ended up in a gunfight, with both of 'em killin' each other? Wouldn't that seem logical to a lawman?" Rawlings gestured. "Now, if worse came to worse and we was captured, why, Laura could tell the law that she led Houston to Brake and they got into an argument and shot each other."

Preacher Rogers, who had been listening to the Dude's startling suggestion, now leaned from his saddle. "My God, Dude, how the hell can you pull off somethin' like that?"

"We'll send word to Nebraska that we have to see 'im," Rawlings said. "We'll tell 'im to meet us someplace in town. Then we'll come into Egleston with Houston, take their guns, shoot both of 'em, and leave 'em dead on the street. Somebody'll find 'em and figure they killed each other in a gunfight."

Now Rogers gasped. "Jesus Christ, Dude, you'd take Brake's life that easy, after all he done for us?"

"Would you rather the bounty hunter took our lives?" Rawlings answered. "If it's a choice between you and Brake, then what? A dead informer or a hangman's noose for you?

"I do regret the need to kill Brake that way," the Dude continued, "but we got no other choice."

"This idea is insane," Roseberry huffed. "We can't kill two men as though they were lambs being led to slaughter."

"It's the only way," Rawlings persisted. "We'll plan this when we get back to the house." Then he whipped his horse. "Hi! let's move."

As the outlaws moved off, Clint Eliot turned to the others. "Do you figure Laura will have a good meal waitin' for us when we get back?"

"Sure," Big Val said. "Ain't she always been good to us?"

"I hope so," Eliot said. "We been on the trail a long time and I'm hungry enough to eat some wild grass."

The quintet continued on for more than two hours, riding down the Johnson County road when they could, and detouring over obscure trails when they neared any points of civilization, especially near the town of Jaycee. They moved wisely, avoiding all people, even in the daytime. Shortly after noon, they emerged from the length of forest deep in the Hole In The Wall country and then splashed across the narrow, shallow creek and onto the open stretch of ground in front of the log structure.

As they trotted toward the tether posts in front of the house, Roseberry frowned. He had hoped to see Laura Renault come out on the porch to greet them—certain she had heard the clods and neighs of their horses. When he dismounted and wound his rein around the post, he saw Big Val Henry suddenly veer his own horse and come back toward him.

"Goddamn, Dude," Henry cried, "the horses are gone."

"The horses?"

"I was gonna take my own mount directly into the stall to save time," Henry said, "but when I got inside I found the stalls empty. That bounty hunter's big bay is gone and so is that Pinto that Laura rode in here."

"What the hell are you talkin' about?" The Dude scowled. "They can't be gone. There was no way that bounty hunter could get outta that room, even if nobody was keepin' an eye on 'im."

Clint Eliot, who had also dismounted, looked hard at Rawlings. "Unless that girl turned him loose and then run off with the bastard." The others looked shocked at the suggestion. Rawlings shook his head.

"She didn't have no use for that bounty hunter. Laura hated him just like the rest of us. She led 'im into a trap, didn't she? There must be some other explanation."

Jerry Roseberry pursed his lips hard. He remembered the exchange of stares yesterday that had hinted of a mutual admiration. And he also recalled that Laura had shown a haughty attitude when he warned her about allowing Pete Houston to escape. The ex-army captain bounded up the porch steps behind Rawlings, across the porch, and into the house. Wild Man instinctively followed and the three men raced through the parlor. When they reached the kitchen, they saw plates, cups, and coffeepot still on the table, untouched and unwashed.

"Son of a bitch!" Eliot cursed. "They didn't even clean up."

Roseberry ignored his companion and hurried

down the corridor and into the ell wing. Rawlings and Eliot were close on his heels. They found the door to the bedroom open with no one inside and Roseberry pounded the heavy portal in angry frustration, then he stood rigid with a tormented look on his face. Eliot went into the bedroom and looked around before he came back to the hall.

"That no-good little bitch!" Eliot cursed. "That dirty whore! I knew we could never trust her, I knew it!"

By now the others had reached the ell wing of the house. Dude Rawlings looked through the open door and into the empty bedroom. He then merely stroked his chin, unusally calm in contrast to Roseberry and Eliot. "Can you beat that?" The Dude grinned. "She even made breakfast for the bastard."

"And probably screwed him all night, while we were gone," Eliot grumbled.

Jerry Roseberry glared at Wild Man, but he said nothing to his fellow outlaw. The ex-army captain suspected that Eliot was right. He turned when Preacher Rogers spoke to him.

"Well, Cap'n, that whole plan a killin' that bounty hunter and Nebraska Brake has gone up in smoke."

"Seems so," Roseberry answered.

"Like I told Eliot at that range when he killed them guards, what's done is done," Rawlings said calmly. "All we can do now is to plan our next move." He shuttled his glance among his four companions. "We've been doin' a lotta worryin'

197

about that bounty hunter gettin' us. Well, it's time we did the huntin'. We've got to get in touch with Brake and Joe Cameron, and if we offer 'em enough, they'll find out where we can get Houston and that double-crossin' wench. Then, we'll run 'em down and kill both of 'em."

"What about the wanted posters?" Eliot asked.

"The hell with that." Rawlings gestured impatiently. "If we could get all the way from here to Spotted Horse without bein' seen, we can sure find that bastard and that bitch without bein' seen. We can't let them do this to us."

"I'd like to get *my* hands on 'em," Eliot said.

Rawlings looked at Roseberry. "Well, Cap, are you in with this? Run 'em down and kill 'em?"

Jerry Roseberry pursed his lips again and then nodded, although he did not speak. Then Rawlings looked at the others. Preacher? Big Val?"

The Preacher also nodded but Big Val soured his face. He liked Laura, he had admired her, and he had always told himself he would protect her if necessary. But now he saw the justice in what Dude Rawlings said.

"We ain't got no choice but to do as you say, Dude," the big man said.

"Good." Then Rawlings sighed. "We had one plan before we got back here, and now we'll have to make a new one. We may as well get to it."

CHAPTER ELEVEN

At about the same hour that Rawlings and his fellow rustlers had returned to their Hole In The Wall country hideout, Pete Houston and Laura Renault were loping into Buffalo. The sun was high now and the heat had drawn perspiration from both of them during the long ride. They had not paused anywhere except briefly in Jaycee to pick up Laura's horse, wanting to put as much distance as possible between themselves and the Rawlings gang. Even when they reached town, they did not stop, but rode directly to the Mercer Hotel stable.

When the duo got inside, Pete unsaddled the three horses and put the animals into the stalls before he gave all three of them a cursory brushing and laid the saddles and reins over stall railings. Then he turned to the girl.

"I'll return the pinto sometime today, but your own horse is fine. If you need to saddle him I'll be glad to do it."

"I won't need it right now," the girl answered. "All I want is to get a good hot bath."

"Then maybe we can go out to dinner later," Pete said. "You must be starved, same as me."

"No," Laura answered. "After my bath I think I'll just rest up." Then she smiled. "You'll need to have a noon meal by yourself."

Pete Houston frowned. There was now a coolness in the girl, an aloofness that had been building all during this several-hour ride from the Hole In The Wall country, and he could not understand it. She had jeopardized her life by allowing him to escape, she had willingly gone to bed with him, and, in fact, had insisted on spending the entire night in that small bedroom. But now she had suddenly reverted to her old aura of vanity and reserve. Perhaps she was trying to cover up a dreaded fear of Rawlings and his outlaws.

Pete Houston had held her hand gently. "I want you to know, Laura, that if you're afraid of Rawlings and the others, I'll protect you."

"Like I said, Mr. Houston, you won't need to do that," the girl answered with a tone of bravado. "I can shoot as well as any of 'em. Besides, with them wanted posters everywhere, they ain't likely to leave that hideout."

"You will be staying here at the hotel?"

"Yes. At least for a while," Laura said.

"I'd certainly like to spend some more time with you."

"We'll see," the girl answered. Then she simply walked out the stable and toward the rear door of the hotel. Pete felt a little piqued, as though his ego had been deflated. Laura was certainly not the same woman he had been close to last night, but then Pete almost grinned. Her attitude now only seemed to confirm his earlier assessment of her. The girl was free-spirited, with a fierce sense of independence, and was obviously unwilling to rely on anyone.

Inside the hotel, Laura Renault again asked the clerk to have Chinaman Charlie draw her a bath, and this time Charlie complied without hesitation or surprise. Nor did he feel the same uneasiness he had experienced during the girl's first visit to his bathhouse. He had even reacted nonchalantly when Laura handed him her clothes. Charlie simply dumped both her riding attire and undergarments into his basket with casual indifference.

Pete Houston himself did not return at once to his hotel room. He walked over to the Rawhide Saloon for a cool pitcher of beer and a thick ham sandwich. He consumed his repast without incident and then returned to the hotel to also ask the desk clerk to draw him a bath. He then went to his room and stretched out on the bed. About ten minutes later, Chinaman Charlie knocked gently on his door.

"Bath is ready for you, Mr. Houston."

"Thank you, Charlie," Pete shouted back.

Soon, Pete had settled in a hot tub, and the warm water soothed his bones and muscles. He relaxed for several long minutes, absorbing the pleasurable soaking, before he washed himself thoroughly. When he finished, he dressed himself in a clean set of underwear, trousers, and laced shirt. Meanwhile, Charlie had polished his boots and taken Houston's soiled clothes to have them washed and ironed.

When Pete returned to his hotel room, he did not dally for long, only long enough to shave and comb his hair. He then put some money into his shirt pocket, strapped on his gunbelt, and left the room.

Two doors away, he stopped and almost knocked on Laura's door, but he then thought better of it.

When Houston left the hotel he walked straight to the cattlemen's association office to see Jane Clemons and Big Jim Simeon. As Pete came out of 14th Street and onto Gillette Avenue, however, Joe Cameron spotted the bounty hunter and gaped. The informant crossed the street for a closer look. The man was indeed Pete Houston.

Cameron stood rigid, almost dumbfounded, and watched Houston continue up Gillette Avenue toward the Wyoming Cattlemen's Association office in Buffalo. Cameron could not believe that the man was alive and meandering around town, for the informant himself had abetted Laura Renault in luring the bounty hunter into a trap and to his death. How could Houston be back in Buffalo only a day later? How had he escaped this well-laid trap? Had the bounty hunter become suspicious on the road south and disposed of Laura Renault instead?

Cameron knew that Houston had not brought in any wanted men today, so what had he been doing for the past thirty hours? The informant could

202

think of only one immediate action: inform Dude Rawlings. He hurried to the telegraph office to send a wire to Nebraska Brake, who in turn would notify Rawlings.

Meanwhile, Pete Houston soon reached the association office and walked inside. Jane Clemons looked up and smiled enthusiastically, a much warmer reception than she had displayed two days ago.

"Pete," the girl cried, "you're back sooner than I thought, and I'm real happy about it."

Houston grinned and then leaned over the counter. "Do you have any Evangelical Circle meetings tonight?"

"No."

"Then, can I see you? I'd sure like that."

"That play is on tonight," Jane answered. "We could have supper and then go to the playhouse."

"That would certainly please me," Pete said. But then, when Jane's face suddenly sobered, Pete frowned. "What's the matter? Did I say something wrong?"

"No, it ain't got nothin' to do with you." The girl shook her head. "I guess you haven't heard."

"Heard what?"

"About that rustled herd last night. A band of outlaws took over three hundred head from the Branden Ranch south a here; drove 'em northeast, they think, but a ranch posse lost the trail. Them rustlers seem to be as sly as mountain cats."

Pete only pursed his lips. He knew that Dude Rawlings and his men had been responsible. After all, he had been at the log hideout when the

203

outlaws left. However, he did not mention this to the girl.

"But that ain't the worst of it," Jane continued. "Them outlaws, whoever they was, killed two guards; just murdered 'em! They didn't kill the horseback guards, though; just tied 'em up. Nobody can figure out why they killed the relief guards at the camp. Ranchers ain't never had that happen before."

"That's real bad news," Pete said, "and I'm sorry to hear that."

"Nobody knows who them outlaws were," Jane continued, "and Mr. Simeon is not inclined to think it was the Rawlings gang. That band has never killed anybody when they stole off a herd."

"Is Big Joe in?"

"No, he took the first stage to Sheridan as soon as he learned about the killings. I guess they'll hold a quick association meetin' today, or tonight, to figure out what to do about them killer rustlers. There was talk that they might even form a regulator posse to find them killers. They'll comb the whole Wyoming Territory, if necessary. How about yourself, Pete? Did you finish your business with that woman? Did you get what you were lookin' for?"

"No, it didn't work out," Pete answered. "She couldn't lead me to anybody who really knew where those outlaws were. So, I came back to Buffalo until I decide where to move next."

Jane's eyes beamed. She was happy that the short association with the pretty girl had ended in failure.

"I'll just pick you up about five, Jane. We'll have supper and then go to the playhouse."

"I'll be ready, Pete."

He leaned close and kissed her, and when he did, she threw her arms around his neck and returned a fervent kiss of her own. Then, she quickly retreated and lowered her head sheepishly. "I'm sorry, Pete. I guess I'm too glad to see you."

Pete kissed her again, squeezed her hand, and then grinned. "I'll see you at five o'clock."

By the time Pete returned to his hotel, Joe Cameron had sent his telegram to Egleston. By two o'clock, Nebraska Brake was galloping out of town and into the Hole In The Wall country. He had come over the trail to within two hundred yards of Devil's Pass when Clint Eliot spotted the informant from his rocky sentry perch. Eliot straightened, stiffened, and aimed his rifle. Wild Man was taking no chances, because the escape of Houston had forced the Rawlings gang to be especially alert. A posse could be coming in here after them at any hour. However, when the sentry recognized the rider as Nebraska Brake, Wild Man relaxed and shouted down to the man.

"Nebraska! What are you doin', comin' in here in such a hurry?"

"I just got a wire from Joe Cameron," Nebraska shouted back. "That bounty hunter is back in Buffalo and wandering around town."

"The Dude will want to know that," Eliot said.

Brake nodded and then continued on. Within an hour he had reached the log house. By the time he dismounted and tethered his horse, Dude Rawlings and Jerry Roseberry had come out to the porch. They stood and watched the visitor hurry up the steps.

"Mr. Rawlings,"—Brake nodded—"I just heard from Joe Cameron and I must tell you I was shocked by the telegram. He said that Houston was alive and just amblin' up Gillette Steet in Buffalo. Goddamn, I thought that bounty hunter would be dead by now. Hell, I got full details on how you was gonna' take Houston. What the hell happened? Did he get suspicious or what?"

"It's a long story," Rawlings answered. "Come on in."

Inside the parlor, the Dude explained how Laura had cleverly lured Houston into the trap, how they had locked the bounty hunter in a bedroom, how they had left Laura alone here while they pulled off the rustling job last night, and how they had returned to find both Houston and the girl gone.

"She musta been charmed by the bastard and turned him loose," Rawlings grumbled. "Maybe even slept with the man all night. All we know is that they left here together sometime this morning."

"I'll be goddamned," Brake hissed.

Rawlings, of course, did not mention their earlier plan to kill Houston in a ruse that would cost the life of Nebraska Brake as well. He looked hard at Brake. "If that bounty hunter is back in Buffalo, Laura must be there, too."

Brake shrugged. "That's probably true. From

what I learned from Cameron, she checked . . . the same place as Houston, the Mercer Hotel, and I'd have to guess that she's stayin' there now. However, Cameron didn't see her with Houston today. The bounty hunter was alone."

"We'll have to get into Buffalo to take care of them," Rawlings said. "They both know too much. We'll have to figure some way to surprise Houston, and that may not be easy, because he surely knows we'll be lookin' for 'im, either we ourselves or some hired guns."

"Well," Brake said, "I know one thing about Houston. He thinks more a that bay horse a his than anything, and Cameron once told me that Houston brushes down that horse every day, even if he don't go no place with the animal."

Big Val, who had been listening to the talk, now straightened his huge frame. "I'll go! I'll go into Buffalo. I'm the one whose picture ain't on any wanted poster. If Nebraska's right, why, I'll just stay hidden in whatever barn that bounty hunter keeps his horse."

"That'd probably be the Mercer Hotel stable," Brake said.

"Then, that's where I'll hide," Henry said. "When he comes in to brush down his horse, I'll get 'im."

The Dude stroked his chin, and Roseberry gestured. "That might be a good idea," the ex-army captain said. "That would be the last thing that bounty hunter would expect—somebody taking him while he's in a stable grooming his horse."

"I was thinking the same thing," Rawlings said.

"Houston knows we'll be after him," Roseberry continued. "That bounty hunter will be wary on the streets, in a saloon, certainly if he's on the trail, and even in his hotel room. But the hotel stable—that would be the last place to find somebody waiting for him."

"Like I said, I'll do it," Henry spoke again.

"All right, Big Val, you do the job for us and there'll be a bonus in it for you," Rawlings said.

"Val," Roseberry said, "don't kill Houston or Laura if you can help it. Bring them both back here."

"Cap, are you loco?" Rawlings huffed. "We already agreed that they have to be killed. She probably confessed everything to that bounty hunter and she'll likely tell the law as well. That means the law will be lookin' for you and Big Val as well as the rest of us."

"It might be better if Val brought them back here," Roseberry insisted. "He's big enough to take them without any trouble. Once they're here, we can find out how much they talked and what we should do about it."

"Goddamn it," the Dude scowled, "you gotta face facts. Laura betrayed us and Houston is our sworn enemy. They're both on the other side now and they've both got to die. Can't you understand that? She don't want nothin' more to do with you, nor with us. You'd best forget 'er."

Roseberry did not answer.

"Big Val, I know that you also have an admiration for Laura, only more like a big protectin' brother," Rawlings continued. "However, you've got to forget any feelings you have, too. You've got to kill 'er. Get into her hotel room and just strangle 'er, nice and quiet, and you could be back here before anybody knows what happened to the wench." When Henry pursed his lips, Rawlings squeezed his face irritably. "If you don't think you can kill that girl, then don't go into Buffalo."

"I'll do it, Dude, I'll do it."

"Are you sure?"

"I'm sure," Henry said. "I'll get myself ready and ride outta here before dark. I'll lope north nice and easy and be in Buffalo before daylight. I'll ride directly to the Mercer Hotel stable and wait for the bounty hunter to come in and tend to his big bay, even if I have to wait all day. And I promise, Dude, once I finish with Houston, I'll take care a Laura."

"Get a bedroll packed," Rawlings said.

By five o'clock, Big Val Henry was well on his way to the Johnson County Highway from the Hole In The Wall country. He rode through the rough country carefully, taking care in the woods and over the rocky trail. Finally, he reached the smooth highway and veered north.

At this same five o'clock hour, Pete Houston was picking up Jane Clemons at the association building, and they walked to the Buffalo cafe for dinner. After spending nearly an hour here, they next walked to the playhouse, where streams of people were also going inside to see the drama *Nellie is Ill*. They had to buck the crowd, but then, outside of saloons, Buffalo offered little nondrinking and nongambling entertainment. Still, Pete and Jane found two seats and settled back to await the rise of the curtain.

As the duo waited, Big Val Henry was loping into Jaycee thirty miles to the south. He stopped there only long enough to eat a quick meal and down a couple of quick beers. Then he remounted and loped north again through the darkness.

All during the melodrama, Jane Clemons alternately laughed, cried, tensed or relaxed as the plot of *Nellie is Ill* unfolded. Occasionally Pete patted her hand or she leaned over and rested her head on his shoulder. The play ended at ten o'clock and now, quite late, Pete Houston walked Jane back to her Durand Boarding House. On the porch, in the darkness, they stood alone and looked at each other before Pete leaned close and kissed her.

Jane retreated slightly and smiled. "I sure had a good time, Pete. I never believed I'd want to be with a man so much as I want to be with you . . ."

"I'm grateful," Pete answered in a whisper.

"I'm glad that business with the pretty woman is over," Jane said. "It is over, ain't it, Pete?"

"Yes," he answered. But, Houston was not certain he was lying, for he no doubt would have taken up again with Laura Renault if she had encouraged him.

Jane moved closer and pursed her lips as she fingered the lapels of Pete's shirt. "I'd like you to come upstairs with me again tonight, but I got to tell you—I ain't in no condition right now for you to sleep with me."

Pete did not answer.

"It ain't that I don't want you—"

Pete stopped her by leaning over and kissing her hard on the lips and then holding her close to him. "It doesn't matter," he said. "Going to bed with you is hardly the reason I want to be with you. That isn't what drew me to you in the first place, and it'll never be the reason for wanting to share your company."

"Pete," Jane asked soberly, "do you love me?"

"I do believe I do," Houston answered, "otherwise I don't know why I'm always so happy to be in your company again."

"I love you, Pete, I know I do," Jane said. "I've got to tell you that I never felt so much jealousy as I did when that pretty woman came into the office lookin' for you; and I was cryin' inside, knowin' you was goin' off alone with 'er. You won't go off with her again, will you Pete?"

"As I said, the business didn't work out," he answered. "There's no reason to see her again." But Houston felt a pang of guilt. He had not been honest with Jane Clemons.

The girl reached up and kissed her companion again. "I'm goin' in now, Pete. I'm quite tired and I got to take care a myself before I go to bed—with my female problem, you understand," she finished with a slight smile.

"Can I see you tomorrow?"

"I'd like that." She kissed him still again. "Good night, Pete." Then she ducked inside the boardinghouse and closed the front door after her.

Houston stood on the porch for a moment and then left, walking back to the hotel. Inside the lobby, he saw three men loitering, businessmen in neat pencil-striped suits. He merely glanced at them and walked up the stairs to the second floor. In the dim-lit hallway he paused before his own room twenty-three and glanced at the hotel-room door two rooms away. However, only a silence came from within room twenty-seven.

After Pete opened the door to his own room and ducked inside, he closed and locked the portal after him. He lit the lamp and the dim glow brightened the room slightly. He then took off his suit coat, tie, and shirt before he washed his face and hands with the water in the basin on the stand. When he dried off, he finished undressing. Then he laid his formal attire neatly on a hanger before he placed it in the closet.

Meanwhile, Pete saw the bundled package in the corner and he grinned. Chinaman Charlie had returned with his chino pants, lace shirt, and underwear, all washed and ironed. As usual, the man had been prompt and efficient. Pete would have clean clothes to wear in the morning.

Pete now turned off the lamp and slipped under the cover, leaving only a pale aura of light coming through the window from the night outside. Houston was tired, but he did not fall asleep immediately. He thought of Laura Renault two doors away, and he wondered what she had done all day. He wondered if she had simply remained in her room, gone about town, or if she was even in this hotel anymore. He could not help worrying about her. Rawlings and his men would surely seek revenge for allowing him to escape.

But then, Pete Houston suddenly realized that he felt only an obligation to Laura Renault, that his infatuation for the girl had diminished. True, he had settled for Jane Clemons when Laura all but rebuffed him. But now, as he lay in his bed, he suddenly felt more desire for Jane. After spending this evening with Jane, he had come away with a warm, satisfied feeling, happy to have been with her, and anxious to see her again. He had not even felt disappointment when Jane told him he could not come up to her room tonight. Thus, Pete now admitted to himself that he was in love with the girl, and that the beautiful Laura Renault had been only a passing fancy.

His thoughts of the two women preyed on his mind for a half-hour, but then he thought of the Rawlings gang and what he could do about them. He knew he would need to be alert, for they were surely out to snare him. He also knew he would have to worry about Laura, for they probably wanted her more than him. But then he remembered Jane telling him about the killings at the Branden Ranch campsite and he knew that it might be difficult to get these outlaws himself. Without a doubt, the cattlemen's association would offer a high price for these killers of the Branden Ranch sentries. Hordes of bounty hunters, lawmen, and Pinkerton men would be out looking for them. Even if such searchers did not know the identity of the culprits, they could round up the Rawlings gang among others.

Houston continued to turn restlessly in his bed but then he shifted his thoughts to more mundane things—getting a good breakfast in the morning, and giving his big bay a thorough grooming. Finally, well after midnight, Pete Houston fell asleep.

While Houston just began his night's sleep, Big Val Henry was well on the road to Buffalo, loping his horse slowly and easily up the Johnson County Highway. In the deep, late-night darkness, Big Val was totally alone on this road. Henry continued on for another three hours and, finally, the silhouette of Buffalo loomed into view. A half-hour later, he was riding slowly up Gillette Street, where the businesses and saloons were all closed and dark. He was alone on the quiet street.

Henry squinted into the darkness to read the street signs until he found 14th, and he loped up this avenue. Every structure on either side of the street was dark, with only a pale light radiating from the Mercer Hotel, because the establishment kept a desk clerk on duty in the lobby twenty-four hours a day. Henry did not go inside, but dismounted and walked his horse through a side gangway next to the hotel to the rear. He suspected that the stable was in the back, as was customary in such lodging places.

The outlaw soon reached the stable and he hoped that Nebraska Brake was correct in stating that Houston probably kept his horse in the Mercer Hotel livery. Henry brought his horse inside and led the animal down the aisle between the stalls. Finally, he grinned when he saw the big

214

bay that he recognized as Pete Houston's horse.

Henry settled his own horse in an empty stall, three places away, and he next got himself comfortable in an obscure corner of the stable. He hoped he would have the patience to maintain his vigil through the rest of the night and into the morning, and even for a couple of days if need be—until Pete Houston came to his stabled horse and Henry could kill him.

CHAPTER TWELVE

Pete Houston awoke well after daylight, almost seven o'clock, when he felt his stomach gurgle from hunger. Again using the water in the basin on the stand, Pete washed himself before he dressed in the clean clothes that Chinaman Charlie had left in his room yesterday. Houston combed his hair, put on his gunbelt, and then left his hotel room. He would eat breakfast first and then return to the stable to groom his horse.

Houston stopped near room twenty-seven, hesitated for a moment, but then rapped softly on the door several times. Laura Renault answered from inside.

"Yes?"

"It's me, Pete Houston. Are you up? Are you decent?"

A moment later, Pete heard quick footsteps and then the click of a key as Laura opened the door. Pete frowned in surprise. The girl was dressed in full riding habit of shirt, jacket, skirt, boots, and her tambourine hat. She had also washed up and combed her long dark hair.

"You look like you plan to go somewhere, Laura."

"I am, Mr. Houston," the girl replied. "I'm leavin' town on the nine-o'clock stage."

"The nine-o'clock stage?" Pete asked. "Why? Where? I thought you'd stay around Buffalo for a while."

"It's best that I leave."

"Look"—Pete gestured—"why not come with me for some breakfast. Then we can talk. I have a suspicion you haven't eaten much in the past twenty-four hours."

The girl shrugged. "Why not."

Pete Houston and Laura Renault came down the front stairs and then into the lobby. As they left the hotel, the desk clerk and three or four loitering men eyed them with interest: a handsome man and a beautiful woman, both dressed neatly, and leaving here together. The hotel patrons conjectured. Were they man and wife? Were they two single people who had spent the night together? Or two people who had simply left their rooms coincidentally at the same time and walked downstairs together? However, none of them said anything as the duo left the hotel.

Gillette Avenue was already crowded by the time Pete and Laura turned into Buffalo's main street, and they literally weaved their way through the heavy pedestrian traffic while heading for the Buffalo Cafe. They walked on the boardwalk for nearly ten minutes before finally reaching the eating place. The cafe was also crowded, but they did find a small table. Pete

217

ordered toast, eggs, and ham, while the girl only ordered toast.

While they waited for breakfast, Pete Houston leaned slightly across the table and studied the girl opposite him before he spoke.

"Laura, are you sure this is what you want to do—leave town?"

"It's best that I do that," Laura said.

"I told you, I'll protect you from Rawlings and the others."

"I appreciate that, Mr. Houston, but I've made up my mind."

"Please," Pete said, "I don't want you to leave. I have a feeling for you and I thought you had the same kind for me. Frankly, I was surprised at how cold you got after we reached Buffalo. And to tell the truth, you don't seem very friendly this morning, either."

"I wanted you, Mr. Houston, and I sure ain't sorry about that. Nothin' would please me more than to have you again, but I want my freedom even more. If I took up with you again, I'd enjoy it too much, and before I knew it I'd become your prisoner, not able to think nor go anywhere, nor do anythin', for needin' you so much. I'd want to marry you."

"That's silly," Pete grinned. "I'd be mighty grateful to know that you'd want to marry me."

"No," the girl said. "You ain't truly in love with me. You must want me 'cause I can satisfy your lust and that's the same thing with me. We ain't really in love, Mr. Houston; we just have a hankerin' for each other. I gave this a lotta

218

thought ridin' in yesterday, and I come to realize that. So, it's best that we don't see each other no more after today."

"I'd miss you," Pete said.

"For a while, maybe." Laura Renault smiled, reached over, and touched Pete's hand. "We both know that what I said is true. That filly, that girl at the association office, she's the one for you. She's decent, a good woman. I'm sure she'd be loyal to you for your entire life."

"How can you be sure of that? You've only seen her once."

"That was enough," Laura said. "I could see the look on her face when I asked her where I could find Mr. Peter Houston. She couldn't stand the idea that you might be involved with some other woman. She'd love you forever. With me"—she shrugged—"we might get along fine for a while, but then I'd get testy because I was tied down to you. Pretty soon I'd come to hate you."

"Is there a chance you're thinking of somebody else?" Pete asked.

She gestured. "There's only one other man besides you that I might have hankered for, and that's Jerry Roseberry. He's been kind to me, and he made them animals in the Rawlings gang behave themselves as best he could."

Pete nodded. "He does appear to be an intelligent man."

"He is," Laura said. "I don't know why he ever took up with them outlaws, anyway. He was a smart man, gettin' all the way to captain in the army. I suspect he coulda gone all the way to general if he stuck it out."

"I guess he was foolish to give up a successful army career."

"I suppose he was like me," the girl said, "figured he could make a lotta quick money if he took up cattle rustlin'." She forced a smile. "I do believe that I'll miss Cap as much as I'll miss you."

Pete only grinned.

The duo ate their breakfast in near silence and left the cafe almost as mutely. They walked slowly back to the hotel, through the main lobby, and up the stairs. Again the desk clerk and a few men in the lobby eyed them with a sense of curiosity. On the second floor, Pete and Laura stopped at room twenty-seven.

"I got to finish packin', and then I got to meet somebody in the stable at eight-thirty," the girl said.

"The stable?"

"Somebody who's buyin' my horse and saddle," Laura said. "I surely won't need them anymore."

"I'm going to the stable myself to brush down my horse," Pete said. "I try to do that chore every day. That bay of mine is a fine animal and I like to take good care of him."

"Then I'll see you there," Laura said.

A few minutes later, Pete Houston left his room and walked through the second-floor corridor to the back. He descended the stairs, left through the rear door of the hotel, and walked to the horse barn. Inside, the patient Big Val Henry stiffened when he heard the sound of footsteps. He had alerted himself twice before this morning, but on each occasion the visitor had not been the bounty hunter.

Big Val again peered over the edge of the stall in which he hid, and this time his eyes brightened. The visitor this time was indeed his quarry. Henry concealed himself again, watching Houston pass by. Then he carefully peered from his hiding place and saw Houston duck into the stall where Pete kept his Bay. Big Val watched Pete take a brush from the wall and begin grooming his horse. The outlaw watched for a few minutes, until the bounty hunter became quite engrossed in his chore. Then, Henry took out his six-shooter and grinned to himself. There was no one in the barn except for himself and the bounty hunter.

Henry tiptoed toward Houston's stall, where the unsuspecting bounty hunter continued to brush down his horse. But Pete stiffened when he heard the click of the gun's hammer. He looked up and saw Big Val Henry standing next to him, grinning like a Cheshire cat, while he pointed the weapon at Pete.

"Well, bounty hunter, this is the end for you."

Pete Houston rose to his feet slowly and looked at the aimed Colt, then squarely into Henry's eyes. However, Pete said nothing and Big Val spoke again. "I came to kill you, as you can plainly see."

Pete took a step forward and Henry, instead of stopping him, retreated slightly, while an uncertainty showed in his eyes. Houston knew at that instant that Henry did not really have the stomach to kill someone in cold blood. Thus, if he was cautious, perhaps Pete might save himself from an impending death.

"Can you really pull the trigger, Big Val?" Pete asked. "Can you just shoot down a man as you would a wild dog?"

"Like I said, that's why I come here. That's why I've been waitin' in this horse barn for four or five hours."

Houston frowned. "How did you know you could find me in here, alone and unarmed?"

"We got out sources," Henry said.

"I do believe you have." Pete nodded. "And I suppose that somebody who told you about my habits is right here in Buffalo."

Henry shrugged. "I guess it don't matter if you know, seein' as how you'll soon be dead. It's a fellow named Joe Cameron. He's got a small house over on Twelfth Street, I believe."

"And he told you I'd be here this morning?"

Henry grinned. "Bounty hunter, we know what you're doin' every hour a the day. We got other people besides Cameron who keep well informed on what you and the law are always doin'."

"But you slipped up, killing those guards on the Branden Ranch job."

"I had nothin' to do with that." Big Val gestured. "Neither the Dude, nor me, nor anyone else intended to kill anybody. Those guards drew on one of us and they was shot. Wild Man killed 'em, and you could say he did so in self-defense."

"Sure." Houston scowled.

"Well, Houston, it won't make no difference to you, 'cause you'll be dead, like I said."

But as Houston took still another step forward,

Henry made no move to shoot, and, in fact, the rustler retreated even again. Pete almost grinned, sure now that the man was not a killer. Henry really had no stomach to simply gun down a man in cold blood. If he shot Pete, the discharge would come from a sudden panic or unexpected move. Houston's mind whirled. He needed to keep talking to the man until he found an opportunity to catch Henry off guard.

"Are you sure that no one saw you come in here?" Pete asked. "If they did, and they find me dead, they'll guess who was responsible."

"Nobody saw me," Henry said. "I got here hours ago, in the dark, and there wasn't a livin' soul about."

"But men have been coming in here all morning to saddle their horses and ride off. How do you know one of them didn't see you?"

"I hid myself real good."

"But those stall railings are open," Pete said. "Someone could have seen you; maybe paid no attention to you, and perhaps thought you were simply some drifter sleeping it off in this barn. But, as I said, if they find me dead in here, those people might remember you well."

Big Val licked his lips, no doubt nervous. Pete Houston had spoken with good logic. But then Henry straightened and aimed his gun sharply. "I can't worry about that no more, Houston. I promised the others I'd do this job, and I aim to do it."

"And after you kill me, then what? Do you intend to kill Laura, too?"

"That's also gotta be done."

"Then get on with it, Big Val," a soft sober voice suddenly echoed from behind Henry. The outlaw turned and froze when he saw Laura Renault standing behind him.

"L-Laura!"

"You got the gun," the girl said, "either use it or put it away." But, as Laura came closer, Big Val retreated. "What's the matter? Can't you shoot?"

Henry slammed himself against the railing of the stall and brandished his six-shooter, his eyes darting between Pete and Laura. Neither of his potential victims was armed, but the sudden appearance of the girl had rattled Henry. The outlaw made no move to fire his Colt, even as Laura and Pete moved closer to him.

"Big Val," Laura said, "you're no killer, and you never will be. You didn't even want to be an outlaw until the Dude talked you into it. I suspect that if you killed one of us, your conscience would burn for the rest a your life, even if you got away free."

Big Val pursed his lips and lowered his head, even as Laura came closer to him. "Big Val, either use that gun or hand it over."

Henry shook his head. "I can't do it, Laura; I can't kill you. No matter what you done or what the Dude says, I just can't do it." As he lowered his arm, Laura took the handle of the six-gun and pulled the weapon away from the rustler's hand.

"Like I said, you ain't no killer," Laura said.

Henry stiffened and once more looked first at Laura and then at Pete. A sudden look of fear came to his face and he finally spoke to the girl.

"What are you gonna do, Laura? What?"

"Nothin'," the girl said. Then, when Henry looked apprehensively at Houston, Laura spoke again. "He ain't gonna do nothin' either."

Houston did not answer.

"Big Val," the girl continued, "have you got your horse here? And did you bring your money with you?"

Henry nodded vigorously.

"Good," the girl said. "At least you had enough sense not to leave your money at that hideout. Get on your horse, ride out; go south, maybe to Colorado or even all the way to Oklahoma. Go back to house paintin'. In a big town like Guthrie or Tulsa, you got enough money to start a real good business."

"The D-Dude'll kill m-me," Big Val stuttered.

"No, he won't," Houston finally spoke. "Everybody in the territory will soon be out looking for him. He and the others will never go free. They'll either come out of the Hole In The Wall country as prisoners or as dead men. You don't have to worry about Dude."

"And you don't have to worry about the law," Laura said, "since nobody's ever identified you as one of the Rawlings gang."

Henry nodded.

"Mount your horse and move," Laura said, "and stay outta trouble when you reach Oklahoma Territory."

"I'm grateful, Laura," Henry said.

"Here, you'll need this." The girl handed the

outlaw his gun. Houston did not protest. Big Val took the weapon, nodded, and slipped the gun into his holster. A moment later, he had mounted his horse and was loping out of the stable. "Good-bye, Laura. I hope you make out well. Even you, bounty hunter." He looked at Houston.

"Take care a yourself, Big Val," the girl said.

Henry nodded and left the stable, veering left. He would ride through town, turn left, and head south. He did, after all, have a three-thousand-dollar bankroll, enough for a fresh start. He did not even look left or right as he traversed Gillette Avenue, but simply continued straight ahead until he left town. He would ride all the way to Oklahoma.

Shortly after Henry's departure, a local Buffalo livery owner pulled up to the Mercer Hotel stable in a buckboard. He alit and walked into the barn to meet Laura Renault. When he saw Pete Houston, he grinned, and he then looked at the girl. "Is Houston here to make sure I don't cheat you?"

"Just a coincidence," Pete said. "I don't think Miss Renault needs me to make sure she dosen't get cheated."

The livery owner nodded. "All right, Miss Renault. I've seen your horse and gear yesterday. It is a good animal, but the gear is only middlin' to fair. I can give you two hundred and thirty dollars for the lot."

"I thought you said you didn't want to cheat me?" Laura said.

"I'll go three hundred." The potential buyer

gestured: "I can't do any better."

"Five hundred dollars," Laura said, "that horse alone is worth that much."

"Five hundred dollars!" the man gasped. "That's outrageous." He looked at Pete. "Tell 'er, Houston. Nobody in his right mind would pay that kinda money for that horse and gear."

"I have nothing to do with this." Pete shrugged. "Your business is with Miss Renault."

The livery owner shook his head. "Miss Renault, you're drivin' an impossible bargain. I can't get five hundred dollars for that myself after I polish that gear and saddle and then groom down that horse. Do you expect me to work for nothin'?" Laura did not answer and the man scowled. "All right, four hundred dollars. That's splittin' the difference. I can't do any better'n that."

"You bought yourself a horse, saddle, and gear," Laura said.

A few minutes later, Laura and Pete watched the Buffalo livery owner lead the horse out of the stable and tie the animal to his buckboard. He then came back and peeled off four hundred dollars and handed it to the girl before Laura signed a bill of sale. Next, Pete watched the man leave the stable with the sheet and with the gear.

"Nice doin' business with you, Miss Renault," the man said as he walked off and placed the gear and saddle on his buckboard. The duo inside watched the man leave before they walked back to the girl's hotel room. There, Pete picked up Laura's bags to carry them to the stage station on Gillette Avenue. They said little to each other

227

as they walked, although the girl occasionally smiled at her companion.

At the station, Pete waited outside while Laura went inside to buy her ticket to Sheridan on the nine-o'clock stage. She then sat on the bench next to Pete. The stage would leave in fifteen minutes, as soon as company hands hitched up a fresh team of four horses.

"So you're going back to Sheridan?" Pete asked.

"Yes. I sent a telegram yesterday to a cousin a mine up there. She sent one right back to me and said she'd love to have me up there again."

"Is that what you want to do?" Pete asked.

Laura Renault shrugged. "I worked in a haberdashery there one time, and now I got enough money to keep a shop a my own. That's what I think I'll do." She smiled at Pete. "Unless you aim to take me in for a bounty. You're the only one who knows I was a part a that Rawlings bunch, although you'd have to prove it."

"You know better than that," Pete said.

"I'm grateful." The girl smiled again.

"Are you sure you don't want to stay here?" Pete asked, gently holding the girl's wrist.

"No, Mr. Houston. I truly want to go back to Sheridan. I want to forget everything that took place in this county. I'll always remember you, but I want to see my cousin again and to open my own business, and yes, maybe settle down like that girl in the association office."

The duo sat and talked here for about another ten minutes, continuing their small chat until a cry came from the station master. "All aboard!

228

Stopping at Story Springs, Station Big Horn, and Sheridan."

Pete and Laura rose from the bench and walked to the stage. She stopped and kissed her companion. "Good-bye, Mr. Houston. It was sure nice knowin' you."

As Pete helped her into the stage, Laura caught sight of Joe Cameron up the street and she stiffened. Pete frowned. "What's the matter?"

"The man in the dark blue shirt hurryin' up the street; that's Joe Cameron. I suspect he's headin' for the telegraph office to let the Dude know that I'm on this stage."

"Maybe we'd better go back to the hotel."

"I'd truly rather be on my way," Laura said.

"Then you go, and don't worry," Pete said. "I'll take care a that Cameron, I assure you."

"I'd be grateful," Laura said.

Pete stepped back and watched the girl settle herself inside the stage. Then she blew him a kiss as the driver lashed the horses. "Hi-yah! Hi-yah!" The stage lurched forward and Pete stood but briefly before hurrying up the street after Joe Cameron.

Houston caught up to the man just as Cameron started into the telegraph office. He gripped his quarry's arm and spun him around just as Cameron was about to open the door. The man froze when he saw Houston standing there, and perspiration quickly dampened his face. His body shuddered from a sudden nervousness.

"You're not going in there, mister."

"W-what do you m-mean?" Cameron stam-

229

mered. "I c-can send a telegram if I like."

But Houston gripped the man's shirt and pulled him close. "A telegram to a partner who might give the information to a rustler named Dude Rawlings? A message that a certain young lady just boarded the stage for Sheridan?"

"I d-don't know what you're talkin' about."

"Look, Cameron, I know who you are, and I know who you work for," Pete said. "Now, maybe you'd like to talk over at the sheriff's office and explain what you intended to do in the telegraph office. I guarantee you, I can tie you into the Rawlings gang as one of their informants."

"Y-you can't do that."

"Now, how do you suppose the law would look on a man who's been giving information to a band of rustlers that also killed two men?"

"T-two men?"

"Don't act dumb, Cameron." Houston scowled. "If you don't know that two range sentries were killed from the Branden Ranch during a rustling caper, why, you must have been buried in some hole for the past two days."

"Maybe I heard a that," Cameron said, the sweat now pouring down his pudgy face.

"And you know that the killers came from the Rawlings gang."

"You can't prove that."

"I've got a witness," Pete said. "But, as long as you're intent on sending a telegram, why, I'll oblige you. Only you send what I tell you."

"W-what you tell me?"

"Unless you want your arm broken, and maybe

230

a bullet through your heart as soon as I strap on a gunbelt." Cameron licked his lips and then wiped his brow. "Who's your contact south of here that carries information to Rawlings?" Pete demanded. "Where is he? Jaycee? Egleston? Where?"

The man did not answer, and Pete wrestled the man's arm behind his back, pulled him up the street, yanked him into a dim, narrow alleyway, and hauled him to a remote, empty backyard behind the telegraph building. Here, Pete shoved him against the wall, pressing Cameron's chest with one hand, while he turned his arm until the man cried out in agony.

"You've got ten seconds to start talking," Houston barked, "or you're going to be lying here with two broken arms and maybe a broken leg as well." The man groaned again, so Pete spun him around, bounced Cameron against the wall, and on the rebound hit him squarely in the jaw. Cameron's head snapped back, drawing blood. The man slithered to the ground, dazed, and in a sitting position. Pete hoisted the man to his feet. "What about it, Cameron? Two broken arms or do you talk?"

"Y-you can't do this," the man panted. "Y-you're as b-bad as they are." But Pete bounced him off the wall again and with the other hand sent a hook to Cameron's jaw that crumpled him to the ground. When Pete lifted the beaten informant once more, Cameron gestured weakly.

"All right, all right."

"Who's your contact."

"Brake, Nebraska Brake," Cameron said. "He

stays at the Egleston Boardin' House."

"If you're lying, I'll kill you."

"I—ain't lyin', I swear it," the man gasped.

Pete Houston then unleashed still another hard fist that left Joe Cameron down and unconscious in the isolated yard. The bounty hunter then hurried through the alleyway and walked into the telegraph office. When the operator looked up, Pete pointed. "The stage to Casper—what time does it leave Buffalo?"

The operator frowned. "Eleven o'clock."

"What time does it reach Egleston?"

"About four," the man answered. "I don't understand, Mr. Houston. You could have found out that information at the stage station."

Houston grinned. "I knew you'd have it here and it saves me time. I want to send a telegram."

The operator nodded. "Where to, Mr. Houston? And who gets it?"

"Send it to Mr. Nebraska Brake, Egleston Boarding House, Egleston." He paused as the operator wrote quickly. When he stopped, Pete continued. "LR girl will be on Casper stage out of Buffalo. Will arrive in Egleston at four for short layover. Don't know what happened to BV or PH bounty."

The operator stopped and frowned again.

"Don't ask questions; just write."

"Yes sir, Mr. Houston."

"Believe BV failed to deliver and BH still here. Signed JC."

"JC?"

"You can send it that way, can't you?" Pete asked.

"Mr. Houston, I can send whatever you like, so long as you pay for it." He quickly counted the words. "That'll be twenty-six cents."

Pete handed the operator a five-dollar note. "If I give you this, will you forget who it was that sent that telegram? And can you also forget what was in that telegram?"

"Yes sir, Mr. Houston," the operator answered with a wide grin. "After all, there's dozens a people who come in and outta here every day, and writin' all kinds a messages. I sure can't remember who all of 'em are or what it was they sent."

Pete returned the grin, tapped the man on the shoulder, and then left the office. He hurried back to his hotel, to quickly pack a bedroll, saddle his big bay, and gallop off to Egleston. He wanted to make certain that he reached that town before the eleven-o'clock stage out of Buffalo arrived in Egleston. Pete was sure that some members of the Rawlings gang, perhaps even the Dude himself, would be waiting there for the stage. Houston wanted to be waiting for these outlaws, rather than having the rustlers waiting for the stage.

CHAPTER THIRTEEN

Pete Houston had guessed right. Less than a half-hour after the deceptive telegram from the bounty hunter reached Nebraska Brake in Egleston, the informant was on his way to Rawlings' Hole In The Wall hideout. Brake was again met at Devil's Pass by a sentinel, this time Preacher Rogers. The rustler soon enough recognized the rider and shouted down to him.

"Brake! What are you doin' out here this time?"

"Some information from Cameron in Buffalo."

"Did Big Val get that bounty hunter and the girl?"

"No," Brake cried back. "I've got to see the Dude and he can tell you all about it." When Rogers gestured, Brake continued on. Within an hour he had dismounted in front of the log hideout. Once again Dude Rawlings and Jerry Roseberry were out on the porch to meet him.

"Have you heard from Cameron?" Rawlings grinned at the visitor. "Did Big Val get that bounty hunter and that traitorous wench?"

"I don't think so," Brake said. Rawlings

frowned, but Brake came onto the porch and headed straight into the parlor. Roseberry and Rawlings followed him and the informant was already seated on a divan by the time the two rustlers came next to him.

"All right, Nebraska, what have you found out?" Rawlings asked.

"To tell the truth, nothin' at all for sure on Big Val and Houston," Brake said. "In his telegram, Cameron says he don't know what happened to Henry and the bounty hunter. I suspect nothin' happened. Big Val musta missed Houston, and for sure he missed the girl. Cameron says that Laura Renault is takin' the eleven-o'clock stage to Casper."

"I don't understand." Rawlings frowned.

"I'm only tellin' you what Cameron said." Brake gestured. "He said the stage reaches Egleston at four, and that's true. The stage'll lay over two hours while they change horses, check the wheels and carriage, and give the passengers a meal. Then the stage will go on through the night and get to Casper in the mornin'."

"How did Henry miss those two?" Rawlings asked. "Are you sure Big Val didn't get Houston and then maybe get caught before he got Laura?"

"I don't think so," Brake said. "If Big Val got Houston and then got caught, why, everybody in Buffalo would know about it, includin' Cameron, and he'd have told me about it in his telegram."

"Then, maybe it was the other way around," Dude Rawlings said. "Maybe Houston got Big Val before Henry could get the bounty hunter."

"I doubt that, too." Brake shook his head. "If that happened, people in Buffalo would know that as well. Nothin' is clear, except that the girl will be on a stage goin' to Casper. I sent a telegram right back to Cameron, askin' for details about Houston and Big Val. I suspect I'll have an answer by the time I get back to Egleston."

"You won't go back alone, Nebraska," Rawlings said. "One or two of us will be there to meet that stage so we can take care a the girl. We'd like to hear from her what happened to Big Val and that bounty hunter before we kill 'er."

"I'll go," Roseberry said.

"No," the Dude said. "You got too much of a feelin' for that female and she might talk you into lettin' her loose."

"Dude, don't you think I realize what she did to us?" the ex-army captain said to the outlaw leader.

"I'm sorry, Cap, I don't trust you," the Dude said. "No, I'm sendin' Wild Man and the Preacher back to Egleston with Nebraska. They can get the girl and bring 'er back. We'll make 'er talk and then we'll take care of 'er."

"Wild Man is the one who can't be trusted," Roseberry said. "You know what he did on the Branden Ranch caper."

"Like he said, they drew on 'im," Rawlings answered, "and I've no reason to doubt 'im."

Roseberry did not answer this time.

A few minutes later, Dude Rawlings called Wild Man Eliot into the parlor and explained that something had apparently gone wrong in Buffalo. Cameron had said he had no idea what had happened to Houston and Big Val. The only certainty was that Laura Renault would be on the stage to Casper, and the stage would reach Egleston at four this afternoon to lay over for about two hours.

"I want you and the Preacher to go into Egleston with Nebraska this afternoon and wait for that stage," the Dude said. "Laura will no doubt get off during the layover. You're to take 'er with as little fuss as possible and bring 'er back here. Wait until she's kind of alone."

"Won't she holler and scream?" Eliot grinned. "She ain't just gonna come alone peacefully. Why, she'll likely fight back like a wildcat."

"Then you'll need to take 'er by force," the gang leader said, "even if you have to hold off with your gun anybody who tries to interfere."

Wild Man grinned again. "That'll suit me fine."

"I'm sure it will," Roseberry said icily.

"Look, Cap," Wild Man retorted, "just because you ain't got the gumption to do what needs to be done, that don't mean the rest of us feel that way."

"Let's not argue." Rawlings gestured to Eliot. "We'll have a noon meal and then Wild Man can be off. You can take some grub to the Preacher at the sentry post, let 'im eat, and then he can be on his way with you and Nebraska."

"Don't worry, Dude," Eliot promised. "I don't know how Big Val got screwed up, but you can be sure that me and the Preacher won't make any mistakes. We'll have that girl back here by dark."

The Dude nodded. "Let's eat."

Meanwhile, in Buffalo, Pete Houston had

packed his bedroll and saddled his horse, and by ten o'clock he had left the Mercer Hotel stable. A few minutes later, he stopped at the association office and ducked inside to see Jane Clemons and Joe Simeon. The girl greeted him with a smile.

"Pete? Have you been busy this mornin'?"

"I guess you could say that," Pete answered. "I got another lead on the Rawlings gang." He screwed his face. "I'm on my way to Egleston and I just thought I'd stop in to let you know."

Jane pursed her lips. "Seems you're always goin' off somewhere."

"I can't pass this up, Jane."

"No, I suppose not." But the chill was still in her voice.

"Is Big Joe inside?"

"Yes."

Pete nodded and then knocked at the door of the private office. Simeon's booming voice responded, "Come in." When Pete entered the room, the association executive grinned and rose from his chair.

"Ah, Pete; good morning."

"Joe," Houston said, "what happened at the cattlemen's association meeting in Sheridan?"

"We agreed to a bounty of five thousand dollars for the capture of the Branden Ranch killers. The reward will be posted sometime today."

"Is that over and above the bounty on the Rawlings gang?"

Simeon frowned. "I guess you could say that, but to tell you the truth, we don't think the Rawlings gang did this. Oh, I admit the job was done the same way"—Big Joe gestured—"but the Rawlings gang always made sure they never killed anybody. We don't think Rawlings himself would tolerate anything like that."

"Unless those sentries tried to resist," Pete said.

"That's a possibility," Simeon agreed, "but we're inclined to believe it was somebody else; maybe a member of the gang who lit out on his own and got up his own band to pull off a rustling job. Maybe somebody like that Wild Man Eliot," Simeon suggested. "From what I hear about him, he's got no conscience at all."

"As I asked," Pete said, "would that five thousand dollars be on top of the bounty already on the Rawlings gang?"

"Yes, but like I said—"

"I have some good information that links the Rawlings gang to those killings," Pete interrupted, "and I'm going down to Egleston now to check it out. I also have information that some of the gang members might be in that town this afternoon, and maybe I can take them."

"Alone?"

Pete grinned. "I'm expecting them, but they aren't expecting me."

Big Joe frowned again. "How did you come by this information? I mean, about knowing the Rawlings gang killed those sentries and that some of them will be in Egleston this afternoon?"

"I've got my sources," Pete said, "just like you have, as the sheriff has, and as a lot of other people have."

"Have you by any chance identified the woman

who was running with that band of rustlers?"

"I think that was false information," Pete lied. "Nobody knows anything about Rawlings gang having a woman with them. It's more likely the rustler was a young kid who was mistaken for a woman. Don't forget, those sentries were in a panic, and they might have believed anything."

"They were pretty sure," Simeon said.

"Well, they were apparently wrong."

Big Joe sighed. "Well, I wish you luck, Pete. Once those posters go out today, every man in the territory with a gun will be out looking for killer rustlers. Just be careful, Pete," Simeon finished.

"I'll do that," Pete grinned.

In the anteroom, Pete again stopped at the counter to speak to the girl. "Jane, I won't be gone long. I should be back sometime tomorrow."

"Are you sure you're goin' to Egleston to find rustlers?" Jane asked coldly. "It ain't that pretty woman you aim to find, is it?"

Pete leaned over the counter and kissed the girl lightly on the cheek. Then he held her wrists. "Jane, the only woman I want to see is you. Now, I'd be a liar if I said I didn't look twice at that Mary Smith. If I didn't, I wouldn't be a man, would I?"

"I suppose not," Jane answered, softening.

"But it was business and it's all over. When I get back, the first place I'll come is here to find you. I just hope you'll be as happy to see me."

The girl smiled and gripped the bounty hunter's hand. "I believe you, Pete." Then her face sobered. "You will be careful, won't you? I don't know how I'd feel if anythin' happened to you."

"Just knowing you'll be waiting for me is enough to make me stay alert." He kissed Jane again lightly on the cheek, but Jane threw her arm around him and kissed him hard on the lips, just as Big Joe came out of his office.

"Jane, I—" but Simeon stopped and grinned. Jane quickly retreated and lowered her flushed face in embarrassment. "I didn't mean to interrupt," Simeon said with a gesture.

"It's all right, Joe," Pete answered. "I was just leaving."

"You don't have to leave on my account." Simeon grinned again. "Jane can come into my office and take dictation later."

"I'm on my way," Pete said.

Both Jane Clemons and Joe Simeon watched Houston leave the office.

By ten-thirty, Pete Houston had left Buffalo and headed south. He would move at a moderate pace, without tiring his horse. He surely wanted to be in Egleston before any outlaws from the Rawlings gang got to the stage station, but he did not want to wear out his animal. Occasionally, however, Pete stepped up his pace, for he wanted to surprise the outlaws, and not the other way around. Houston did not worry about any potential bushwhackers on the Johnson County Highway, for he was certain that if Dude Rawlings had accepted the contents of the fraudulent telegram, the outlaw leader would concentrate on getting Laura Renault in Egleston.

Houston rode south for the rest of the morning,

reaching Jaycee about one o'clock, where he stopped for a quick noontime meal of a sandwich, soup, and coffee. He then continued south, and by two-thirty he saw Egleston ahead. Pete urged his horse into a fast trot and within ten minutes was loping into town. He passed the boarding-houses and saloons as he weaved through the heavy afternoon traffic. When he reached the stage station, he saw only one man there, the clerk who would meet the stage from Buffalo at four o'clock.

Pete only studied the station and continued on, finally veering his horse off the main street and into the Egleston Livery. The owner eyed him with a mixture of uncertainty and suspicion, for he recognized the visitor as the notorious bounty hunter Pete Houston. Pete pursed his lips, piqued by the recognition.

"Can I leave my horse here for a few hours?" Pete asked. "Maybe overnight?"

"Yes." The man nodded. "But it'll cost you two dollars."

"I know," Pete said, dismounting from his horse.

The man leaned forward and grinned. "Everything is high in Egleston, mister. I think you know that."

Pete extracted a wad from his shirt pocket and the man's eyes widened. However, he said nothing as Pete handed him two dollars. Then Pete held out two more bills. "One is to make sure you take good care of that bay and the five is to keep your mouth shut."

The man frowned.

"To make sure you don't tell anybody I came in here with this horse; to make sure nobody knows I'm in town."

"It ain't none a my business why you come to Egleston," the man answered, taking the extra money. He then watched Pete extract his rifle from the saddle scabbard and then pat the horse on the nose. The horse neighed gratefully.

"I must warn you," Pete said, "if anybody learns that I came in here, I'll hold you responsible."

"Mister"—the man grinned—"you're one man I don't want to mix with. Meanwhile, I'll take good care of your bay. I know how much he means to you; everybody does."

Pete nodded, waited until the owner led the horse into a stall, and then left the livery stable. Houston now walked slowly up the street, cradling his rifle in his right elbow. Soon, he reached the stage office, where he sat on the empty bench outside, straightened his legs in a slouching position, and tipped his Stetson down below his eyes. However, he had not been sitting there for five minutes before he felt a slight kick to his leg. Pete looked up to see Egleston Police Chief DeLisle looking at him.

"What are you doin' here, Houston?" DeLisle barked.

"Sitting on this bench and minding my own business."

"Violent business is the only kind you seem to have." DeLisle scowled. "Is that what you aim to do today? Cause more trouble like you did the last time you was here?"

"I'm just waiting for the stage."

"The stage!" DeLisle huffed. "What kinda bullshit is that? The stage ain't due in for a couple of hours." Then he leaned down and grinned. "You're wastin' your time. You ain't gonna find no wanted men in Egleston today. They're all stayin' clear a this town since them killin's at the Branden Ranch. You may as well go somewhere else."

"I told you; I'm waiting for the stage."

"Bullshit!" DeLisle cursed again. "You're a goddamn liar. Now I'm tellin' you, get on your way."

"I'm not breaking any laws by sitting here, am I?" Pete asked. "And I've never heard of the Wyoming Stage Company having a rule against somebody sitting on a station bench. Do they have such a rule, Chief?"

"Goddamn you, Houston. I'm warnin' you, if you cause any trouble again, I'll lock you up for sure. You're lucky I got rounds to make or I'd stay here and watch you all day. But I'll keep an eye on you." He gestured threateningly.

"You do that, Chief."

As DeLisle walked away, grumbling, Houston again slumped on the bench and tilted his hat over his eyes. He sat thusly for almost a half-hour, nearly falling asleep in the afternoon warmth. However, the clodding cleats of four horses alerted him and he looked quickly to his right, where he saw three men loping toward the stage station, with the fourth horse saddled but rider-

244

less. Pete did not recognize one of the riders, but he saw clearly that the other two horsemen were Wild Man Eliot and Preacher Rogers. Pete quickly guessed that the empty horse was for Laura Renault. His deception had worked. Houston left the bench and ducked into a niche next to the stage office.

Here, the bounty hunter waited cautiously and watched Eliot and Rogers dismount, while the third man remained in his saddle.

"Nebraska," Eliot gestured, "take the horses up the street to a tether post. You can come back as soon as that stage pulls in."

"We don't want to waste any time." Rogers pointed to Brake. "As soon as that wench gets off that stage, we want the horses ready, so we can mount her up in a hurry and get outta town."

"Don't worry, Preacher," Brake said. "I'll be back before the stage driver even reins up."

Pete watched Brake trot away, moving only about a half block up the street, where he tethered the horses while remaining in the saddle. Then, Pete saw Clint Eliot and Preacher Rogers sit on the bench. However, Wild Man had only been there a few minutes before he rose to his feet.

"We got lotsa time," Eliot said. "I'm goin' to the Salt River for a cold beer."

Rogers gripped his companion's arm. "You heard what the Dude told us. Stay put; don't go no place. We can't have anythin' go wrong on this, and we all know that you're the type who finds trouble wherever you go."

"Ah, hell." Eliot waved his arm. "I ain't gonna

245

get in no trouble. Why don't you come along? You must be pretty thirsty, too."

"No. I'll just sit here."

"Suit yourself." Eliot shrugged. "I'll be back before you know it."

Preacher Rogers watched Eliot move off and then he himself slouched on the bench. Houston eyed first the man on the bench and then Eliot moving up the street. A moment later, the bounty hunter left his niche and followed Eliot, making sure that Wild Man did not see him. Nebraska Brake, meanwhile, remained with the horses, and when he saw Eliot he leaned from his saddle. "Wild Man, where are you goin'?"

"Just to get a cold beer," Eliot said. "I'll be back to the station shortly."

Brake did not answer, but only watched Eliot pass through the swinging doors and into the Salt River Saloon. Pete had also been watching Eliot, and now the bounty hunter checked his six-gun, slipped it into his holster, and then headed toward the saloon. Eliot had made Houston's job easier, for now Pete could take the outlaws one at a time.

Because men were coming in and out of the Salt River, Brake didn't notice Pete duck into the saloon. When Houston got inside, he saw Eliot and three others at the bar drinking beer. The bounty hunter came within several feet of Wild Man and then cried out:

"Eliot, I'm taking you in."

Wild Man stiffened, turned, and stared when he saw Pete Houston standing a few feet away. He then grinned, however. "Houston! You son of a

246

bitch! What are you doin' here? I thought Big Val took care a you."

"Hand me your gun nice and easy, Eliot, and there won't be any trouble."

But Eliot moved away from the bar and stared hard at the bounty hunter, grinning again. "Why don't you come and get me."

Those about the bar quickly scattered, with the bartender ducking down, the patrons hurrying to the other side of the room, and those at tables near the bar quickly deserting their chairs and also darting to the other side of the room. Houston and Eliot now stood alone as the bounty hunter came closer.

"Give it up, Eliot."

"Suck my prick, bounty hunter," the outlaw disparaged Houston.

"Are you the one who killed those sentries?"

"Yeh, I killed 'em, although it ain't none a your goddamn business," Eliot boasted. "They tried to draw on me, and anybody foolish enough to do that against me ain't got no right to live." Wild Man then lowered his right hand toward his holstered gun. "I ain't afraid a you one bit, you bastard. If you want a chance to save your life, why, you'd better draw your gun. Otherwise, you'll die standin' there."

"I have no desire to kill you, Eliot," Pete said. "If you come along peacefully, you'll get a fair trial."

"Shit, there ain't no such thing as a fair trial for men like me." Then, Eliot took one step back and reached for his gun. He had barely hoisted the weapon from his holster before Pete Houston had extracted his own Colt and fired two shots almost point-blank into the outlaw's chest.

The two hits lifted Wild Man Eliot almost off the barroom floor and then spun him around. He staggered drunkenly, uncontrollably, while spewing blood covered his chest and dripped in heavy drops to the floor. A wide-eyed, startled look had cemented itself on Wild Man's face before his countenance softened lifelessly and he crumpled to the floor—dead. Houston came forward and rolled him over on his back with his foot. Then he looked at the bartender, who had now risen from his crouching position.

"Get this body to the morgue. I'll pick it up later."

The bartender nodded.

Those in the Salt River Saloon stared at the slain Wild Man Eliot and at the departing Pete Houston. None of them said anything, but all of them knew that the dead man had guessed badly when he thought he could outdraw the bounty hunter.

By the time Pete got outside, a small crowd of people were loitering in front of the saloon, drawn there by the sound of gunfire. They quickly split, as if with an axe, to allow Houston a passage. Most of the curious group glanced at Houston, then at the saloon and then back to Houston, but none said anything. And now, as Pete headed back toward the stage station, Nebraska Brake, from atop his horse, saw the bounty hunter walking.

Brake gaped in astonishment, horrified to see

Houston in Egleston, and certain that Houston had fired the shots inside the saloon, probably to kill Wild Man Eliot. Brake left two horses tethered, and galloped up the street with the other horse before rearing up in front of the stage station. Preacher Rogers rose to his feet, surprised by the sudden appearance of the informant.

"Mount up, Preacher, and let's get the hell outta here."

"What are you talkin' about?" Rogers scowled.

"That bounty hunter's in town and I think he just killed Wild Man in the Salt River. He's comin' back now—after you, I'd guess."

"W-what?" Rogers hissed.

"This whole goddamn thing musta been some kinda trap. I don't think that girl'll be on the stage at all. I think Houston somehow got Joe Cameron to send that telegram so's he could set a trap for you."

"Son of a bitch!" Rogers cursed.

However, as the rustler started for the waiting horse, Pete Houston came within ten or fifteen yards, and he opened fire with his rifle. The two shots just missed Rogers, who ducked behind the horse. Meanwhile, Brake reared his own horse while he yanked out his own six-gun, fired twice, and then galloped away—alone. The shots missed Houston, who now aimed his Winchester and fired. The shot grazed Brake's temple, but he continued on and soon veered off the street, obviously terrified. Brake rode slowly back to his boardinghouse, where he would stable his horse and then lock himself in his room.

Meanwhile, Preacher Rogers darted back and forth behind the horse while he sought a good shot at the approaching bounty hunter. However, Houston fired an occasional rifle shot that forced Rogers to remain hidden behind the animal. The horse neighed nervously, jerking and rearing, while Rogers held onto the saddlehorn. Finally, Rogers fired. The two wild and inaccurate shots from his Colt missed badly, but prompted the horse to rear in panic, yanking itself free of the rustler before the animal bounded off.

Now, Ralph "Preacher" Rogers stood alone and exposed on the street, his smoking gun in his hand. Crowds on the street watched the bounty hunter come closer to the outlaw before Houston cried out:

"I'd prefer to take you alive, Rogers."

"You no-good bastard," Rogers shouted, "you ain't takin' me anywhere."

Then, as Houston came cautiously on, Rogers raised his six-shooter and fired. However, Houston had anticipated just such a move and he had already lurched out of the way and flattened himself on the dirt street. Before the Preacher could aim his six-shooter again, Pete unleashed two shots from his Winchester. Both struck home, one in the head and the second in the chest. Rogers bounced backward as blood smeared his face and chest. Then, he collapsed to the ground, jerked once, and lay dead—like a discarded, contorted mannequin.

As Houston approached his fallen adversary, the crowd came forward. Chief DeLisle and one of his policemen jostled their way through the mob and came up to the bounty hunter.

"Houston, you're under arrest!" DeLisle cried.

Pete turned to the Egleston police chief. "I tried to take him alive, but he wouldn't have it. So, I had no choice."

"Goddamn you," DeLisle cursed, "I knew you'd bring more trouble to this town; I knew it. Now I'm takin' you in."

"On what charge?"

"Murder, or killin', or at least disturbin' the peace."

"Every man there"—Pete gestured to the crowd—"knew that I wanted to take these men peacefully. And you know those two men have bounties on their heads, so I had a right to take them." He scowled at DeLisle. "Are you going to tell the Wyoming Cattlemen's Association that you arrested me for running down two wanted men?"

"You bastard," DeLisle muttered, "All right, you got 'em. Now pack 'em up and get outta town."

"I'm not leaving town," Pete said. "I've got some other business in the morning. You can take him to the mortician, too." Houston gestured toward the slain Preacher Rogers.

"You're gonna stay here tonight?" DeLisle growled.

"That isn't against the law, is it?"

DeLisle merely mumbled, ambled away, and motioned to a pair of onlookers. "Take this body to the mortician and tell 'im to keep it there until this bounty hunter claims it tomorrow." Then, DeLisle and his officer walked off, while Pete started up the street.

When the crowd had cleared, Pete Houston walked up the street until he reached the Egleston Boarding House, where he knocked at the door. He soon heard footsteps before an elderly man opened the door. "Yes?"

"I'd like a room for the night."

The man studied Houston and then craned his neck to look into the street. "I don't see your horse. Do you have one?"

"It's at the livery stable. I'll pick it up in the morning."

"The only room I got is the west corner, upstairs, facin' the street. But it's one a the best in the house and it'll cost you two dollars."

Pete nodded, peeled off a pair of one-dollar bills, and handed them to the man. "That should cover it."

The man nodded and led Houston upstairs, shaking his head. "I don't know why you took your horse to the livery. He's a robber. You coulda kept your mount in my barn for fifty cents."

"Well, what's done is done."

The old man nodded and then led Pete down the hallway to room six on the second floor. As he fumbled for a key to open the door, Nebraska Brake heard the noise in the hallway and opened the door slightly to peer outside. He blanched when he saw Pete Houston, ducking back into his room.

When Nebraska heard only the plodding footsteps of the elderly man, he came out of the room and followed the manager downstairs.

"Jed," Nebraska said, "that man you just put into room six—how long will he be there?"

"Just tonight, I guess." The old man shrugged. "He said he was tired, was gonna do a little business around town this afternoon, get himself some supper and then get a good night's sleep. He asked me to wake him up at six tomorrow morning because he's got important business. Personally, I don't know of any kinda business that would have a man get up that early."

"I'm obliged for the information, Jed," Brake said.

The informant returned to his room, put a fresh dressing on his gazed temple, and then hurried to the stage office, which had now opened to await the four-o'clock stage from Buffalo. He spoke to the man inside. "Can you tell me if a Laura Renault is on that four-o'clock stage?"

The man went through a sheet on his list. "Accordin' to the manifest that came by telegraph from Buffalo, there ain't no such Renault among the passengers. In fact, all of 'em are men, six of 'em, and all going on to Casper."

"Thank you," Brake said. "She must be takin' tomorrow's stage."

Brake hurried back to his boardinghouse, saddled his horse in the barn, and quickly left. He loped swiftly out of town, heading for the Hole In The Wall country. He had plenty of news for Dude Rawlings, but all of it bad—except for one. Pete Houston would be sound asleep tonight in room six of the Egleston Boarding House. Rawlings would never find a better opportunity to kill that bounty hunter.

CHAPTER FOURTEEN

Twilight had come to the Hole In The Wall country by the time Nebraska Brake reached the log structure. As usual, he tethered his horse in front of the house, where a light already glowed from the parlor. A moment later, Jerry Roseberry answered.

"Nebraska! What are you doing here?"

"Is the Dude inside?"

"You must have serious news to come out here at this time of day."

"I have, and it's all bad."

By the time Nebraska seated himself on a divan in the parlor, Dude Rawlings had come in from the kitchen where he had been preparing some supper for himself and his fellow outlaws. He frowned when he saw his informant.

"I wasn't expectin' you, Nebraska. I thought I'd be seein' Wild Man and the Preacher with that wench here just about this time. How come you're here?"

"I can tell you, Mr. Rawlings, everything that could went wrong," Nebraska said. "That bounty hunter is slicker than any of us thought. Your two men are dead. Houston killed both a them. They was supposed to be waitin' to get the girl from the four-o'clock stage. Instead, the bounty hunter was waitin' for Eliot and Rogers. He killed Wild Man in the Salt River Saloon and then got the Preacher at the stage station. He nearly killed me, too; grazed my temple as you can see." He showed the Dude his bandage.

"Goddamn," Rawlings hissed.

"That girl never was on that stage," Nebraska continued. "I checked at the station, and the telegraph manifest from Buffalo only showed six men passengers on the stage. It seems that Houston somehow got Joe Cameron to send me that telegram fulla misinformation, and that bounty hunter set a real nice trap for your boys."

"I'll be a son of a bitch!" the Dude cursed.

"What about Laura?" Roseberry asked. "Where is she? Did she come into Egleston with Houston?"

"No, I'm sure a that." Nebraska shook his head. "I don't know where she is; maybe still in Buffalo."

Rawlings looked hard at Roseberry. "Cap, you know what this means? We ain't got a band anymore. There's just you and me left. We don't know about Big Val, but I suspect that bastard Houston did him in, too."

"I think we'll just have to give the entire thing up, Dude," Roseberry said. "We should cleanse this place of any money and valuables and leave the territory."

"That's easy for you to say," Dude said. "They

ain't got your picture on any wanted posters. I need to be real careful."

"It's still the best course," the ex-army captain said.

"Cap's right, Mr. Rawlings," Nebraska said. "Them new wanted posters for the Branden Ranch killin's will be all over Wyoming Territory by the end a the day or tomorrow at the latest, and I heard the bounty'll be five thousand dollars. Why, every man with a weapon will be comin' into Hole In The Wall and shootin' anything that moves."

"All right." The Dude nodded. He looked at Roseberry. "We'll take whatever cash those others left here and anything else worthwhile. We'll split it down the middle. Then we'll pack our saddlebags and git. For myself, I'll just head west, maybe to California. You can go wherever you want, Cap, since they ain't lookin' for you."

"I do have one other piece of information, good information," Nebraska said. "That bounty hunter is stayin' in Egleston tonight. Fact is, he's right in my own boardin'house and takin' a room on the upstairs west corner. You could reach the room easy from the front porch roof. I heard 'im tell Jed that he was dog tired and he needed a good night's sleep."

"Goddamn." Rawlings grinned. "That means that by midnight or so, he'd be so sound asleep that even a dynamite blast wouldn't wake 'im up. We could kill 'im right in his bed."

"I'd say so," Nebraska answered.

"No, no." Roseberry shook his head vigorously.

"There's no longer any reason to worry about Pete Houston. Our game is over, Dude. Why take any chances? The best thing to do is to simply pack up and leave."

"It's that bounty hunter who ended our game," the Dude pointed out, "and the least I can do for all our boys who've been killed or captured is to kill that goddamn Houston."

"Dude," Roseberry said soberly, "you said it yourself—what's done is done. Everybody who enlisted in this band knew he took a chance. They lost. We're alone, but with considerable money. Forget this obsession for revenge. Let's just clear out and get fresh starts somewhere else."

"You can clear out," the Dude said. "From what Nebraska says, I got a chance to kill that man, and I ain't gonna pass it up."

"It's foolish, Dude," Roseberry persisted. "Why commit murder, especially against that bounty hunter? Houston has surprising influence in this territory. If you kill him, the cattlemen's association will do anything to find his killers. I must remind you, Dude, the association has substantial money and power. They can hire the best to run you down."

"I've made up my mind, Cap," the Dude answered.

"Well, you'll have to do it without me."

"Then, that's how it'll be," Rawlings said. He looked at the visitor. "Nebraska, are you willin' to throw in with me on this tonight? Get that bounty hunter right in his bed? I'll pay you a couple a hundred dollars."

"I owe that Houston somethin' after he nearly killed me, and two hundred dollars would be a damn good stake."

"Then, we'll go after that bounty hunter together," the Dude said.

For the next two hours, Dude Rawlings and Jerry Roseberry ransacked the log house premises, pawing through dresser drawers, under mattresses, inside closets, under beds, or inside bags. They extracted whatever they could find of value that had belonged to the other members of the gang. They found considerable worthwhile jewelry as well as some eight thousand dollars in cash, mostly belonging to Preacher Rogers and Wild Bill Eliot, and some that had been in the possession of Frank Sparks and Pedro Anias. However, they found nothing belonging to Big Val Henry or Laura Renault.

"I can understand that wench takin' all her money with her since she planned to run out on us," the Dude said, "but I'm surprised at Big Val. Maybe he never intended to go to Bufflao to kill her or the bounty hunter. Maybe he just meant to run out on us."

"It makes sense," Roseberry agreed, "especially since there's not a hint at all that he contacted Houston or Laura in Buffalo."

When the two men finished, they filled extra saddlebags with their loot. The Dude abandoned his efforts in the kitchen to cook supper and instead decided to leave for Egleston at once. He and Nebraska Brake walked to the barn and saddled the Dude's horse while Rawlings tied the extra saddlebags to the animal. When he finished, Rawlings loped into the open clearing in front of the porch and looked at Roseberry, who stood on the steps.

"Well, Cap, it was nice workin' with you," the Dude said. "I'll be headin' west as soon as I take care a that bounty hunter. I'll be all right. It's easy to make out when you got enough money. You take care a yourself, hear?"

"I still think you're making a mistake."

"So long, Cap," Rawlings said. Then he veered his horse, trotting across the clearing and then through the shallow creek. Nebraska followed on his own mount. Roseberry stood rigid, squinting into the darkness until the two men disappeared into the depths of the trees beyond. Then Roseberry sighed and walked back into the log structure.

In the parlor, alone, an eerie feeling gripped the ex-army captain. It was all over, and only the memories in the place remained. He recalled when they had first banded together in this ornate structure that the Dude had built with money from a bank robbery. An eagerness and anticipation had gripped all of them. He remembered the comradeship, the big plans, the activities—and, yes, even the friendships. Now, they were all gone: McIver and Sparks in jail; Rogers, Anias, and Eliot dead; Big Val somewhere in the broad endless territories of the west, and, worst of all, Laura Renault. The ex-army captain missed her the most. He wondered where she might be now, what she had been doing, how close she had really been to Pete Houston. This last thought bothered him the worst. He could not bear the idea that she had even kissed him, much less shared a bed with the bounty hunter.

Roseberry slumped on the divan and stared at the quiet emptiness about him. In retrospect, he wondered if all this had been worth it. True, he had over eight thousand dollars in his possession and perhaps another one or two thousand in valuables, but all of it ill-gotten. Still, he realized that Eliot, Rogers, and the others would have picked his own pockets if he had been slain or been put behind bars. So, his conscience did not bother him. The ex-army captain sat meditating for nearly an hour, but then a sudden panic gripped him.

No! He could not allow Dude Rawlings to kill Houston, even though Roseberry had no love for the bounty hunter. The ex-captain could not have the man murdered. From a practical point of view, such a killing would endanger his own well-being. The cattlemen's association would hunt viciously for the killer, and they might put enough pressure on the jailed McIver or Sparks to make them talk and involve Roseberry.

If nothing more happened, however, Roseberry could lead a serene future. He had plenty of money and he could do well with it: start a ranch or open a thriving business. The law didn't know he had been a part of the Rawlings gang. Only Houston knew this, but if he talked, it would be the bounty hunter's word against Roseberry's. In a court of law, who would believe Houston's story that he had been lured into a trap by a woman, taken to this log structure where he saw Roseberry, and then had been freed by the same woman who had snared him? Such a tale would sound too ridiculous.

The ex-army captain wasted no more time. He dressed in neat riding clothes, packed a bedroll with extra attire, picked up his own extra saddle bag, and headed for the barn. There, he saddled his own horse, loaded the animal with his gear, and then left the stable. He paused on the open area and stared at the now-deserted log house. He felt a tinge of regret—a luxurious place like this abandoned. He was half-tempted to put a torch to the place, but then he shrugged. The hell with it.

A moment later, he loped away, crossed the narrow stream, and disappeared into the depths of the forest. However, the horse stepped into a hole and Roseberry dismounted to check. The mount was all right, but the animal had almost torn off one of its shoes. Roseberry cursed. He could not continue on, especially in the dark. He needed to walk the animal carefully back to the log structure's barn and replace the shoe. He sighed in resignation. There was nothing he could do to stop Rawlings. He would simply return to the log structure and leave the Hole In The Wall country at first light.

Dude Rawlings and Nebraska Brake arrived in Egleston about ten o'clock, for the ride out of the Hole In The Wall country had been quite dangerous at night and they had needed to move slowly and warily. They tethered their horses in front of the Salt River Saloon and spent the next couple of hours drinking while they worked up courage to kill Houston in his sleep. If anyone in the saloon had recognized Rawlings as the head of the now-defunct rustler gang, they made no effort to do anything about it. Nor did anyone attempt to engage the Dude in conversation. Then, shortly after midnight, Rawlings and Nebraska Brake left the crowded drinking place, remounted their horses, and loped up Main Street before turning into Avenue A and heading for the Egleston Boarding House.

The duo dismounted several doors away, tethered their horses, and walked softly up the sidewalk until they reached the boardinghouse. Nebraska pointed to the window on the west corner of the second floor, the bedroom of Pete Houston. The Dude nodded, checked his gun, and motioned to his companion. Together, they shimmied up the porch post and onto the roof, moving stealthily in a crouched position toward the window. Rawlings gestured again, directing Nebraska to one side of the window while the Dude set himself on the other side. Rawlings would quietly open the window and signal. Then, both men would burst into the room and shoot the bounty hunter as he slept.

However, the Dude had underestimated Houston. Pete had gone to bed, all right, but he had kept his six-gun with him under his pillow. The bounty hunter suspected that the man he had grazed today might likely warn the remaining members of the Rawlings gang and that they in turn might try to kill him. Remembering that Big Val Henry had chosen the Mercer Hotel to ambush him, Pete had resolved to take no more chances, not even in this quiet boardinghouse bedroom.

While the two would-be bushwhackers had approached the window quietly, and even though Houston slept soundly, his unconscious mind had remained alert. The squealing movement of the window being raised was enough to awaken him. Pete squinted to his left and saw the shadow of a man outside. Then, easily, he pulled his six-shooter from under his pillow and aimed it at the silhouette. As soon as the shadow had lifted the lower pane fully open and moved toward the inside of the window, Pete fired two quick shots that sounded like deafening explosions in the dark, serene, quiet night.

The two bullets hit Rawlings squarely in the neck and chest and he bounced backward into a sitting position on the porch roof. A startled look came from his small gray eyes as blood poured from his neck and torso. Then, he simply doubled over, rolled off the roof, and fell to the sidewalk below.

Nebraska Brake stared in horror at his fallen companion and for a moment he crouched stiffly, stunned by the unexpected turn. Only the sound of the squeaking bed as Houston moved inside brought Nebraska out of his near trance. Brake scrambled across the porch roof, quickly shimmied down the post, and raced up the street. He mounted his horse, took the reins of the Dude's horse, and darted away, the galloping hooves echoing through the night like a herd of wild stallions.

Luckily for Nebraska, Pete Houston had not rushed to the window to look outside after he shot Rawlings. Pete could not be sure that others were not also on the porch roof, so he had approached the window slowly and carefully before rising from the floor to look cautiously outside. By that time, Nebraska had already reached the horses.

Pete Houston now climbed out of the window, crossed the roof, and squinted down at the bloodied body of Dude Rawlings.

The shots and the galloping horses had awakened others in the Egleston Boarding House and several lamp lights went on, including that of the house manager Jed. A moment later, Jed and five others came onto the porch and looked in surprise at the dead man on the sidewalk. Moments later, Pete Houston had joined them.

"What happened?" Jed asked.

"The man there tried to kill me," Pete said. "He climbed to the roof and opened my window. But, I heard him and shot him first."

Someone quickly shimmied up the post and found Rawling's gun on the roof before he shimmied down again. "Here's the man's weapon. I guess he never got a chance to use it."

"Was there anyone else up there?" Jed asked.

Houston shook his head. "I didn't see anybody else by the time I came out of the window and onto the porch roof. If there were others, they got away."

"There must've been more of 'em," one of the roomers said. "I heard them horses galloping off. They musta got scared off after you picked off the first one," he said to Houston.

"Who was he, mister? Do you know?" somebody else asked.

Pete nodded. "Dude Rawlings. He led that band of rustlers. He's the last of 'em."

"Hey, ain't Rawlings got a price on his head? A big price?" another of the loitering men asked Houston.

Pete nodded again.

"Then you've earned yourself a good stake." The man grinned.

"I'll have to get that body over to the mortician," Pete said, "and I'll take care of things in the morning."

"We'll help you," somebody said.

Pete Houston accepted the offer before he went back upstairs to fully dress himself. By the time he returned outside, Jed himself had hitched up a buckboard, while two roomers had hoisted the body of Rawlings to the wagon's platform. Then, Houston boarded the wagon and rode with Jed to the mortician. Jed banged on the door, hard and long, until somebody inside finally answered.

"Goddamn, what's goin' on? Wakin' up a man in the middle a the night?"

"We got a dead man for you," Jed said.

"Good Lord!" the mortician gasped. "That's the third today." He sighed. "All right, bring 'im

265

inside. We can put the corpse with the others."

As they entered the building, the bounty hunter turned to the mortician. "My name is Pete Houston. I've been authorized by the Wyoming Cattlemen's Association to bring in members of the Rawlings gang, dead or alive. All three of them belonged to that gang. I'll make arrangements in the morning to take the bodies back to Buffalo. If you have any charges, why, you can bill Mr. Joseph Simeon of the Buffalo branch of the Wyoming Cattlemen's Association."

"Goddamn, so you're Pete Houston, that bounty hunter." When Pete nodded, the mortician continued. "You can tell Mr. Simeon there will be charges. I can't board these dead men and ready the bodies for shipment for nothin'."

"I'll tell him," Pete said.

Within a half-hour, Houston and the others had returned to the boardinghouse, where all went back to bed. However, the bounty hunter again slept warily, and again with his gun at his side.

Pete slept relatively late, until well after seven. He shaved, washed up, and dressed. He would get some breakfast, lease a buckboard, pick up the bodies of the three rustlers, and then haul the corpses to Buffalo. Pete left the boardinghouse, and by the time he reached Main Street, crowds were loitering in front of the post office. They were reading the cattlemen's association posters that now offered a $5,000 reward for the killers of the two sentries at the Branden Ranch and also listed the rewards for members of the Rawlings gang, $2,000 for the leader and $1,000 for the others. Pete felt elated. He would collect $4,000 when he reached Buffalo, and better still, he had completed his own mission, before hordes of gunmen poured into the Hole In The Wall country.

Houston ducked into a local cafe to eat a breakfast of eggs, toast, ham, and coffee. He then started up the street toward the livery stable to get his horse and to rent the buckboard. But an ambusher was waiting for him. Half-hidden at the side of a building was Nebraska Brake with an aimed rifle in his hand. He had watched Houston go into the cafe, and he now waited patiently for Pete to come up the street toward the livery stable. Nebraska watched Pete until he came within easy range, then Brake raised his rifle, aiming carefully.

However, from seemingly nowhere, a voice cried out: "Houston! Look out!"

Pete reacted instinctively, stopping neither to look nor to answer. He dove into the street and flattened himself on his stomach before two rifle shots echoed through the morning, missing the bounty hunter but crashing through a storefront window. The rattled Brake came out of hiding and tried to aim again at the prostrate Houston as Pete tried frantically to extract his own six-shooter from his prone position. But then another shot rang out. Nebraska stiffened before falling into the street, a spew of blood saturating his back.

Houston rose to his feet and stared in awe, before he saw Jerry Roseberry riding toward him with a smoking rifle in his own hand. Pete considered what had happened as a crowd gathered about the dead man.

"He was going to kill you from ambush, Mr. Houston," Roseberry said.

"Rawlings is dead," Pete said soberly.

"Then, there's been enough killing," the ex-army captain replied.

"I'm grateful, mister," Pete said. "I owe you my life."

By now, Chief DeLisle had arrived, and he stared down at Brake before glaring at Houston. "Jesus Christ, another corpse?"

"He didn't do it," someone in the crowd said. "He done it." The man pointed to Roseberry. "But he had no choice. The dead man tried to kill this man from ambush." He pointed to Houston. "You can't blame somebody for savin' a man's life."

DeLisle grumbled.

"For whatever it's worth, Chief," Pete said, "I'll be leaving town shortly; going to Buffalo. I've no more business in Egleston."

"Thank the Good Lord." DeLisle clasped his hands. "That's the best news I've heard in a week." He then gestured to some spectators. "Take the body over to the mortician."

When the crowd dispersed, including DeLisle, Pete Houston looked again at Roseberry. "Why did you do it?"

Roseberry shrugged. "As I said, there's been enough killing."

"I owe you one," Pete said. "I'm going to forget I saw you out in the Hole In The Wall country. And if it's any consolation to you, Big Val and Laura are all right. Henry went south to get a fresh start."

"And I suppose I needn't ask you about Laura," Roseberry said. "I suspect she has it real bad for you, risking her life to set you free."

"You're wrong, Captain," Pete said. "She thought she liked me, but she found out she really didn't. As a matter of fact, when I last saw her, she expressed a gratitude for you. She said she might have been ravaged by some of those gang members except for you."

"I had nothing to do with killing those sentries," Roseberry said.

"I know that," Pete answered. "Wild Man Eliot confessed to the killings."

"It's not in my nature to kill anyone unless I have to."

"I suspect that men like Eliot or Anias might have done a lot more killing if it hadn't been for you."

Roseberry nodded. "Laura—is she all right?"

"I don't know if she'd appreciate it, but I'll tell you anyway. She went north to Sheridan. She intends to stay there with a cousin until she can open some kind of business, a dress shop I think. I know she has a lot of respect for you, Captain, and if you aren't set on where you intend to go, maybe you ought to go to Sheridan."

Roseberry grinned. "I'm thankful for the information. I believe that Sheridan is as good a place to go as anywhere." He doffed his hat. "Good-bye, Mr. Houston."

"I wish you luck, Captain," Pete answered.

Houston stood in the street and watched the ex-army captain move off. The bounty hunter remained there until Roseberry loped out of town and onto the Johnson County Highway. Then, Pete sighed and continued his walk toward the livery stable. Inside, he got his bay and leased the buckboard before heading for the mortician's place. Within another half-hour, he was riding northward with three blanketed bodies on the rear of the wagon.

People on the street stared as the bounty hunter moved out of town. No doubt many of them were glad to see him leave, and none more than Chief DeLisle, who stared from the doorway of his small jail. The Egleston police chief did have one solace. A host of people at the Salt River Saloon yesterday had heard Wild Man Eliot confess to the Branden Ranch killings, and now the last of the Rawlings gang was leaving town. That would end the business, and DeLisle would see no hordes of trigger-happy searchers swarming through Egleston.

Pete Houston rode leisurely northward for the remainder of the morning and into the afternoon before he pulled up the wagon in front of Sheriff Red Angus's office. The sheriff came outside, looked at the three dead men, and then grinned. "Goddamn, Pete, you hit the jackpot on this last trip."

"That's the end of the Rawlings gang, Sheriff."

The sheriff frowned. "I do believe there were at least a couple of more in that gang, but I don't

270

know who they are. But, with their leader dead, I suppose that any survivors of that gang ain't likely to do any more rustling." He shook his head. "I still can't get over that report about a woman bein' with 'em. Pete, are you absolutely sure you never heard of a woman with the Rawlings bunch?"

"No, Sheriff," Houston lied again. "And I can also report to you that after I got these three members of the gang in Egleston, there was no more sign of any remaining members of that gang in the area."

"All right." The sheriff nodded. "We'll write off the gang. Come on inside. I'll give you vouchers for these three corpses on the buckboard and you can collect the bounty from Big Joe Simeon." Pete Houston waited until Angus had made out the vouchers.

Later, when Pete presented the slips to Simeon, Big Joe again needed to have a fund transfer, since he did not keep $4,000 lying about the office. He also told Houston that he might be entitled to $5,000 more if they verified the story that Wild Man Eliot had indeed been the killer of the Branden range sentries.

When Pete finished his business with Simeon, he returned to the Mercer Hotel to stable his horse, take a bath, and shave. He then donned neat clothing, and at precisely five o'clock he picked up Jane Clemons at the association office. They went to the Buffalo Cafe again for dinner and they then ambled to the park to sit and talk during the balmy evening. By nine o'clock, Pete was walking Jane back to her boardinghouse.

"I'm so glad you're back, Pete," the girl said.

"The business with the Rawlings gang is a over," Pete answered, "and I think I'll just stic. around town and take it easy for a while."

"It'll mean we can see a lot more of each other, Pete," Jane said, snuggling close to her companion. She then looked up at him. "That girl . . . Are you sure you haven't seen her again?"

"I'm sure," Pete said. "In fact, I think she may have a beau of her own looking for her."

"Are you my beau, Pete?" the girl asked.

"I hope so." He grinned.

Soon, they reached the Durand Boarding House and walked up to the porch. The side street was quiet and peaceful at this time of night. So, alone on the porch, Pete leaned forward and kissed Jane Clemons lightly on the lips. The girl threw her arms around him and kissed him hard. Then she retreated slightly and smiled at Houston.

"Pete, you can come upstairs with me tonight."

"I'd like that," Houston answered in a soft whisper.

Jane Clemons hooked her arm through Pete's right arm before she opened the front door. Seconds later, they disappeared inside, leaving only an empty, nighttime stillness on 13th Street.